PARTS UNKNOWN

PARTS UNKNOWN

A DEVLIN KIRK MYSTERY

REX BURNS

VIKING

VIKING
Published by the Penguin Group
Viking Penguin, a division of Penguin Books USA Inc.,
375 Hudson Street, New York, New York 10014, U.S.A.
Penguin Books Ltd, 27 Wrights Lane,
London W8 5TZ, England
Penguin Books Australia Ltd, Ringwood,
Victoria, Australia
Penguin Books Canada Ltd, 2801 John Street,
Markham, Ontario, Canada L3R 1B4
Penguin Books (N.Z.) Ltd, 182–190 Wairau Road,
Auckland 10, New Zealand

Penguin Books Ltd, Registered Offices:
Harmondsworth, Middlesex, England

First published in 1990 by Viking Penguin,
a division of Penguin Books USA Inc.

1   3   5   7   9   10   8   6   4   2

LIBRARY OF CONGRESS CATALOGING IN PUBLICATION DATA
Burns, Rex.
Parts unknown / Rex Burns.
p.   cm.
ISBN 0–670–82912–9
I. Title.
PS3552.U7325P37   1990
813'.54 — dc20   90–50043

Printed in the United States of America
Set in Times Roman
Designed by Bernard Schleifer

*To Terry
and
The Pirates*

PARTS UNKNOWN

1

"It won't take that much time, Dev." Bunch propped a gigantic shoe on the cold vanes of one of the radiators that flanked the arched window and its wrought-iron rail. The glass reached up from the office below and curved to a halt a foot from the ceiling. In its middle, a couple of panes were cranked open to catch any air, but all that came in was a whiff of diesel smoke from the trucks snorting in Wazee Street below. "You know what a missing persons case is: a few phone calls, a little leg-work, and we find the guy sleeping at his girlfriend's house."

I knew what this missing persons case was, and a detective agency couldn't survive with that kind of business. "How much did Mrs. Gutierrez say she'd pay?"

"She's a friend of the family, Dev. She doesn't have that much money. And it took a lot for her to get up the nerve to ask me in the first place. I can probably wrap the damn thing up in twenty-four hours flat."

"Let her go to the cops. They'll wrap it up for free."

Bunch explained with exaggerated patience. "Mrs. Gutierrez doesn't want to go to the cops. The kid is her cousin's nephew or some crap like that, and he's only been in the States a few months."

"Meaning?"

"Meaning he's an illegal. Meaning the cops are out!"

"Bunch, we haven't had a decent case in over six months. We're barely keeping our butts away from the alligators with a little insurance stuff, and even that's falling off. Now you want to take a case for free?"

"Jesus. You know what you sound like? A goddamn accountant. Prissy, you know? Pursed-up lips like a puckered anus, telling the secretaries not to sharpen their goddamn pencils because it wears them out faster."

"Dammit, Bunch!" That stung. It stung because it was true: I was beginning to feel like a prissy accountant. The in-box held half a dozen unopened envelopes with grinning plastic windows and fat with convenient preaddressed return envelopes. I didn't have to open them to know what they wanted, and a glance at the return address was enough to tell me how much. It seemed that lately I spent more and more time totaling columns of figures and arriving at the same dismal conclusion.

Some security agencies feasted on bad times; they went into the skip-trace game and made a tidy profit on debt collections. The Vinny Landrum Agency was doing fine. But who except Vinny Landrum wanted to be like Vinny Landrum? Even as Bunch and I watched the old accounts close out and the new ones fail to appear, we held out against debt collecting. For one thing, we were too vulnerable in the debt we owed; for another, industrial security was our game, something we did better than the competition, and we were building our reputation on it. What would happen if we were out of the office chasing a deadbeat, or in court swearing the husband of wife A was screwing the wife of husband B, and had to turn down a big company?

But along with so many other businesses that relied on the oil money, which for years made Denver a boomtown, Kirk and Associates had fallen on hard times. And if the drying up of that oil and its wealth hadn't brought a genuine bust, it sure as hell let the air out of a lot of bank accounts. Including ours. The insurance surveillance wasn't regular and it didn't pay nearly as well, but it did bring in enough to cover the rent. And the jobs were quick, leaving us free for that big call that never came. Fortunately, the corporation still had enough in the bank to provide half-salaries for Bunch and me. But the season was a dry one, and long. And now Bunch was talking about taking on charity work.

"Look, Bunch, you know we're getting the leftovers because we're available. If one of the insurance companies calls and we're tied up on a nonpaying case, they're going somewhere else. Just like that, they're going to dial another number, and we lose them and any other cases they might bring. All for the sake of sweet charity."

"You even talk like a goddamn accountant. How come you're not squawking about the bottom line or the margin of profit?"

"Because I can't find the bottom line anymore! And do you really want to hear about our margin of profit?"

"No."

"Damn good thing."

"But I'm tired of sitting on my butt waiting for the lame to walk and the dead to rise."

That's what most of this insurance work was: lurking around to catch accident victims who claimed permanent and total disability, yet who managed to change the tires on their cars or paint their houses or even jog along country lanes. All it took was a telephoto lens, some skill at cover and concealment—and a lot of patience, which, for world-class security agents, neither Bunch nor I seemed to have in sufficient supply. I, too, felt the drudgery of it. Still, it paid. I reminded Bunch of that.

He squashed one fist inside the palm of his other hand; his knuckles made a muffled rattle, like pebbles dropped into a wooden barrel. "I told you, Dev. Mrs. Gutierrez is a friend of the family. Even if she can't pay a cent, I'm not going to turn down a friend who asks for help."

"Goddamn it, the kid's probably back in Mexico! He's homesick, he hopped a bus, he went back. That's all."

"He's not from Mexico. He's from El Salvador—the whole family is. They're political refugees, and there's not a damn thing left for him to go back to. Besides, the Mexicans don't want him either."

"Doesn't he have a green card?"

"He doesn't qualify. Our government says El Sal's a fine place to live. Nobody should want to leave El Sal, they say."

Bunch's silhouette, as tall as mine but twice as wide, blotted out the view across the low brick warehouses and small factories of Wazee Street. Beyond them, the haze-faded mountains west of Denver lifted in ridges one behind the other. Earlier in the summer, the distant slopes were shadowed dark with pines and green grass fed by runoff. But this late in September, the runoff had ceased and the slopes had turned to patches of pale brown streaked here and there with darker smudges of forest. Above that, snowfields glimmered dusty white. They were big enough to survive until the next snows, and some of them had been around long enough to earn the name of glacier. But from this distance, it was hard to think of that white as cool and fresh. Instead, they were unreal places of escape—tantalizing but forbidden.

"I expect Costello to call soon, Bunch—"

"You've been saying that for a week."

"—and when he does, it'll be a twenty-four-hour surveillance. You know that."

"Fine. When he calls you, you call me. I'll come. Simple."

"Why don't you wait until we know for certain? Costello said he'd call this week and let us know."

"Because he hasn't called yet. Because he might never call. And because Mrs. Gutierrez is worried. Really worried, Dev. It's been over ten days since she heard anything, and nobody knows what happened to him. Nobody at work, nobody at his apartment house. She telephoned his boss and even went by to talk to people in his apartment."

"Oh yeah? When did she see him last?"

"A week ago Sunday. But he usually phones two or three times a week, drops by on weekends, has Sunday dinner with the family. That kind of thing. She's the only relative he's got in the States, and that's one of the reasons he came to Denver. And why she feels responsible for him."

"He just went to work and didn't come back?"

"That's what she says."

"You've talked to the employer?"

"No, Devlin. I have not talked to the employer. What in the hell do you think you were bitching about just two minutes ago? That's one of the things I want to do this afternoon—talk to the employer. But you're telling me it'll take too much out of your goddamn pocket."

"Well, it can wait—" The ring of the telephone cut off my words, and I picked it up quickly. "Kirk and Associates."

"This here is Drayton Coe?" The voice had a rising inflection and an accent that was soft on r's and long on vowels. Virginia maybe, or Georgia. "I'm the vice president for facilities at Hally Corporation?"

I didn't recognize either name, but he sounded as if I should. So I said, "Of course, Mr. Coe. What can we do for you?"

"We have this little problem of theft and vandalism of company property—I see you people do industrial security. Does that include putting in security devices and such?"

"It certainly can, sir. In fact, you couldn't have called at a better time—our specialist in electronic surveillance just came in from another job. I can have him drive over right now and talk with you, if that's all right."

The drawling voice said that would be nice, and in fact, the sooner the better. Coe gave directions and I jotted them on a pad for Bunch. He glanced at the address and smiled. "It's not too far away from where Mrs. Gutierrez' nephew works."

"Bunch—"

"Hey, prissy-purse, cool out. I can swing by there after I talk to this Drayton Coe. Won't cost you a dime, and I can find out about Nestor."

"Nestor?"

"That's the kid's name: Nestor Calamaro."

The Hally Corporation, the Yellow Pages told me, was a firm that manufactured paper goods of all kinds and was located in

Northwest Denver in what used to be a residential district for meat plant workers, when there had been a meat-packing plant and when there had been workers. I hoped that the job wouldn't be one of those quick, low-profit installations of sensors and alarms—not a job to be scorned, but not one to rely on for a palpable income either.

Bunch left the office whistling; he would find out for certain what Mr. Coe and his company needed. I stayed behind with the bills and the silent telephone, and listed the items we could, if necessary, begin to sell off. Our fax machine, a Panasonic UF-250, was our last major purchase from what was—though we didn't know it then—our final big job. It wasn't doing much for us right now and, as the newest piece of office equipment, probably had the best resale value. In fact, I was dialing the office supply company to see what they'd offer when Uncle Wyn, game leg stumping heavily, knocked and opened the door.

"Jesus, Dev. It's like a tomb around here. Business still that bad?"

"Still that bad, Uncle Wyn." I got up and swung the desk chair around for him, and held it as he gingerly let himself down. The only visitors' chair had soft cushions and a raked back and was too hard for him to get in and out of.

He grunted and propped his arthritic knee with the stout cane. "Going to rain sure as hell. I used to laugh at old cooters who claimed they could tell from their arthritis. But by God, I know now they were right. And this is what I get for laughing at them."

"We could use some rain. The month's been a dry one. Everyone's complaining."

"Don't know what the hell everyone expects, living in a high desert like this." With another grunt, he shifted his weight. "Now tell me outright, are you going to make it or not?"

That was the question I'd been asking myself off and on for weeks now. And I didn't know the answer. "We're skating on the edge, Uncle Wyn. I had a call yesterday from an insurance company canceling another job. But Bunch just went out to look at some possible installation work."

"Lose much yesterday?"

"Well, it would have covered the overhead for another month."

"I see." He rubbed a finger across a scar on the back of his right hand, a memento from one of the thousands of cleats or foul balls that had bounced off him during his days as a professional catcher. "You need some help, I'm here."

"Thanks, Uncle. I might call on you if things get bad enough. But we have a good chance to make it. It's just that things could be a little better, that's all."

"I told you once, I'll tell you again: I think it was dumb to pay me back so soon when you didn't have to. If you hadn't done that, you'd have a lot left in the bank—it could've been making money for you all this time for when you get in these slumps."

"But it's good to be free and clear, too. Even when there's not that much that's clear." And when the failure of my business wouldn't mean loss for our major investor.

"Hey, I wouldn't put the squeeze on you. You know that."

"I know, Uncle Wyn. And I didn't mean it that way. I meant it feels good to me—I feel better about having debts paid off, no matter who it is I owe."

"Yeah. Your daddy was that way too, God rest his soul. Me, I could owe somebody and lose no sleep over it. He couldn't. It bugged him for some reason."

My uncle had taken my father's place when he was murdered, and in a way I had taken the place of Uncle Wyn's children, who, following their own lives, had moved away to the East and West coasts.

"Trouble was, he also lost sleep when somebody owed him. Thought everybody ought to feel the way he did." The heavy-featured head wagged back and forth. "Don't sweat it, I say. You lend somebody a little, they don't pay you back, you don't lend them any more and they stay clear of you anyway. Cheap lesson, and you get rid of lousy company. Good deal all around."

"Maybe it's genetic. I'm the worrier. Bunch could care less. If we go bankrupt, he'll whistle to the next job."

"He's got the right attitude."

"His name's not on the letterhead."

"It wouldn't make any difference if it was. He's a good ol' boy."

He was that, and as an ex–professional football player, Bunch shared with Uncle Wyn a view of the world that I wasn't privy to: life as a contest. A serious one, demanding full commitment perhaps, but fundamentally without any purpose except what the players themselves agreed to.

"I know you don't like to hear this, Dev, but I could use you in my own business. I'm getting pretty old, and this damn arthritis . . ." He caught the note of complaint in his voice and stopped. "Anyway, none of the kids are interested in it, you know that. But I'd like to keep the business in the family."

"I appreciate the offer, Uncle. But it's premature on two counts—one, you're not ready for the retirement farm yet, and two, Kirk and Associates isn't ready to quit yet."

"Yeah. 'Two counts.' I keep forgetting you got some law school. Well, your old man was stubborn too. Ma said all us boys got Dad's bullheadedness; I guess you got it too."

The difference between stubbornness and foolishness was the outcome. If Kirk and Associates survived, I'd be labeled stubborn and maybe admired; if it folded, foolish. But as I'd told Uncle Wyn, we weren't dead yet, and the telephone might ring any minute with a client who needed help and, more important, who could pay for that help.

But of course, it didn't. The afternoon dragged on, and Uncle Wyn hung around as long as his arthritis would allow, talking baseball and relatives. When he left, I sat and gazed out the window at the snowfields that freckled the distant peaks and wondered if taking a vacation would save a few bucks. No.

Camping in the office would be cheaper than camping in the hills, and I wouldn't chance missing that telephone call.

Gradually, the sounds of Wazee Street below our window grew louder with the increasing restlessness of quitting-time traffic. Overhead, the sculptress who had taken the place of the piano teacher pushed her acrylic creations back and forth across her studio. I never did understand why they had to be moved periodically or why she preferred working in the afternoons and evenings, but the muted thunder of casters punctuated every day about this time. There had been a period when we were too busy to notice that the piano teacher's business had collapsed and she had moved out and the sculptress had moved in. Now the occasional rumbles emphasized the silence of the office.

I had just trimmed the blinds against the afternoon sun when Bunch came back, wiping at his sweaty forehead with a wad of handkerchief.

"Good God, it's hot. And not a sniff of breeze."

"Uncle Wyn's leg tells him it's going to rain."

"Hope to hell his leg's right. But I wouldn't bet the house and kids on it."

"What's the Hally Corporation want?"

Bunch shrugged and settled on the corner of the desk, which creaked in protest. "They're not all that sure. Probably end up with a closed-loop system, the kind any home security outfit can install. If they want to do the job right, it's going to cost a hell of a lot more than I think they're willing to pay."

Usually that meant the client would have a major retrofit—a lot of companies put up their facilities or bought cheap and then decided they wanted to add the kind of security system that should have been built into the structure initially. "Did you explain it to them?"

"Yeah, I explained it. But the guy's a real asshole—the kind who knows everything and listens to nothing." Bunch caught my expression. "Don't look so worried, Dev. I was my usual smooth self. Yes, I explained the options—the quick fix versus the right way. He said he'll talk it over with his boss or whoever and let us know. A day or two, he said."

"He sounded over the phone like he was in a hurry."

"Maybe so. But he sure slowed down when I gave him a ballpark figure. He's got people stealing him blind from the grounds and warehouse, but he's more worried about the security costs than the losses. Hell, it wouldn't be the first time somebody went through the motions and called themselves covered."

That was true enough. Penny-wise, and so on. "I suppose you went by the place where what's his name, Nestor, works?"

"A packing plant over in Swansea. Apple Valley Turkeys. No valley, no apples, plenty of turkeys. Including the guy I talked to. Says Nestor just stopped coming to work. Never picked up his paycheck, never signed out of the retirement fund. Just flat disappeared."

"How much did he leave?"

"Three hundred seventy-two dollars and fourteen cents. A week and a half's pay, plus the seven hundred in the pension fund."

We both knew what that meant: an unplanned disappearance. "Nothing in the John Doe file at Denver Police Department?"

"I thought you didn't want me wasting time on this one."

"A little legwork here, a couple phone calls there—that's all it should take you, Bunch."

"Boy, you never forget a thing you don't want to forget." He gazed down into the heavy traffic and whistled a half-audible tune between his teeth. "I just hope it's not what I hope it's not."

"Did he have any enemies?"

"None the employer knew about, which means jack-shit. I didn't get a chance to talk to any people he worked with. Guy wouldn't let me on the floor."

"Maybe we can do that tomorrow."

"Oh?" I felt his gaze. "What's this 'we' stuff, white man? Aren't you afraid it might cost you a dime?"

"Damn. I forgot all about that." Bunch was going to do what he wanted to anyway; if I was along, maybe I could keep the lost time to a minimum. Besides, I was bored out of my gourd too. "Can you find out who's working homicide at DPD tonight?"

"I already did. It's Ashcroft."

I led the way to the door. "Let's go talk to him."

My car was an Austin-Healey 3000 whose temperament became volatile on hot days in heavy traffic. But if the old girl didn't like the long idles of rush hour, Bunch liked her even less. For one thing, the car was too small for both of us; for another, he thought it was yuppie kitsch. "Next thing, you'll be telling me what kind of goddamn running shoes to wear, or the right color patterns for my jogging suit." I told him I liked the car for two reasons: one, it was too small for both of us, and two, yuppies didn't drive museum pieces that looked so ratty. Besides, if I kept it moving enough so the undersized radiator could do its job, it was quick to dodge through the lumbering sedans and trucks and easy to park when there wasn't much curb space available. Bunch preferred his Bronco, which he said was big enough to let him sit without hitting his head and heavy enough not to pull to one side when he rode alone. And I have to admit that as the Healey lurched over the dips near the Police Administration Building, the shocks groaned and thumped in an agony that questioned its service.

"Do you know Ashcroft?" In the several years since Bunch had left the force, a series of different administrations had speeded up changes in personnel.

"I met him in the patrol division, but he was over in District Four." Bunch shrugged, his shoulder bobbing against mine. "He might remember me. We'll see."

I pulled the Healey into an open spot reserved for municipal judges. The courts closed at five, and the judges' cars were gone by one minute after. Now a picket line of red and white warning signs watched over the empty curb. Down Fourteenth Street, a swirl of traffic swung around the greenery and Greek columns of Civic Center Park, with its winos and teenaged prostitutes of both sexes. Even this early they could be seen posing on the lawn just off the sidewalk, selling their flesh and hungrily eyeing faces in the stream of traffic that drained out of downtown. The main pickup time would come a little later, when dusk started to make details hazy, and the johns, bolstered by after-work drinks, felt less conspicuous in the dimness. But business was business, even in the sale of self, and a good hustler didn't let a chance pass without trying. If luck was with them, they could turn enough tricks before prime time to cover the day's overhead. Then the rest of the evening would be, so to speak, pure gravy.

Nearer, a man pushing a grocery cart of belongings shuffled across Fourteenth Street and slowly sought the shade of an alley. A few steps behind him and ignoring the blat and hurry of traffic, a black and white dog, tongue and tail drooping in the heat, followed closely. Bunch eyed the man, who was draped in a heavy coat despite the temperature. "What do you think trickled down on him?"

"It wasn't what the politicians promised."

"Come on now—that's his chosen lifestyle: shopping cart chic."

"Could be *our* chosen lifestyle if we don't get a few clients. Paying clients."

"Jesus. You and your one-track mind."

Across the car-filled parking lot reserved for people the city paid, bands of black windows, like eye slits in a visor, emphasized the towering block of the holding jail and the slightly smaller monolith of the administration building. The few stray figures around its entrances were dwarfed by the weight of the concrete above, and—in a weak attempt to soften the expanses of bare stone slabs linking the two buildings—a fountain splashed feebly against the trapped and radiating heat. The facade spoke of rigidity and power and especially of an unimaginative adherence to fact and rule. It was a stifling and a restrictiveness that had driven Bunch out of the police and ultimately into Kirk and Associates. It was the same burden of bureaucracy and bullshit that had made me leave the Secret Service. As we approached the glowering overhang above the glassed-in lobby, I could sense Bunch tighten himself against its atmosphere.

Ashcroft waited for us in the offices of crimes against persons. A tall man with narrow, curving shoulders, he accepted the fact of private investigators but he didn't relish it. "You gentlemen want to come this way?"

We followed him past the night clerk and into offices filled with two rows of metal desks. They were empty, the night shift already on the streets. Ashcroft, saying nothing, gestured for me and Bunch to find empty chairs.

"You gentlemen want to see the John Doe files, that right?"

"That's right." Bunch ignored the chairs and sat on one of the glass-topped desks. "How do you like the new chief, Ashcroft?"

The homicide detective glanced up from the file drawer. "Fine. I'm sure he'll be a fine chief. You gentlemen got a description of your missing person?"

Bunch sighed—so much for old times and small talk—and nodded. "Hispanic male, medium height, slender build, twenty-six years old. Has a four-inch scar on the inside of his left forearm. Probably wearing a work shirt and blue jeans." He handed the detective a tinted photograph of a young man smiling whitely at the camera. A scrawl in a lower corner read, "*A mi tía con amor.* Nestor."

He hefted a pile of manila folders from the drawer and set them on a desk. "Here's the Hispanic John Does. The photograph probably won't help much—most of these were pretty messed up by the time we found them."

"Right." Bunch divided the stack into two piles and shoved one my way. The photograph in the first file showed a nude man lying faceup on a gurney, suspended in a darkness that the flashbulb did not pierce. Puncture wounds made dark blotches in the paleness of his stomach, and part of his neck gaped open and glistened wetly in the flash. The face, distorted yet empty, showed lividity marks as well as the slightly double chin of a man older and heavier than Nestor. I turned to the next file.

It took a while; there were a lot of photographs and—as Ashcroft said—some of the faces pictured had lost a lot of detail. I was half aware of the silence of the large office, a silence intensified by the tiny buzzing of fluorescent lights and then broken by the occasional jangle of a telephone. Once in a while, another detective walked between the rows of desks and eyed us with brief curiosity before talking with Ashcroft. From down the hall, the quack of the duty clerk's television set made a constant background murmur. Bunch was more practiced at this type of identification, and he finished first. Ashcroft, trailing a telephone wire, talked to someone about an investigation and refiled the cases as we finished.

"What about the metro and state lists?" Bunch asked.

Still talking on the telephone, Ashcroft nodded and pulled more manila folders from a rack to lay on the desk. These were verbal descriptions rather than photographs. Filed chronologically, the lists covered unidentified bodies found in the cities and municipalities that surrounded Denver, as well as elsewhere in the state and region. We turned up two whose descriptions and probable dates of death matched Nestor's, one over in Alamosa and one north of Denver in Weld County.

"You gentlemen have any success?" Ashcroft finally hung up the telephone.

"A couple possibles."

"Yeah?" The detective looked over my shoulder. Then he grunted, disappointed that the possibles weren't from his caseload. He gathered up the scattered folders and refiled them, then walked us back through the offices to the elevators. It was less courtesy than security, but now that we were leaving, he felt friendly enough to attempt a smile and some light banter. "You gentlemen can have the missing persons jobs. They're nothing but headaches—a big waste of time."

"That's what I keep telling Bunch."

2

A telephone call saved the long drive to Alamosa; their John Doe had been identified and claimed by relatives from California. The other was in the county hospital's morgue at Brighton, an hour's ride north of downtown. It was also an hour's ride back.

This time Bunch drove his Bronco. "You didn't have to come along, you know." He poked buttons on the radio, looking for his favorite country and western station.

"Somebody has to keep you out of trouble. You can't do it yourself."

The unidentified body was Hispanic and looked about the same age as Nestor. But the description had failed to mention that the deceased was missing his left eye and ear. "Hell, we didn't know," shrugged the sheriff's deputy who had led us toward the body. "He got killed in a fight. It wasn't until after the autopsy we found out they were missing before he was beat up."

"For Christ's sake," said Bunch, "you can see how old the scars are—the goddamn things are healed!"

The officer's neck grew red and he glared up at Bunch. "You know this greaser or not? If not, quit wasting my goddamn time!"

"We wouldn't have wasted our own goddamn time if you knew your goddamn job."

"Come on, Bunch. Let's not waste any more goddamn time."

The officer yanked the rubber sheet over the victim's face. "Fucking rent-a-cops!"

"This is what the taxpayers get for their money? Jesus, no wonder private enterprise is taking over."

Now the big man swerved the Bronco out of I-70 traffic onto the York Street ramp. The black of prairie surrounding Brighton had given way to clusters of lights that marked shopping centers and malls and finally became the steady flicker of city-glow. But here, beneath the elevated freeway and its concrete sky, the lights were dim and distant, and the brightest of them came from the modest neon of an occasional neighborhood bar. Interspersed among the black emptiness of fenced storage yards, a few small houses showed some life after dark. But most of the area had been cut up for commercial use, and the shops were closed for the day: salvage, electrical repair, automobile painting, generator rebuilding. It was one of those old, dying neighborhoods whose residential role had been sold out to industry, and what houses were left for people to live in were ill kept, grimy, and forlorn.

"There it is—that two-story on the corner." I pointed toward the narrow frame house whose lapped siding was punctured by two rows of windows.

"Looks like an army barracks."

Mrs. Gutierrez had reluctantly given Bunch her relative's address. It was, she said, a place where a lot of her countrymen roomed, because the owner, Senora Chiquichano, was Salvadoran and the refugees felt more comfortable with their own people.

"By refugees, she means illegals?"

Bunch shrugged. "That's my guess."

We looked at the gabled end of the building. A tiny covered porch marked the entry, and four windows—two up and two down—were the only relief in the end wall's blankness. The patch of lawn had long ago surrendered to bare dirt. A few scraps of paper rolled in the night wind across a sparkle of broken glass to catch on a sagging and well-used tricycle. From somewhere in the swaybacked building came the wail of a baby, and through another thin wall we heard the inevitable chatter of a television with its canned laughter and bouncy, happy advertisements. The torn screen door hung half open into a hallway smelling of urine, and the light from a dim bulb at the far end showed a row of doors leading away beneath stairs that lifted into the shadows of the second floor.

"You want to take the upstairs?" Bunch jerked a thumb upward. "I think I'm too heavy. I might fall through."

It wasn't that farfetched: I felt the floor joists tremble and quiver as I climbed the creaky stairs. At the first door, my knocking was followed by a tense hush. Then a voice asked, *"Quién es?"* and I sensed a figure hovering behind the gritty wood.

"I'm looking for Mr. Calamaro, please."

"No hay." Then in half-English, *"No es* any Calamaro *aquí."*

"He's a man who lives downstairs. Room four. *No soy la policía, no soy la migra. Abierte, por favor. Es muy importante."*

Whether or not he believed I wasn't the police or immigration, he was curious. A lock rattled, and the door opened the length of a chain to show the dark eye and pockmarked flesh of a man somewhere in his late twenties. Despite his youth, he looked as if he had been working since he could walk. At his knee, another brown eye peered upward, this one above the smooth, round cheek of a child.

"The man is missing. Disappeared. His aunt, Senora Gutierrez, asked me to look for him. Do you know Mr. Calamaro?"

"A little bit. No much."

"Can you tell me when you saw him last?"

"Maybe last week. Two weeks. I don't know."

"Did he seem worried? *Aprensivo?"*

"No sé. We no talk much, you know."

"Aren't you from El Salvador too?"

"No!" A flash of anxiety crossed the eye, and the door wavered.

"Wait!" I shoved one of Kirk and Associates' business cards through the closing slit. "If you see Calamaro or hear anything about him, please call. It won't get you in trouble—I'm not the police." The door shut, leaving a tiny corner of white cardboard trembling against the paintless wood.

From the hallway below came the brief rumble of Bunch's voice and short silences marking the timid responses to his questions. Then a rattle of knuckles on the next door. I figured he was having the same luck I was.

Some doors wouldn't open, some did. But the answer was the same: No one knew much about anything. I left a trail of business cards and met Bunch in the sour-smelling hallway downstairs, where he picked the rusty lock on number four. For such a large man—ex–professional football player, ex-cop—he had surprisingly nimble fingers, and in the occasional lock-picking races that we staged to pass long days in the silent office, he usually won.

The door cracked open and we found the light switch. A single unshaded bulb lit up a cubicle filled mostly by a sagging double bed without a headboard. A closet had been added to one corner of the room, built of ill-fitted boards and closed with a grimy curtain dangling from a shower rod. A chest of drawers, scarred and with some of the glass pulls missing, took up most of the remaining space. In the other corner, a small stand made of an apple crate held a washbasin, a glass that sported a toothbrush, and a brightly flowered towel—Calamaro's purchase, most likely. On the shelf below sat a cracked glass pitcher with a smiling Kool-Aid face frosted on it.

Bunch looked in the closest. I looked under the bed and pulled out a scuffed suitcase whose cardboard corners had frayed.

"A couple shirts, a couple pairs of pants. Nothing in the pockets."

"Suitcase is empty."

Bunch began going through the lower drawers of the chest. I looked through the pair of uppers.

It didn't take either of us long. "Find anything?" he asked.

"Some socks, a few bandannas. Some papers."

"Jesus—chartreuse socks?"

I glanced around the room. The dominating color of the thin walls was weary brown, and even the ceiling, once white, had leached to a dead gray. "Maybe it was his way of fighting back."

"Man, if this place is better than what he left in El Salvador . . ."

I spread out the small pile of papers I had found in a corner of the drawer. One was a letter in Spanish, difficult to read because of the formal ornateness of the penmanship, but signed, in a different and less florid hand, "Maria Cristina." His pay stubs for the last six weeks had been carefully stacked, and additions and subtractions in pencil marked the blank spaces on the slips. The patient's copy of a health claim form from Warner Memorial Hospital dated four weeks ago, a smudged calling card from Friendly Used Cars, a wallet-sized calendar with days carefully x'd off, a gas station map of Denver and Colorado, an RTD flier with bus schedules and routes, a worn deck of cards.

"What's the last day crossed off?" Bunch asked.

"Monday, two weeks ago."

"So he didn't come back Tuesday night."

That fit with the possible time of his disappearance. "Unless he crossed them off before he left in the morning."

Bunch shook his head. "His boss said he punched in and out on both Monday and Tuesday."

The medical form was a list of the standard-fee codes for various blocks of services. The referring doctor was number 139, the patient was number 3006188, the services provided were numbers 85031, 83002, and 84550—all of which supported the trend toward more personal relationships between doctor and patient. One item without a code number was checked with ballpoint pen: Pus-Wound-Lesion. Most of the numbers referred to tests of body fluids, especially blood.

"Did his boss say anything about a visit to the hospital?"

Bunch was looking over my shoulder. "No. Why?"

I pointed to the date on the form. "It's a weekday a month ago. He'd have taken time off from work."

"Good, Dev—I wondered if you'd spot that. I may make a detective of you yet."

"Right. Thanks." We took a last look around the small room, aware of the voices—human and electronic—on the other side of the thin partitions that had been tacked up to make Nestor's cubicle. As Bunch said, it was hard to imagine that El Salvador was worse. He relocked the door, and I led across the square of dirt toward the Bronco.

"Sssssst."

"What'd you say, Dev?"

"Wasn't me." We paused, waiting for the sound to come again.

"*Señores, por favor.*" From a corner of the building where the shadows lay deepest, a blurred face leaned toward us. "Please, misters."

"What's your problem?" asked Bunch.

He was slender and work-stunted, and his face was creased with worry. "Is true you are no policeman?"

"Yeah," said Bunch. "That's true. You're the guy from room eight, right?"

"*Sí.* You look for Senor Calamaro?"

"You know where he's at?"

"No, senor, I'm sorry." He listened, glancing back over his shoulder for sounds beneath the steady rush of traffic off the nearby elevated freeway.

"What's wrong?" I asked.

"You are no the police?"

I handed him a card. "*Detectivos privados.* We're looking . . . *buscamos solamente Señor Calamaro.*"

The Spanish relaxed him a bit, and he said something too rapidly for me to understand.

"A little slower, please."

"Can you help me too? *Es mi esposa.* My wife."

"Is she sick?"

"No, señor. Desaparecida—gone."

On the other side of the apartment wall, a television voice blared out and was cut quickly. The man's eyes widened and he sank back into the shadows, a dim outline against the pale boards.

"We'll drive around the block," said Bunch. "Meet us on the corner."

I repeated the words in Spanish, and the man nodded and glided out of sight. A few minutes later, the headlights picked him up perched on the old redstone curb. A lifted hand shielded his eyes from the glare. He slid quickly into the rider's seat.

"What are you afraid of?" I asked.

"La patrona." He took a deep breath and groped in a shirt pocket to offer a pack of cigarettes. We declined, and he put them away without lighting up. "She don't like it that we talk to Anglos."

"Go ahead and smoke if you want." Bunch steered the Bronco to a stretch of empty street and pulled over in the shadows of a high, wooden fence.

"Thank you." A match flared for an instant, bringing the sharp worry lines of the man's face out of the darkness. *"Mi esposa*—my wife—she is gone. I don't know where. I come home from work, she is gone. Nobody knows where. *Desaparecida."*

"Did she leave you?" asked Bunch. "Run away?"

"Oh no, senor! Where she go? To who?" He drew deeply on the cigarette cupped in his palm and sighed a cloud of smoke out the window. "We are illegals. All of us. Where can we go?"

"Did she go south? Home?" I asked.

"No, senor. We don't have the money for that. She don't want to go back anyway. She likes the States." He added politely, "We all like the States."

"So you didn't check with the police?"

"No. If I go to the police . . ." He shrugged. "But she is gone. I don't know what to do—who to talk to. I told *la patrona.*

She say she look, but nothing. Nowhere—no one. My wife!"
The voice caught and stifled itself, embarrassed to show emotion.

After a moment, I asked, "Was she sick? *Enferma?*"

"*Fué embarazada.*" He saw my puzzlement. "*Embarazada.*"
His hands made a swelling motion in front of his stomach.
"*Niño*—baby."

"Pregnant," I told Bunch.

"You keep her barefoot in winter too?" he asked.

"*Cómo?*"

"*Nada,*" I said. "How many months?"

"*Siete.* Seven."

"The landlady—did she ask at the hospitals?"

"*Sí.* Everywhere. Nothing."

"Ask him if he's got a photograph of her," said Bunch.

He replied before I could speak. "*Fotografía? Sí.*" Fumbling
quickly in his wallet, he handed us a small tinted school picture.
A girl who looked about sixteen smiled widely at the camera,
her eyes large and dark with the excitement of being photographed.

"When was this taken?"

"Eighteen months ago. Before we start north."

"Did you talk to the neighbors around here? *Los vecinos?*
Ask them if they saw anything?"

La patrona, sí. Yo, no. She don't like for us to talk to nobody." The thin shoulders bobbed again. "*La migra.*"

Bunch sighed, not without satisfaction. "How much you
going to charge this guy, Dev?"

I sighed too. "The same rate Mrs. Gutierrez is paying—call
it twofers."

We spent a few more minutes getting names and dates clear.
He was Felix Frentanes and his wife was Serafina. She had
disappeared six weeks ago Thursday, and the last trace anyone
had of her was when the woman across the hall in number seven
saw her headed for the corner market with an empty shopping
bag. Felix had waited for more information, growing distraught

as the night passed, until he had taken a chance on his landlady's displeasure and asked the shop owner if he knew anything. But the owner said no—he didn't even remember waiting on her the day before.

"What apartment does the landlady live in?"

"No here." His hand flapped vaguely at the surrounding dark. "Somewhere else. She comes Saturdays. To get *los* paychecks."

"The paychecks?"

"She makes the . . . *cambio.*"

"Cash? She cashes the paychecks?"

"*Sí.*" Another shrug. "Without the identification cards . . ." The worried look came back. "You no talk to her, yes? You no tell her I talk to you, please?"

"Okay by me," said Bunch. "But we got to talk to the people in the apartment."

I explained to him that we couldn't do much without asking people questions. Then, resigned, he nodded. "Will they tell *la patrona* we're asking about your wife?" I added.

A tilt of the head that meant probably. Most of the people in the apartment wouldn't tell, he said. But a few—those who got something extra from the woman—acted as her eyes and ears and told on those who disobeyed *la patrona*'s rules. She would hear of it sooner or later. But he was more worried about his wife than about any punishment from *la patrona*. That was why he had dared to talk to us in the first place. Seven—eight months pregnant, now. No English, no money, no relatives, no friends. And, in this alien and frightening city, adrift somewhere. Or worse. And for her, as for him and the others like him, there was no appeal to the law. He was right to be worried.

3

The telephone answering machine's light was winking red when I arrived at the office in the morning, and the message was a welcome one for a change: "This is Allen Schute with Security Underwriters in New York. I have a job for you if you can handle it. Would you please give me a call before noon your time?"

I dialed the area code and local numbers Schute had recited—a Murray Hill exchange, meaning midtown Manhattan—and worked my way past a receptionist and a personal secretary to the man himself. I hadn't done any jobs for Security before, but I'd heard of them: a big underwriter who, for a percentage of the moneys saved, would determine if an injury claim was false. And apparently they'd heard of us; Schute wondered if Kirk and Associates could take an assignment on short notice. I allowed as we might.

"We've received a tip about a claimant in a motorcycle accident who's just moved to the Denver area. We'd like to clean this one up as soon as possible—we're facing a statute of limitations on it."

I said fine and we settled on the fee schedule, and Schute gave me the particulars. One William "Billy" Taylor, who claimed permanently debilitating leg and back injuries as the result of a car-motorcycle collision, had recently left the metropolis of T's Corner, Virginia, and moved to the Denver area. He was supposed to be looking for work as a roofer.

"With a bad leg and back?"

"That's what we hear from his ex-girlfriend. She's the one who tipped us off that he submitted a false claim. Now, she may or may not be telling the truth; they had a big fight and she ended up in the hospital, I understand, with a few broken bones and a craving for revenge. But we did have our doctors look at him following the accident, and they suspected then that he was faking it. But you know about back injuries—they can't be determined with any accuracy, so we went ahead and settled out of court. Christ, the way juries are making awards nowadays, we were afraid to take it to court. Which he knew, of course."

"Do you have a local address?"

Schute gave me all the information he had, which wasn't that much. Taylor's mailing address was a rural route near Erie, Colorado, a small town about forty miles north of Denver. His ex-girlfriend said he was staying with some motorcycle buddies there. Schute read off a list of Taylor's known acquaintances in the Denver area and mentioned Ace Roofing as a possible source of information. "Apparently it's run by a buddy of Taylor's who moved out there a couple years ago. After he got off parole."

"What was he busted for?"

"Moonshining. No big thing among local law enforcement in that corner of the state. But the feds get pretty excited about it."

"Do you have a description of Taylor?"

He did, and was delighted to learn my office had a fax machine. A few minutes later, the machine murmured and then beeped the arrival of a three-page police file, which noted that Taylor—thirty-two years old, five eleven, one eighty-five, black hair and blue eyes—was affiliated with a group whose interest in motorcycles was not solely recreational. In fact, it edged into the criminal. Fortunately, I didn't have to arrest the guy; all I had to do was photograph him on the job or on his motorcycle, thereby demonstrating his ability to lead a normal life. But to do that, I had to find him.

Erie, Colorado, was named after Erie, Pennsylvania, because of the coal mines that meandered under the surrounding prairies. The seams had played out decades ago, and except for the name of a bar and a handful of relics in local museums, there was no reference to mining anymore, and no one made their living at it. I cruised down the cracked and ragged pavement of the town's single main street: A small pizza restaurant, a fast-food drive-in, a liquor store, and four or five bars. The rest of the town's income came from highway maintenance work, schoolteaching, and, especially, jobs outside the community.

Aside from a few kids riding bicycles up and down the lone stretch of lumpy pavement, the town seemed deserted. Over many large store windows boards warped from long weathering, and rock facings whose stains hadn't been blasted for years said the town was a quiet eddy out of the mainstream of progress and development. The dirt streets wandering off between houses implied that was the way the residents liked it. Maybe they had found a set of values different from that of hustling, hungry Boulder just across the county line; then again, maybe they hadn't. Most of the homes were small bungalows huddled under large cottonwoods, but here and there newer apartments ruptured the tree line, stark and boxy and hinted of pending change.

At the north end of the street, I found the post office. It was the newest structure in town and looked like the central warehouse of a lumberyard, with its low-pitched roof, wide eaves, and freshly stained boards. The woman behind the counter scratched a pencil in her heavily dyed black hair and said, "Just a minute," when I showed her Taylor's address and asked where it was. She came back with a county map glued to a square of cardboard and covered with plastic film.

"Here we are." A smudge of ballpoint ink was "here." Her

finger traced a line of road. "You go down Briggs—that's right out front there. Where it turns east, go down to County Road Five and turn south maybe half a mile. You'll see the mailbox on your left—says 'Wilcox,' but they're the original owners. Don't live there now."

"Do you know Mr. Taylor?"

The blue-black hair shook no. "Only people I see regular are those with boxes or who use general delivery."

I thanked her and followed the ragged and lumpy asphalt strip around to the graveled county road. A thin haze of dust hung over the glare of dirt and stone to powder the weeds that filled the roadside ditches. Treeless land rolled gently toward the horizons. Here and there were patches of dark green corn or silage crops watered from narrow irrigation ditches, the glint of aluminum siphons leading off between rows from the water running down the concrete slit. But for the most part, the land was brown and dry and empty of everything except an occasional wire fence that swung past like a long pendulum anchored to some point at the edge of sky. To the west, ranges of mountain, blurry with dust and heat, lifted abruptly from the yellow of prairie to the blue and gray of icy rock. Already, clumps of white clouds rose like billows of smoke from behind the farthest peaks, and by early afternoon they would build into towering thunderheads that would sail, stately and slow, toward Kansas. That was the rain promised by Uncle Wyn's arthritis, and if the prairie was lucky, a curtain of water from the dark bottom of one of those swelling columns would sweep across the cracked and gaping clay. Aside from a white-chested hawk that hung wagging above a gentle rise of land, I was the only thing moving in the shallow bowl formed by the grassy ridges.

The mailbox, anchored in a rusty milk can, had the route number nailed to the upright and the name Wilcox painted in faded red on the metal. Beneath it dangled an orange newspaper box labeled "*Times-Call.*" A two-rut road led across a narrow cattle guard and wound over a knoll to make a pair of dimples in its crest of tall, dry grass. I pulled the rented Subaru

onto the weedy shoulder and walked up the lane. The heavy
sun pressed down on the tawny swell of earth, and the grass
sang with the high-pitched keen of insects.

From the ridge, the ruts led down into the next shallow valley
toward a cluster of dull tin roofs surrounded by a small stand
of cottonwood trees. I squatted in the high grass, using binoculars to study the farmyard and buildings. The house itself was
a roofed basement whose walls lifted about four feet above the
earth. It was the kind that people built to get started, moving
into the basement and planning—if the floods didn't wash away
the crops or the drought blow them away—to eventually add
a main floor and then maybe a second one, and to rise in the
world with the house.

Apparently, things worked out for the original owners only
enough to justify a peaked roof over the basement and a porch
lined with rusty metal chairs in the shape of seashells. Close to
the house, a blue pickup truck sat in the shade of one of the
trees, and as I watched, a large German shepherd plodded
listlessly toward the house and disappeared under the porch.
Beneath another tree were the shadows of motorcycles, possibly
four or five. From this distance, they looked heavy and fast and
had the bulk of Harleys. On a rise beyond the broken-down
corral, the wide dish of a satellite receiver aimed into the hot
sky. Surrounding the little island of trees and roofs, the dry
prairie stretched bare and vacant. It was a lousy place to live
if you wanted rich, green fields and neighbors close enough to
visit. But it was fine if you were afraid someone might want to
sneak up on you. And a hard one for surveillance if you were
the sneakee. I shot half a dozen pictures with the telephoto just
to prove to myself I'd been here, and then crept back over the
ridge and down to my car.

Driving the dirt section roads that carved the county into
large squares, I circled the farm looking for alternate ap-
proaches. To the north, a tall radio tower flashed its warning
strobes every few seconds to fend off low-flying airplanes, and
farther east—too distant to be heard—I glimpsed the rectangles

of semitrucks gliding up a rise on I-25. After a while, I swung that way and joined the river of traffic back toward Denver, mulling over the problem of surveillance.

I reached the office after lunch. Bunch was in the small cubicle that served as workshop and storage room for his electronic equipment, and he told me he was sketching out a closed-circuit loop system for the Hally Corporation. "That's what they decided on, so what the hell. It's their loss."

It was what we were afraid of—quick work and low profit. "How big's the plant?"

"Just one building. I'll draw up some options, show them the different degrees of protection. But don't be too cut up if they stick with the cheapie." He finished rolling a spool of sensor tape. "What's with the new insurance job?"

I told him about Taylor and the farm, and he nodded glumly. "More squat-and-peek work." Then he perked up. "But, hey, what do you say we try a night gig? That way we can check out the infrared gear. From what you say, it'll be harder than hell to eyeball the place during the day, anyway."

It was as good a plan as any, and it was nice to see him finally eager to do some insurance work. I handed him the list of Taylor's known associates. "See what you can find out from Dave Miller on these people. My guess is some of them have local records."

Bunch glanced over the names and grunted. Dave Miller, of DPD's vice and narcotics section, was Bunch's contact in the police by virtue of being his ex-partner. Miller would do favors for me, but not as readily as he did for Bunch.

"Did you talk to Nestor's co-workers?"

Bunch nodded; he'd been busy while I was up in Erie. "They didn't tell me much more than we already knew. He showed up on Tuesday, worked all day, didn't show up Wednesday."

"He was seen leaving the plant?"

"At four thirty-seven."

"Somebody timed him?"

"No." Bunch glanced at his small notebook. "One Arnold Castillo was getting on his bus and saw Nestor. The bus usually makes its pickup there at four thirty-seven, and the driver swears she was on time that day. Of course, they always say that."

"Nestor rode the bus?"

"He walked. Told people it was for his health, but they think it was to save a few bucks. Poor bastard."

"Did you go over the route?"

"A little under two miles from the plant to his apartment house. At most a forty-five-minute walk each way."

"Anyone along the way notice him?"

"Haven't checked that out yet. I figure I could use a little help."

Why not? I'd spent the morning wandering around the prairie; might as well spend the afternoon wandering around Denver. Detectives walked a lot. "We ought to make another visit to missing persons, too, for Serafina Frentanes," I said.

Bunch paused as I locked the office door. "Oh yeah? Listen, Dev, you got to start cutting back on the charity cases. We won't have time for anything else if you keep that up."

Surveying Nestor's probable route home used what little was left of the afternoon. It didn't take long for folks to look at a photograph and shake their heads no. And much of the route was past the mesh and board fences of light industry or down streets busy with commercial truck and car traffic, so that residents closed the fronts of their small houses against the noise and did most of their living at the back. Bunch and I parked in the shade of the elevated freeway near the apartment building and compared notes.

"Some people remembered seeing him now and then, but nobody could say anything about last Tuesday," he said.

That was the sum of my information, too. "Back to homicide?"

"Might as well start there."

The sergeant who cleared us through the flimsy security gate of the lobby remembered Bunch. "You making a fortune rattling doorknobs now, Bunchcroft?"

"We're helping the citizens of our fair community, Baker. Supporting law and order, protecting the Constitution, safeguarding the flag."

"Yeah. And ripping off people who don't want to show their faces around a police station, right?"

"Helping people in distress, and—believe it or not—doing it for no money."

"Right. I sure believe that."

We went up the oversized elevators to the crimes against persons office. "I never did like that bastard when we worked the same precinct. Always had a smart mouth and nothing to back it up."

"He's making more money than we are."

"A lot of people are doing that, Dev. It doesn't mean they're not bastards."

That was true and left little to argue. The elevator doors slid open to an empty hallway, and we followed it down to the CAP office. The civilian receptionist who handled the evening shift made us wait for Detective Sergeant Kiefer, a stocky man whose horn-rimmed glasses and sweater made him seem more like a college student than a cop. "You say it's a Hispanic female, Dev?"

We knew each other, and that saved a lot of time. Many cops—maybe most—have little affection for private detectives, even those who might bring the answer to a missing persons case or an unidentified corpse. "Serafina Frentanes." I described her and showed Kiefer the photograph. "She's an illegal."

"You check with immigration? Maybe they grabbed her and hustled her back across the border before she dropped the kid."

"Yeah," I lied. "We looked into that. They don't have anything on her." But they would if we brought her to their attention. And on Felix as well.

"Ah. Well, I don't remember a stiff like that. Seven months pregnant—I'd remember something like that."

From what I knew of the man, he remembered every corpse he investigated, and the paper record bore out his statement. Bunch and I rode in silence down the elevator and paused outside Police Administration to look over the surging traffic.

"You think the disappearances are related, Dev?"

"I don't think Nestor and Serafina went off together, if that's what you mean. Nestor would have needed every cent he could grab. Besides, she disappeared before he did."

"Yeah. It doesn't make sense. But it is a coincidence."

And coincidences were suspicious. "Did you ask his employer about the hospital visit?"

"Cut himself on the line. Happens a lot, I guess. All anybody knew, he went back to work that afternoon so he wouldn't lose any hourly. Come on, I'm starved. We'll swing by Warner and then grab something to eat."

The records office clerk at Warner Memorial Hospital was polite but firm: no access to files without authorization by the patient or his designated representative, which in most cases meant either the employer's personnel officer or a representative of the insurance company responsible for verifying treatment and costs.

"Honey, the man's missing. He could be hurt bad or in trouble. We're trying to find him."

"He was properly discharged from this hospital, mister, and don't you call me 'honey.' I don't have to put up with that from you or anybody else!"

"Crap, they're getting touchy." Bunch turned his Bronco onto Colfax Avenue and headed toward Bannock Street and a medium-cheap restaurant we both liked.

"I don't think 'touchy' is the word you want."

"No touch-ee no feel-ee, that's for sure. Damn women's lib."

"Suave is in, Bunch. Neanderthal is out. You should wear your hair long and blow-dried and be sensitive. Glasses would help too."

"Yeah? Next you'll be telling me to take a bath."

"This is September, isn't it?"

"Come on—you know I take one every other Saturday." He led the way into the restaurant. "Change my socks, too, every New Year's."

One of the virtues of the restaurant was its food: another was its prices. But speed of service was something else, even this early in the dinner hour. We managed to get back to the office in time for me to make the last pickup with a special delivery letter to the business office of Warner Memorial Hospital from Kirk and Associates' Medical Underwriters. The ornate letterhead looked satisfyingly impressive—one of an arsenal of Kirk and Associates' supposed endeavors—and the message requested verification of charges and services on one Nestor Calamaro, whose claim was submitted on . . . case number . . . dates of service, etc. I even thoughtfully included a prestamped return envelope for their convenience.

While I did the work, Bunch took time for a jog along the Cherry Creek bike path on his more or less daily run of four or five miles. In my mind's eye, I could see the winding concrete ribbon that meandered along the creek's banks, sheltered by occasional small trees and by the high retaining walls that channeled the course away from the boulevard straddling it and provided mural space for graffiti artists. I should have gone with him; I needed to flush out my system with a good sweat. But instead, I made an appointment to visit Mrs. Chiquichano, owner of the barracks that had housed the two missing people.

She lived in the Bonnie Brae area, a settled neighborhood of formerly medium-priced houses, some of which were now in the several-hundred-thousand-dollar range. Her address was a Tudor cottage with sharply pitched roofs, windows peeking from shaded gables, stucco walls bearing trellises of ivy, and bay windows that reached out to gather in sunshine. A yardful of mature trees brought shade and foliage up to the eaves, and a brick walk wound from the street past a large blue spruce to the front door. It looked like something photographed for *The American Home,* and the house, like the manicured lawn, showed the care of someone with a lot of time to work it or a lot of money to have it done right. Even as I parked and stood a moment looking, a dark-haired woman was finishing up the Cadillac parked in the drive, wiping a chamois across the gleaming black of the long hood and bending to scrub at a speck of something on the chrome hub.

"Mrs. Chiquichano?"

Wordless, she bobbed her head toward the house and silently watched me cross the spongy lawn, go up the walk, and rap with the iron knocker. Another Latin woman finally opened the door. This one, too, was short and had rounded Indian features. "Yes?"

"I'm Devlin Kirk. I called for an appointment to see Mrs. Chiquichano."

"Please to come in. This way, please." The woman led me into the entry and gestured at a living room that was overcrowded with deeply stuffed armchairs, end tables crowded with doodads, lamps shaded with brocades and tassels, heavy, patterned curtains across the windows, a variety of rugs, paintings with florid gilded frames, and even—where space allowed—potted plants that struggled for light in the gloom. The rhythmic, sleepy tick of a large clock echoed sinuously from behind a bamboo chair whose intricate back spread like a peacock tail. "Please to sit down. I will call the madam."

It seemed safer to stay mobile; I stood. A few minutes later, the sound of heels clacked on the occasional strip of wood floor that peeked out at the edges of carpets.

"Mr. Kirk? You said you had important business with me?"

She, too, was short and with her wide face and high cheekbones could have been an older sister of the other women. Older and more responsible and in better command of her English. Hers was a bearing of authority, and she verged on careless scorn when she dismissed the maid who had let me in.

With a quick gesture, she ordered me to a chair. Her hair was pulled back into a knot and held by a pair of long needles. It showed streaks of gray that swept past her ears.

"I'm looking for Nestor Calamaro, and I wonder if you might be able to tell me anything about him." I handed her a business card with its little logo for Kirk and Associates, Industrial Security and Private Investigations.

She wasn't impressed. "About him?"

"If he had any friends—what he did in his spare time. Anything that might give me an idea where he could be."

"What is your interest in this one?"

"His aunt is worried about him. She hired me to look for him." I smiled. "I understand you come from the same village in El Salvador?"

The black eyes stared back without warmth. But beneath the hardness was caution. "Not the same village—the same region. My home was a farm, not a village."

"I understand, too, that Nestor was an illegal immigrant."

She set the card on the gleaming corner of an end table that held a large potted fern, a sparkling ashtray of cut glass, an oval picture frame with what looked like an old sepia wedding photograph, and a ceramic miniature of a shepherd girl with blond hair and a blue frock. "I don't know about that. I rent rooms. I don't have to ask for the documentation to rent rooms."

I nodded at the woman servant, who was pushing a noisy vacuum cleaner down the strip of carpet that led from the front door through the entry. Apparently my shoes had tracked in some dust. "Does she work for you?"

"And I do not have to answer no questions from you, Mr. Kirk."

"No. No, you don't, Mrs. Chiquichano. That's true. And I'm not trying to threaten you. I'm only trying to find a man who disappeared and whose family is worried about him."

"I do not know what happened to him." She stood and I did too.

"Did he owe you any rent when he disappeared?"

For the first time she smiled a bit, a grim clench of cheek that stretched her lips across the unevenness of her teeth. "My boarders pay in advance."

"And you take care of the rest of their money too, is that right?"

"I do not know what you mean." Her hand pushed the air and me toward the door. "I work for my living. I work hard to make my living in this country. I do not know who you talked to, Mr. Kirk, but nobody can say not one evil word about me. I come to this country, I work hard, now I have my business. Many people who don't do so good are jealous of me and they talk, but none of it is true."

"That's fine, Mrs. Chiquichano. It's always good to see the virtues of capitalism rewarded. But a man has disappeared—someone you are familiar with—and you don't seem too curious about where he might have gone."

"It is not strange. Every now and then someone disappears. Especially if they are undocumented. Especially if immigration finds out about them."

"You think that's what happened? Immigration got him?"

"It happens all the time. I told you, I get my rent in advance."

"Have any other people recently disappeared from your apartment house?"

She shook her head. "No."

"But I heard about a woman a month or so ago. I heard you were asking the neighbors about her."

Mrs. Chiquichano's face hardened into something like a Mayan stone carving, and her eyes were equally expressive. "I said no, Mr. Kirk. Good-bye."

"Do you think immigration got her, too?"

The door closed firmly. The woman polishing the Cadillac stopped again to silently watch me walk back to my car. In the rearview mirror, I could see her stare after me as I drove away.

———

Bunch steered the Bronco onto the shoulder of the dirt road and turned off the lights. We sat for a few minutes to let our eyes adjust to the black of empty fields, and gradually we could see that the blackness wasn't quite so absolute. To the west, where Boulder lay against the foothills, a vague glow gave dim silhouette to the nearest rise of earth. Behind us, over Denver, the sky was even lighter. And to the north a string of strobe lights periodically made a tall exclamation point in the night.

"How high you think that radio tower is?" Bunch asked.

I squinted at the blue-white flash of lights. "Oh, just a rough guess: nine hundred ninety-eight feet, three and a quarter inches."

Bunch looked at me.

"I read up on it when I was looking for surveillance sites—it's some kind of experimental tower for the Bureau of Standards. Just under a thousand feet high."

"What kind of experiments?"

"They bounce radio waves off it from Boulder, for one thing. And there's a platform at the top to study air pollution patterns that come up the I-25 corridor."

"You wanted that for surveillance? Man, I definitely would not go to the top of that thing!"

I hoisted the monopod for the telephoto and the battery pack for the night scanner. "They wouldn't let us anyway. And it's pretty secure at night—I checked it out. So we're stuck on the ground."

"Good." Bunch nodded. "A quick trip in, a few shots, a quiet sneak out. That's the civilized way."

We had parked on a section road that, we estimated from the crisp new Geological Survey map, was directly behind the old Wilcox farm and about a mile distant. Bunch took our bearings from an engineer's directional compass, and we crawled between strands of barbed wire and started across the weedy prairie. What had looked smoothly rolling during the day was uneven and rough in the dark, and despite the heavy leather of my hiking boots, I could feel the occasional jab of cactus spines against my ankles. A narrow but deep gully cut a black line at the base of the first hill, and we wandered along its lip in the dark searching for handholds to scale down the bank. Somewhere ahead a coyote gave a quavering bark, and off to the north beyond the flashing tower another answered, three quick yips and a long, dying howl. Once, we stumbled across some bird's nest and the night exploded into startled screeches and a drumming of frantic wings. In the distance down the ravine, a rabbit squealed its life away as an owl or coyote or fox found its supper.

"Should be up here not too far," I said.

Bunch wiped the sweat from his eyes and lifted his cap to welcome the night breeze that brushed across the rise of land. "I don't see any lights yet."

"Won't, until we're almost there. It's in a little valley and surrounded by trees."

"Just one dog?"

"That's all I saw."

"I hate dogs."

We crossed the next low ridge and stumbled downhill and then began climbing again. From the top, I could see the wink of house lights clustered like a handful of sparks in the dark below, and beside me Bunch grunted in satisfaction. "I was beginning to doubt you, Dev."

I had been wondering too; the dark makes time and space different. "That's damned insulting, Bunch. In fact, it hurts deeply."

"Sorry about that." He stood spraddle-legged. "Wait a minute before we move in—got to bleed the old lizard." I heard the splash of urine against the hard earth. "Okay—ready for action."

We moved cautiously down the slope, worried not about being seen but about being heard by the German shepherd, which no doubt cruised the farm when it grew cool enough to move around. Easing to within thirty yards of the farmhouse,

I set up the monopod and camera, and Bunch plugged the battery pack into the infrared scanning device. Through the scope, objects came out of the darkness as pale green silhouettes—a cluster of motorcycles parked under a tree, the same pickup I'd seen earlier, the sides of the house with its illuminated windows and doors like fuzzy black squares in the green. Bunch adjusted the telephoto lens and shot a few pictures of the vehicles and their license plates; then, slowly, we moved the awkward equipment closer to look for people.

"See that dog anywhere?" he asked.

"Not yet."

The farmyard was level and packed and free of weeds and rocks. The remnants of horse smell drifted out of the barn on the mild breeze, and overhead the dry clatter of cottonwood leaves sounded like the patter of a light rain. From the farmhouse came the deep pulse of a stereo, and an occasional figure moved past the stubby, unshaded windows that ended just above ground level.

"See Taylor?"

"Can't see much of anybody yet."

"Maybe the dog's inside."

"Just keep that can of dog repellent handy," I said.

A spring creaked and the back door slapped as a female figure came up to ground level to toss something from a basin into the dirt behind the house, her gestures a ragged movement of blurry green in the scope. Then the door creaked and slapped again. Bunch and I, camera ready, eased up to the house through a pale blue glow thrown by the mercury vapor light high on its pole. Crawling to the window ledge, I shot a quick series of pictures of the room, catching a bearded man sprawled on a couch and staring numbly at the flicker of television. Another, whose beard was cropped close to his face, tilted a beer can. In the background, a woman with stringy hair wearing a loose Mother Hubbard dress hauled a baby across the room on her hip and said something to one of the men, who might have been Taylor. Unfortunately, the photograph would also show that he wasn't moving and actively able.

"Shit, Dev, look out!"

Behind me, with a single deep bark, the German shepherd bounded from the darkness around the barn and raced through the steely gleam of the farm light. I ran from the window and sprinted hard toward Bunch, who threw a stick at the dog and then sprayed a cloud of repellent toward its open mouth. I heard a voice shout something, and a door banged open to the sound of running boots.

"This way, Dev."

I dashed toward Bunch's voice, the dog barking crazily now and whining and trying to run after me even as it stumbled to rub its eyes and muzzle and writhe in the dirt. Behind its contorted shadow, a smaller one zipped fast along the ground, legs blurred with speed.

"Watch it, Bunch!"

"Oh, shit—" He held the spray can out behind him as he ran, knees lifting high to pull his legs away from the almost silent lunge of jaws. "Oh God, I hate dogs!"

I grabbed the monopod and night scope and raced up the ridge. Bunch labored behind with the power pack and cameras. The can sputtered into an empty hiss, and he swore and threw it hard at the feinting shadow at his heels and swung the battery case by its strap, trying to hit the dog. From the porch of the farmhouse, the heavy boom of a shotgun spurted flame our way, and I heard something angry whistle overhead. I ducked and plunged across the ridge and then down and up the gully on the other side, scarcely aware that Bunch was cursing and struggling after me.

On the other side, I paused and saw him dragging one leg as he ran. From that leg hung a small form almost horizontal to the ground, flopping with each long stride.

"Bunch, you have a passenger!"

"Laugh, damn you, Kirk! Just keep laughing, goddamn you!"

"Kick him loose."

"I can't—it's a pit bull!"

"Hold it, Bunch—hold up." I kicked the dog hard in its ribs, and it coughed twice and chewed deeper.

"Owww! Quit it—you're making him mad!"

"Hold still!" Jamming the leg of the monopod at the back of its jaws, I twisted the animal's mouth open, and Bunch yanked his leg away. The dog growled and swung after me, the teeth a rip of white against the black earth.

"Bunch, where the hell are you going?"

"I ain't staying here!"

He was gone, leaving me to back away from the snarling dog, which sprayed saliva and blood as it rushed to get past the sharp monopod leg and make acquaintance with my own. "Bunch!" I jabbed at the dog's chest and it yelped, pulling back, and I charged after it. The animal turned into the dark and I did too, running under the weight of the equipment and hearing a growling breath circle around me. Wheeling once more, I held the dog at bay as I stumbled backward and dueled with its teeth. "Bunch, you son of a bitch, help me with the goddamn fence!"

"Nobody helped me."

"I'll dump this crap. So help me God, I'll leave all this stuff!"

In the distance behind one of the long, dark ridges, I heard the snarl of motorcycles like hornets swarming from a nest. Bunch pulled the Bronco down into the ditch and up close to the fence and leaned out the window to grab the gear.

"Not the monopod—not yet!"

"Christ, I hate dogs."

I jumped on the aluminum running board and made a last savage jab at the rabid-looking beast, feeling the metal leg hit something that resulted in a very satisfying yelp. "Go—goddamn!"

He did, the vehicle rocking up on one side as he floored the gas and surged across the ditch and onto the gravel road. Behind, blinded by dust and falling farther and farther back into hazy darkness, the pit bull tried for one last bite of me or the tire or anything else it could sink those jaws into.

"Stop a minute, Bunch! Let me get in—hold up, goddamn it!"

He slammed on the brakes and I scrambled in, tossing equipment and looking back for the snap of teeth. "Okay—go!"

"Did you get the battery pack?"

"No—you had it."

"I put it on the hood. Damn thing must have fallen off."

A line of bobbing headlights crested a ridge in the black far behind us and dropped out of sight. "Can't go back, Bunch. Here come the boys."

"Shit." He lurched the Bronco forward, and we drove without lights and peered through the dark for the next section road that would lead back toward I-25.

"That goddamn dog still chasing us?" Bunch used the gears rather than the brakes to slow for the hard turn.

"Yes," I said without looking. I didn't have to look.

"Dogs!" He reached down and groped around at something below the dash.

"Will you watch the road, Bunch! You're doing sixty miles an hour without lights!"

"I'm watching. My goddamn leg's chewed halfway to the bone and hurts like a bastard."

"I hope the dog wasn't rabid."

"He wasn't. Just high on crack. Damn, that hurts. Goddamn dog bites really hurt."

We scratched from the gravel onto pavement, and Bunch flicked on the headlights and stepped harder on the gas. At the next intersection, we turned onto a county highway and slowed to blend with the occasional car or pickup truck. A few minutes later, a pair of motorcycles came up fast, and we watched in the rearview mirrors as they rode beside each car for a few seconds to check it out and then speeded up to the next.

"Duck down—they're looking for two people."

I slid into the darkness beneath the dash, my knees tight against my chest. The rattle of engines pulled up to the driver's side and hung there for a long time. I saw Bunch glance toward them, and his hand hovered over the Python Magnum slung in its holster riveted beside the steering column. Then the engines revved and the bikes pulled away.

"Two of them," he said. "They split up to go both ways on the highway."

"You're getting blood all over the floor mats."

"Like to have that dog's guts all over the mats." He muttered something else.

"What?"

"I said it's too bad about the battery pack."

"I'm not going to complain about the cost, Bunch."

"That's not the problem."

"What's that?"

"It has our name on it."

4

The reason the battery pack had our name on it was that Bunch couldn't bear the thought of losing one of his toys. When I reminded him that we were on an operation and it wasn't wise to have traceable goodies, he reminded me that I'd said there was only one dog. "I mean we weren't exactly planning to haul ass like that, were we?" Maybe they wouldn't find it, he said. If they did, maybe they wouldn't associate it with the snoop on the farmhouse, he said. I said maybe we could go back and get it. There were a lot of maybes but, he said, that wasn't one of them—not in the dark, not with that pit bull waiting, and not as sore as his leg was. In fact, the doctor at the hospital's emergency room wanted to start rabies shots immediately.

"No way!" Bunch pulled himself to a sitting position on the examining table and started fumbling at the hospital gown. "No way are you going to stick me in the belly with a goddamn needle!"

The doctor, eyes wide behind thick glasses, looked up at the towering man and backed out of reach. "It doesn't have to be right away—we can wait a little. Can you bring in the dog? You won't need the shots if we know the dog's not rabid."

"He wasn't rabid, just pissed off. Tell him, Dev."

"He looked rabid to me." I smiled at the doctor. "Of course, it was real dark."

"Dev—"

"Mr. Bunchcroft, rabies is a very serious disease and it can be fatal. The health department will need to observe the animal for ten days to be certain it wasn't rabid." He pulled off his rubber gloves and tossed them in a can. "If the dog isn't available, you should start postexposure treatment as soon as possible, for your own safety."

"How soon you need that damn dog?"

"Certainly within the next twenty-four hours."

He was still limping the next morning, but a night's rest and a long soak in Epsom salts had taken the infection from the leg and even a lot of the soreness. Now he felt ready to do a little work. His first chore was to show Drayton Coe the plans for installing the cheapest alarm system in the Hally building. He would also show Coe the more expensive alternatives, advising a central reporting system that used long-range radio. The combination of a local alarm and a radio-based central reporting system would give the best, if most expensive, security. And perhaps Coe might like such options as emergency call buttons installed at strategic locations to provide backup for the night watchmen.

"While I'm out, I'll swing by and talk to some of Mrs. Chiquichano's friends and neighbors."

"What for?"

"Wouldn't you like to know why she lied to us about Serafina's disappearance?"

A whiff of mendacity was usually the odor of something hidden, and Bunch was right to follow established procedures to investigate the woman. But other things were more important. "You're going to do that after you see Coe, right?"

"Right, Dev—absolutely right. Always money before pleasure." He limped out, a satchel of equipment bumping against the door frame.

I turned to my morning's business—running the initial report on Taylor through the word processor. I left out the most exciting—if embarrassing—elements and was doing the printout when I had a telephone call from an Agent Roybal of the U.S.

Immigration and Naturalization Service. He verified who I was and said, "Just a moment please."

"Senor Kirk? It's me—Felix Frentanes. You remember me?"

"Sure. Have they picked you up, Felix?"

"Yes. They let me make use of the *teléfono*. You can come now, yes?"

"Yes, certainly. Where are you?"

"Momentito, por favor."

Agent Roybal's voice came back and told me the address of the INS detention facility. It was in Aurora, just east of Stapleton Airport. "Are you his employer, Mr. Kirk?"

"No. Just a friend."

"If you want to visit him, better hurry. We'll be shipping him to Texas this afternoon."

"I'm on my way."

Felix was very apologetic when I saw him, but—more—he was worried. His anxiety made his Spanish rattle faster than I could understand, and I had to keep telling him to slow down, until he finally settled into a mixture of languages. We sat in an interview room, institutionally bleak and stripped of anything that might be used as a weapon or a tool. The decorations were Justice Department signs warning in Spanish and English that damaging government property would result in fines or imprisonment or both. The man smoked nervously and flicked the ashes into the small cardboard dish serving as a tray. "My wife, Senor Kirk—have you found anything?"

"Not yet. We're still looking and asking questions, Felix." I reminded him, "It's only been a day, and these things can take a long time."

He nodded, eyes sad and focused on the tip of his cigarette. From the compound outside came a garbled squawk of loudspeakers, and from a boom box somewhere down a corridor the bouncing jangle of *ranchera* music. "I don't know . . . I don't know . . ." He sucked hard enough to make the tobacco crackle and flicked the ash again.

"Don't know what, Felix?"

"Maybe I should not have asked you for help, Senor Kirk. These people will maybe send me to Mexico." He shrugged and smiled. "They think I'm Mexican. But the Mexicans will know I'm not." He inhaled again. "Maybe they'll just let me go. Maybe they'll send me back to El Salvador." He rubbed thumb and forefinger together. "It depends on how much they want."

"Do you need—?"

"No, senor, *muchas gracias*. It's just it could be a long time before I can get back. My wife . . . the baby . . ."

"Give me an address in El Salvador, Felix. If they do send you all the way down, at least I can write you if we find out something."

He smiled ruefully. "You have to write it for me—I don't know how."

I copied the name of his village and a priest's name to send letters to. Felix said the village was in a war zone and he hoped it was still there, and he hoped he wouldn't be sent there— young men were arrested and put in the army as soon as they stepped off the plane in San Salvador. But it was the best we could come up with. That and my business card, which he carefully tucked into a worn cloth wallet. "Can't you petition to stay, Felix? Claim refugee status?"

Another small smile. "It wouldn't do any good—and besides, I don't have money for the lawyer. This way, they don't know I'm Salvadoran. Maybe I'll be lucky. Maybe they'll just take me across the line and let me go."

"Does your wife know anyone at all in Denver that she might get in touch with? Any names at all?"

"No one. Just Senora Chiquichano. But that woman is why I'm here."

"What's that?"

"How else does *la migra* know? They come to the plant, they ask for me by name and for my green card. Now my employer, he must pay many dollars in fines because I don't have the permission. If I get back here, he will not hire me again."

Frentanes shook his head. "How else do they know about me? Who else would tell them?"

I thought that over. "Was it because I asked about Serafina?"

"Yes, of course." He picked at the crumpled cigarette butt. "But she will pay too—that woman. A little, anyway."

"*La patrona?*"

"*Sí.* No more . . ." He shrugged, unable to find the American word. "*Mordida.*"

"Graft? Take?"

"Take—*sí.* She takes from my pay fifteen percent for finding me the job. Now no more fifteen percent."

"Every month?"

He nodded. "And maybe no *propina* from the boss for the one who replaces me." He saw my puzzlement and explained. "I think the boss pays *la patrona* for getting us. She's a . . . *cazadora de cabezas,* you understand?"

"Headhunter? She brings in workers for other employers?"

A tilt of the head. "I think so, yes. She told me the job waited for me. That's why we came here, Serafina and me. The apartment, the job, the medical approval—all in order for when I get here."

"What's the medical approval?"

"*El doctor.* The examination for working with food, you know?" He fished in that frayed wallet to show me a carefully folded form that certified Felix Frentanes was medically qualified to work in food processing. An illegible signature rode over an inked stamp that said "Associated Medical Pavilion" and bore a date several months old.

"Did you work at the Apple Valley Turkeys plant with Nestor Calamaro?"

The man looked a bit shamefaced as he nodded. "But we don't know each other real good—*la patrona* doesn't want us to know each other. She said it's best that way if *la migra* gets somebody, then they can't tell about the others."

"Mrs. Chiquichano arranged for the medical exam?"

"Yes."

"But nothing for Serafina?"

"No. *La patrona* knows *una partera* . . . a . . ."

"Midwife?"

"*Sí.* But it wasn't time to call her yet." He stared down and shook his head. "I want to find my wife. I need your help to find her. Now, maybe, I might never find her. If she was sent to Mexico . . ." He looked up and wiped quickly at a wet spot that had dropped onto the oily compound of the tabletop. "The Mexican police—what they do to us foreigners from the south! Especially the women."

"Do you think immigration picked her up already?"

"I can't ask. What if they haven't? Then they know she's here, and they look for her." He inhaled deeply again and stubbed out another butt. "Just like she would not telephone me if she had been caught. She would protect me too."

"You didn't tell *la migra* about Senora Chiquichano?"

"No! The others at the apartment, they would be picked up— if immigration learns about *la patrona,* she will tell them about all the others. You must not tell them either!"

The law, which was supposed to protect citizens, was, for someone who wasn't a citizen, simply another avenue of extortion. But Felix didn't need to be told that. We wished each other good luck, and the black warden led him down the pale green hallway toward the security fence that closed off the distance. Tall and broad-shouldered in a tailored khaki uniform, the warden dwarfed the smaller figure whose bowed legs moved rapidly to keep up with the long strides of his guard.

Agent Roybal waited for me in the receiving room. "Step into my office, Mr. Kirk." I did, and it wasn't coffee and doughnuts he offered but my Miranda rights. "Anything you say can and will be used against you in a court of law."

"What the hell for?"

"Aiding and abetting an illegal foreign national. You're looking at five years in the pokey, mister. And a twenty-thousand-dollar fine."

"Wait a minute—he didn't tell me he was here illegally. And

just what kind of aiding and abetting am I supposed to be doing?"

"I think you're a coyote, Mr. Kirk. I think you're one of these people who make their living providing illegal workers to employers. And I think Felix Frentanes can be convinced to tell us all about you if we don't send him back to El Salvador."

"How do you know he's not Mexican?"

Roybal didn't hide his disgust at the question. "I've been in this business for fifteen years, Mr. Kirk." Then he smiled, the whiteness of his teeth contrasting with the glossy black of a thick mustache. But there was little cheer in the sight. "And, Mr. Kirk, I think I've got you by the balls."

"I only met the man yesterday."

"That's what you say. We'll see what he says."

"You've warned me of my rights, Agent Roybal. Does that mean you're putting me under arrest? I want to have this clearly stated: You are arresting me for visiting a detained illegal alien who telephoned me with your permission and—with your prior knowledge—asked me to come down here to talk to him. Is that right?"

The man's brown eyes studied mine. To stop me for questioning, to use the Miranda to try and frighten me—that was one thing. But to make the legal move of actual arrest with all its related laws governing due process and entrapment was something else.

"Be damned sure you want to do this, Agent Roybal. Because a false arrest charge won't look good on your record."

"You're, by God, threatening me?"

It was my turn to smile. "I'm explaining the ramifications of what you're trying to do. Any lawyer can see the possibilities of entrapment and false arrest in this. Of course, you will be called as a witness at the trial and asked to state your probable cause for my arrest. And we both know you have none. Now, am I under arrest?"

The man leaned back in his chair, and I could see the deep anger that comes when arrogance of office is denied. His plan, so clear and effective at the outset, had suddenly been muddied and snarled by an uncooperative prey.

"Just what the hell is your relationship with Frentanes, Mr. Kirk?"

"I'm a private investigator. He asked me to find his wife." I added, "Nobody needs a green card to talk to a PI."

"When was this?"

I told him. "She was seven months pregnant—eight, now. Frentanes is worried that when he gets shipped south, he'll never see her again."

"He knew the risks—they both did when they sneaked into the country."

"It's the man's pregnant wife, Agent Roybal. And you know why they came here."

"I hear a lot of sad stories, Mr. Kirk. But my job is to catch them and send them back. And to pop anybody who aids and abets them while they're here." He leaned forward on his desk, heavy shoulders pushing his collar up around a thick neck. "Now, why don't you just tell me the fucking truth and stop crapping around. You do this on commission, don't you? You deliver people for employers to hire, don't you? You get so much for each body you deliver and a cut of the chicken's paycheck, don't you?"

Deliberately I pulled out my wallet and showed him my PI identification card. In Colorado that doesn't mean much, because the state doesn't have a licensing program for the business. But it did look impressive and it did say I was a member in good standing of the Private Investigators Association and the World Association of Detectives. "Check the Yellow Pages, Roybal. And the DPD. Here." I tossed him a business card. "Call my office; check with my landlord and see how many years I've been renting an office; check with my bank and see how long I've had an account. Hell, if you're not going to believe what I tell you, then you go out and do it the hard way."

He rested his chin on a meaty fist as he stared at me another few seconds. Then he scratched a thumb in the bristles under his jaw. "What did you find out about her?"

"Nothing, yet."

It was an answer he seemed to expect. "That woman is an illegal alien too, Kirk. It's your duty as a citizen to notify the Immigration and Naturalization Service if you know her whereabouts."

"Is that how you found Felix? A citizen did his duty?"

The brown eyes narrowed again. "No. An anonymous tip. It happens all the time—some illegal gets pissed off at another illegal or owes him money, they drop a dime." He added, "And then the deportee scrambles around with his coyote to cover his job until he can sneak back, Mr. Kirk. Or makes arrangements for his wife and kids to hide out while he's gone."

"I don't know where Frentanes' wife is, Agent Roybal. I don't have any leads at all. She simply disappeared. For all I know, you people have already rounded her up and deported her."

He kicked back in his chair, and swiveled to a computer terminal, and punched in a code. "Frentanes. First name?"

"Serafina."

"Date of birth?"

"She's around twenty, maybe eighteen, and she disappeared about a month ago." Felix wouldn't like it, but *la migra* either had her or they didn't, and there was only one way to find out. If they'd already arrested her, it made no difference if I spilled her name. If they hadn't, then it was up to me to find her before they did.

Roybal scrolled a series of names across the screen and then shook his head. "We didn't process her, not in the last two months anyway. You have a physical description?"

I gave him as much as I knew and he searched another file, this one shorter. "No local hospital or morgue filings either. Did you check with the police?"

"Yeah. No Jane Doe matching her description." I was

tempted to mention Nestor's name, too, but thought better of it. The agent already suspected me of running a smuggling operation; no sense letting him know I had wider acquaintance among the illegals.

Roybal shut off the terminal and swung back. "Maybe she got tired of her old man and went off on her own."

"She was seven months pregnant."

"These things happen. My wife, she gets a little nuts around six months." He stood, signaling an end to the interview. "There's a whole anonymous population out there—nobody knows how many thousands of people live out of sight totally undocumented. Until they end up in jail or a hospital or we find them, they stay that way." Opening the door, he nodded for me to leave. "Well, Mr. Kirk, I may or may not believe what you've told me, but you believe this: If you find that woman and if you in any way help her to avoid arrest, you're going to jail. No ifs, ands, or buts, mister, you are going to jail. Is that clear?"

It was clear. What wasn't clear was where Serafina went and just how I was to find a missing person who had no official existence anywhere.

The afternoon sun lay in a warm arc on the floor of the office. I lowered the venetian blinds and tilted them against the glare before listening to the answering machine. The first voice was a crisp reminder about an overdue bill and made polite mention of ruined credit ratings and collection agencies. That was all Kirk and Associates needed: a knock on the door from one of our competitors whose life was brightened by chasing dead-beats. Vinny Landrum. With my luck, the skip-trace would be good old Vinny, who qualified as a PI because his immediate family spent a total of five hundred years in prison. I wrote out a check, calculating it would arrive at the bank one day after the retainer from Security Underwriters.

There weren't many other calls. A few people wanted to give us something for nothing: the chance for a free car, a trip to

Aspen to see time-share condos, a six-months free subscription. This last was a computer voice that must have made a conquest of my answering machine because the whole spiel was taped. Only one caller was a potential client. He wanted an estimate for debugging his office. I wrote that one out for the firm's electronics genius, Bunch. There were also several calls that left no message and clicked into silence at the end of the tape.

I had three months left on my health club membership, which stood a very good chance of not being renewed. There was no sense wasting it. And even less sense sitting around a silent office. Besides, I and the Healey both needed a workout, and it was a pleasure to lower the ragtop and have a little fun going through the gears and letting the pipes rap against the closed glass of the air-conditioned cars we wove among. The body of the Healey 3000 showed filigrees of rust holes, but beneath the hood, a Cinderella of gleaming chrome and polished aluminum charm purred sweetly. The twin carburetors demanded a lot of tinkering to keep them in sync—all SUs did—but when they were tuned, they were very, very tuned, and the smooth, head-snapping acceleration that came from a light jab on the gas pedal made it worth the time.

Susan, Bunch's girlfriend, used to say the Healey was my surrogate for female companionship, and I had come to realize that it would have been better if that had been so. Because the way things turned out, Susan was dead, and Bunch still hadn't gotten over it. But that had been a couple years ago, and neither Bunch nor I talked about it anymore. Not that we talked much about it then. As Uncle Wyn told Bunch at the time, the ones you love live on in your heart, and you have them with you always. He didn't have as much consolation for me—the one I had loved lived on in the women's state pen, and all I had left in my heart was a bitterness and sense of betrayal I was still trying to get rid of. And gradually I was managing to. I learned that I couldn't let someone like that influence the rest of my life; she had her shot at it once and that was enough. But sometimes, alone with the wind whistling across the cockpit and the rumble of the exhaust stirring memories of our good times in the Healey, I wondered what it might have been like.

Boring.

That's what it would have been like. As boring and colorless as the cars we threaded among, and I was a lot better off by myself and doing what I wanted. Such as worrying about the future of Kirk and Associates. Such as sweating a stack of bills on the office desk. Such as thinking like a goddamn accountant. Maybe it wouldn't have been all that different after all. But— and I shifted down to make the turn from Cherry Creek Drive onto Colorado Boulevard—it made no difference now. As Uncle Wyn had said, that ball game was over. It didn't pay, he said, to lie there in the dark and play over and over the errors of a game that was already in the record books. It was something that had cost him a lot of sleep when he was a young catcher; but none of it did a damn bit of good once the umpire tossed the first ball for the next game.

Not that he would say life was fun and games—a cliché like that sent Uncle Wyn's eyes rolling up until only their whites showed. But there was some truth for him in the idea of ending a thing with the neatness of a final inning. And telling yourself you could begin over with the scoreboard empty and waiting. It was a truth he tried hard to convince me of, anyway.

Midafternoon was a good time to work out at the health club, a remodeled supermarket that had been expanded to include a swimming pool and saunas as well as the usual arrangement of exercise machines. Most of the clientele wouldn't arrive until after working hours, and those who were there tended to be models trying to stay in shape between gigs. Their shiny Lycra stretched where it should stretch, and their ponytails bobbed saucily as they ran around the indoor track. It sure beat watching television while you pumped iron, and it was sad to think all this might end in a few weeks.

Bunch was waiting by the time I returned. "That tall blonde— was she there?"

"Oh, yeah! Wearing this new skintight silver thing that just . . . wow!"

"You're telling me she wasn't there."

He was right; she wasn't. "What about the Hally job? What'd they decide on?"

"Nothing, yet. Coe said he'd call us in a day or two."

"You showed him all the options?"

"Yes, Dev. I showed him all the options. And the prices. And the benefits of going with the better equipment. But I don't think he was impressed. The guy's cheap, that's all."

Well, I hadn't really counted on any money coming from that direction anyway. "What about Senora Chiquichano's friends?"

"I don't think she's got any." He lurched out of the swivel chair and limped over to lean on the wrought-iron rail that guarded the lower half of the window. The traffic below in Wazee Street was heavy and loud with the day's final deliveries, trucks returning to their garages, commuters taking shortcuts to and from the Valley Highway. Bunch closed the glass air panel against the noise. "Her neighbors don't know much about her. She moved into the place maybe a year ago. Stays by herself, doesn't cause any problems, keeps the house and grounds very neat. She didn't return the visits a couple people made to welcome her to the neighborhood. She's self-employed."

"Doing what?"

"Runs a small-time janitorial service—Olympia Janitorial—and my guess is she uses a crew of illegals and pays them maybe fifty cents an hour and all the cigarette butts they can carry. One of the neighbors figures she has plenty of money because there's always somebody working around the place—doing the yard, washing her car, handyman stuff. And she has a maid who lives in. That's it."

"That's it? She doesn't have any extra income from somewhere?"

"Aside from her apartment building? If she did, I'd know

about it. I checked out the realtor who sold the house. She says Chiquichano financed her loan through Citizen's Bank and Trust and paid a third down with a certified check. The people at Citizen's wouldn't give me any information from her loan application—said it was confidential."

"We can fix that." I thumbed through the stationery file for the Kirk and Associates Credit Service letterhead. Professional courtesy between moneylenders opened a lot of doors.

Bunch went on. "Public records lists her as the sole owner of the place where Frentanes lives, and they say she's paid her taxes and assessments."

"Lived. Felix doesn't live there anymore."

"What's that mean?"

I told him and he stared at me for a long moment, putting things together. "Felix thinks Mrs. Chiquichano turned him in to immigration?"

"It makes sense. It's a good way to get rid of him, and it happened just after we talked to her about Serafina."

"But we didn't say Felix told us. Maybe we found out from some of the people who live near the apartment—people she asked about Serafina."

"And maybe that's what she told Felix she did. Maybe she and Felix were the only two who knew Serafina was missing."

He grunted. "She lies to you about Serafina. Now she gets rid of Felix. Why?"

"Why indeed."

Bunch, restless and hobbling, went to the brick wall and leaned stiff-armed against it to do slow, one-armed presses while he pondered. "I'm beginning to get the feeling, Dev. I think we should have another talk with Mrs. Gutierrez."

"Not so fast. Did you see that note about the guy who wants a debugging estimate?"

"Yeah. I already called him. I go by tomorrow to take a look at his office."

On the way over to talk to Nestor's aunt, we discussed last

night's adventure and the possibility of recovering the battery pack. "Heard anything from the bikers yet?"

"No," I said. "Some anonymous calls on the recorder, but that could be anyone."

"Probably didn't find it. It's probably still there in the ditch."

"How's the leg?"

"Stiff and bruised, but no infection. I'm not worried about rabies."

"It's supposed to take a few days to show up."

"How do you know?"

"I did some reading on it. Two, three days from now, after the wound starts to heal, bam! Then it's the needle in the belly routine."

"I hate needles worse than I hate dogs."

"Then we'd better make some plans," I said.

"I'll think about it," he said.

Mrs. Gutierrez was in her forties, stocky, with glossy black hair and high cheekbones that showed a strong mixture of Indian. The hair, braided and then twisted up into a tight coil, showed no gray yet; and despite the worry in her eyes when we spoke of Nestor and Serafina and Felix, her face had the plumpness and color of good health. Bunch and I towered over the woman so much that we both had to be careful not to step on her. When she offered us a seat on the overstuffed couch facing the large television screen, we sat with relief.

"I wrote to his mother in case he went home, but she thought he was still up here." From an end table, she lifted a flimsy air letter bright with foreign stamps. "They've heard nothing from him. They're very worried."

"Is it possible he and Serafina Frentanes went away together, Mrs. Gutierrez?"

She gave that some thought, half listening to the sounds of children that filtered through the thin walls of the tiny house. Then the tight coil shook no. "I don't think he even knew her. He never mentioned anyone who lived there except Senor Medina—the man who lives across the hall. They talked a lot about El Salvador. They played cards sometimes." She added, "Besides, Nestor has a sweetheart in Ibarutú. Maria Cristina. He was always talking about her—how long it would be before he had enough money to return and buy a farm and marry her, how long the war would last, whether he should bring her to the States." The head shook again. "He would not go with another woman, I'm sure."

"We didn't think so, Mrs. Gutierrez," said Bunch. "It's just something we have to ask."

"I understand, but it's impossible." She went into a long amplification of what she'd said, describing the relationship between Nestor's family and that of his intended. Maria Cristina Quiroga, whose line was related to Nestor's by the marriage of his great-great-aunt to her great-great-uncle. "And besides, Nestor was very much worried about finding another job if he was fired from this one for not having the papers. He was working very hard to earn enough money so when things get better in El Salvador, he can go back and buy a farm. He just wouldn't up and leave a good job."

Bunch broke in. "What can you tell us about Mrs. Chiquichano?"

"Ah, that woman!" Mrs. Gutierrez settled back in the armchair with its patches of crocheted doilies. "She's not from Ibarutú, I can tell you that. Her family lived on a ranch somewhere up in the mountains, and the only time they ever saw civilization was once or twice a year when they made the trip down for a saint's day. They were poor—even for El Salvador, they were poor. But look at her now!"

She went on to describe Mrs. Chiquichano—born Hernandes—as a girl, growing up in feed sack dresses and shoeless as a chicken until she was in her teens. If the woman had any schooling at all up in those godforsaken mountains, it was only what little someone in the family could provide or what she could learn herself. There were rumors about her chastity or lack of it too, but then, those country girls were often treated like animals, so if they acted that way it was only to be expected, and Mrs. Gutierrez didn't even want to think of what might have gone on. But when she was sixteen, she was given in marriage to Senor Chiquichano, a friend of her father's and even older by a handful of years. His death during one of those quick, violent raids by either the army or the guerrillas left the young widow on her own. She quickly sold the property left by her husband and, wearing straw sandals and carrying her only pair of shoes in a plastic bag, boarded a bus headed north. Somehow she got her immigration papers and ended up in Denver, writing once a year to her family and sending occasional photographs of her car, her house, herself in the finest clothes. It was her success, in fact, that led many from Ibarutú and the surrounding province to come to Denver, including the younger Mr. and Mrs. Gutierrez.

"She rents rooms only to people from El Salvador?"

"I think so. You understand how it is—people when they first come north are very, very frightened. Especially"—she hesitated and looked from me to Bunch—"especially if they are undocumented. I'm sure many of those rooming there are undocumented. Like Nestor."

"She knows this?" Bunch asked.

"Of course. That's how she makes her money."

"You mean she charges them extra?"

"Yes." And to provide them their false Social Security numbers so they could get the jobs, which she also arranged for. And to cash their paychecks when they lacked identification. Senora Chiquichano was a legal immigrant, and the others huddled behind the aegis of her legality—for a fee. Mrs. Gutierrez looked down at her hands with their tightly intertwined fingers. "I wanted Nestor to stay with us—my husband and I both asked him to. But he said no. He said he wouldn't want to make our home any smaller than it already is. And there was the problem of the danger."

"How's that?"

"Immigration. If we were caught with him living here, we could go to jail or be deported."

"Wouldn't Mrs. Chiquichano be deported too?" asked Bunch.

"Yes. That's why she charges so much, she says: to pay for the risk she's in."

The risk wasn't all that great—the courts would have to prove she knew they were illegals, and no law required landlords to ask their renters for documentation. Ironically, the Gutierrezes were in greater danger by being relatives of the illegal than someone like Chiquichano, who exploited them but could claim ignorance of their status. "Can't they rent a room somewhere else?" I asked.

The woman's rounded shoulders rose and fell. "They're afraid to trust anyone else, Mr. Kirk. Maybe someone else would demand even more. She's greedy but at least she speaks their language and knows their people. She's from their country. To frightened people, that means a lot."

"How much did Nestor pay?"

"Most of what he made. She gave him forty dollars a week from his paycheck for personal expenses and savings."

He netted around two hundred a week, I remembered, which meant he was paying as much as six forty a month for the closet-sized cubicle. Bunch and I had talked to about twenty occupants, and if the rents were comparable, then the income from that dump of an apartment house came to over twelve thousand dollars a month. Most if not all of which would be unreported to IRS, and little of which went back as property taxes or overhead. Add to that the other fees the woman extorted or any additional roomers we had missed, and that run-down rabbit warren suddenly began to look like a gold mine.

"No wonder she can afford a couple maids and a gardener."

Bunch shook his head. "I bet she doesn't pay them."

Mrs. Gutierrez nodded. "Nestor told me—she brought two women into the country from a farm up near her father's place.

She promised to teach them English and give them a place to stay if they work for her for five years. She does the same to get workers for her cleaning business."

"A fine old American tradition: bond servants."

"Sounds more like slavery to me," said Bunch.

"Is she bringing many more people from Ibarutú to Denver?"

"I don't know, Mr. Kirk. The village—" The shoulders lifted and fell again. "Ibarutú's in the guerrilla zone now. The government's trying to move everybody out of there, so they don't protect them from the rebels anymore. The rebels take food and money from the people and shoot them. So there aren't many people left in the village now." She added, "But a lot of people want to get out of El Salvador, and a lot of people know about Senora Chiquichano."

Which was why they suffered and why they paid what they did to Mrs. Chiquichano and others. And why they would protect the exploiters who might, even for such a price, save the family members who were still down there. What was money for if you weren't alive to spend it? Still, Nestor was worth about six thousand a year to his landlady, and unless she found another illegal willing to be extorted, Mrs. Chiquichano would have a hard time renting that cracker box room for six forty a month. Add to that the loss of income from Felix and Serafina, and you were talking a healthy pocketful of change each month. "Felix Frentanes was picked up by immigration at work this morning. He thinks Mrs. Chiquichano tipped them off about him."

"Ah." Her head nodded emphatically. "It's something that woman would do."

"How do you know?"

"She tells them—she told Nestor if he didn't pay what she asked, if he made a disturbance or drew attention to himself or started getting too friendly with strangers, she would make a telephone call. She said she had friends in *la migra,* and all she had to do was make one telephone call. He would be arrested. Like that!"

"She's a real barracuda," said Bunch.

"*Vinchuca*," said Mrs. Gutierrez.

"What?"

"Nestor said they call her *la vinchuca*—it's an insect that sucks people's blood while they sleep. Very poisonous."

On the way out to the car, I asked Bunch why *la patrona* would be willing to turn in somebody like Felix who was so happy to pay so much.

"A couple reasons, maybe. She can replace him easily, or somebody's willing to pay more for that rathole of a room."

"She was already out Nestor's rent. Then she turned in Felix. That adds up to at least twelve thousand a year loss, plus what she loses on skimming from the paychecks."

"She must have a waiting list."

"Or maybe Felix represented a danger that could cost her a lot more if she didn't get rid of him fast," I said.

"What the hell kind of danger would somebody like Felix be?"

"He keeps asking questions about his wife. He brought us in."

"Yeah." His little finger dug at something in his ear. "The wife that Mrs. Chiquichano says isn't missing." Bunch squeezed into the Healey's seat and cursed both the car and its owner under his breath. "We're back to that again, aren't we?"

We were. But the only thing that was clear about what we had come back to was that Mrs. Chiquichano seemed to be some kind of focal point of questions about a faintly possible link between Serafina and Nestor. "You want to get something to eat before we drive up to Erie?"

The sun was about fifteen minutes above the wall of mountains when Bunch guided the Bronco slowly down the road we had raced across the night before. We searched for telltale signs of disruption in the loose dirt along the weedy ditch.

"Is that the place?" Bunch pointed to a freshly scraped stretch of berm.

"If it is, I don't see the battery pack."

He got out and walked back and forth, peering into the ditch, then climbed back in. "I don't think it's the right place. I think the hill was steeper."

"Maybe we should just look for that pit bull."

"And maybe we can run over the son of a bitch."

"Naw, he'd just rip the tires off."

I asked, "Are we going to snatch the dog?"

"Goddamn it, I don't have rabies!" He stopped the car again. "Besides, I'm working on it." Getting out, he studied the torn earth and looked around at the prairie and the fencing beside the gravel road. "This has to be the place, Dev. There's where I drove into the ditch to pick you up. And there's where we pulled out."

I got out too, and yes, it did look vaguely familiar. To the north the strobelike flash of that tall tower flickered against the clear evening sky like steady lightning, and to the west the ridge of brown fields crested to close off any view of the mountains. But their shadows had stretched this far across the prairie, bringing that early and long-lasting daylight to soften the rolling earth and cool the air. I began pushing through the knee-high weeds and grass in the trough of the ditch; Bunch strolled along the higher bank, head turning this way and that.

"Hey, hey!" Bunch trotted down into the weeds and pulled up the leather carrying case for the battery pack. "Look what I found!"

"Great!"

He opened it and checked the batteries and then began looking around.

"What's wrong?"

"The ID tag. It must have ripped off."

"Let me—" That was as far as I got. Between Bunch and me the earth exploded in a ripping pop, and an instant later came the sound of a shot, the tight crack of a high-powered rifle. Bunch flopped into the weeds and I sprinted back behind the automobile. Crawling into the front seat, I stayed low as I started it. A second shot thudded into the car's window and tore into the seat back, sending a spew of stuffing across my face. Leaning out of sight, I steered by a glimpse of road and kicked open the rider's door for Bunch to jump for. He did, eyes wide and mouth an angry line as he dived across the seat, and I floored the gas to scratch gravel into a cloud of dust. The sound of another shot echoed from the ridge, but where the bullet went I didn't know. Bunch, peeking above the windowsill, said, "Oh shit," and I glanced over to see, racing down the ridge like a line of Indians, half a dozen motorcycles bouncing wildly and trailing plumes of dust as they angled to cut us off.

"Turn around, Dev. Turn this fucker around!"

Slamming the wheel over and the brake down, I spun the car in a one-eighty skid and we headed back. The dust churned behind us and blanked out the mirrors, but the pop and rattle of straining motorcycle engines came clearly from beyond the cloud.

"It was a trap, Dev. The bastards were waiting for somebody to come for that case."

"You just figure that out?"

"If you're so goddamn smart, why didn't you think of it before they shot at us?"

"I did. I just didn't want to worry you."

Ahead, the county road disappeared over a rise of ground, and beyond that was the paved highway leading east to I-25 and west to Erie. If we could get to the town, we'd at least be within shouting distance of a peace officer. Bunch was already on the mobile phone dialing the highway patrol from our list of emergency numbers and glancing back through the dust to tell me he could see them coming.

I swung onto the pavement. The car rocked up on two wheels and laid rubber as I floored the gas, and we sailed clear of the ground across a series of ripples in the tar. Beside me, I heard Bunch report gunfire and a car chase by motorcycles to a dispatcher, and then he hung up quickly. A sudden roar at my window, and in the mirror I saw a bearded face half hidden by a leather motorcycle cap as a cyclist lunged forward from the pack.

"Bunch, get the camera! It's him—Taylor. Quick, get a shot!"

"What camera? We didn't bring the goddamn thing!"

I swerved hard to cut across his wheel and he dropped back and hung like a hawk, ready to dart forward again and probably fire a pistol in my ear. The road tilted down sharply, and in the small valley ahead I saw the trees and roofs of the village and a set of emergency lights flashing red and white under the tree limbs and between buildings.

The dust had blown away and we could see the motorcycles close on our rear bumper. I slammed on the brake, and they exploded into darting, roaring confusion as they tried to avoid the crash. One spun across the pavement and up the berm to sail gracefully out of sight behind an embankment; another shot past us, his face open in a screaming curse as the high handlebars wobbled at the edge of control.

"Watch it, Dev! That's Taylor—that's our meal ticket. Don't cripple the fucker."

A solid thud told me one didn't make it, and I glanced in the mirror to see a cartwheeling motorcycle fling its rider in a burning slide down the pavement and into the weeds beside the road. Stepping on the gas again, I roared downhill toward the welcome flash of lights on the patrol cruiser that wailed toward us.

"They're backing off, Dev—they're pulling out."

5

Whether or not the officer believed in our innocence, the bikers had worse press than we did, and there was no evidence to show we had contributed to the assault.

"I stopped by the side of the road and the next thing we knew, we're getting shot at . . ."

The officer looked up from his report. Behind him on the wall of the small concrete block building that was the highway patrol district headquarters, a detailed map of the region charted every road and public right-of-way in different colors and varying types of lines. From a back room came the sound of a bored voice talking on a telephone.

"You just happened to stop there. Why?"

"Trying to find a Mr. William Taylor." I showed him my ID. "We're working for an insurance company. We think he filed a false claim."

"Ah." The officer leaned back into the creak of his swivel chair. "So you went looking for him?"

"We went looking for where he lives. We didn't go on their property. In fact, we didn't even know that was their property."

He looked as if he didn't believe us. "Well, if you're not going to file charges, Mr. Kirk, there's not a hell of a lot we can do about what occurred this afternoon, is there?"

"If we file charges, it'll come out we were looking for Taylor. We don't want to alarm the suspect."

"It's pretty plain you alarmed the whole damn bunch, now ain't it?"

"We didn't know they were there, Sergeant." Bunch raised a hand palm out. "Scout's honor. We really didn't know they were there."

"If we had," I added, "we sure wouldn't have stopped."

"Well now, that much I can believe." The sergeant finished his report and shoved a copy toward us for a souvenir. "The arresting trooper didn't see anything except a traffic violation by one of the bikers, who was parked in the middle of the highway for some reason trying to start his vehicle. The rest claimed they were only out for a ride and weren't chasing anybody. You won't swear to them doing anything, but there's that bullet hole in the window of your car. And somebody called in an alarm claiming somebody was being chased and shot at."

I shook my head, innocent. "We didn't see who shot at us, so we can't swear it was one of the gang. You know there's no sense going to court with nothing stronger than that."

"Yes. Well now, that's so. But if I was you two, I wouldn't go near their place again. Like it or not, they got a right to do whatever the hell they want on their own land. And to kick anybody off that land they don't invite on—or whoever doesn't have a warrant. And so far, the sheriff hasn't had any call to file a warrant on them."

"Why are they so touchy?"

"Because they're up to something." It was obvious to the sergeant. "They're growing pot or making LSD or some crap like that out there. But until there's enough evidence for a warrant, the law gives them every right to do it until they're caught. And you people be real smart to stay the hell away from that place, insurance scam or no. That's not a bunch of Boy Scouts out there; they've been linked to more than one homicide and beat the rap every time." He fished around in a desk drawer for a business card. "Here's Sheriff Hoveland's number. Next time you want to go out there, you see if he can take you. Save you a lot of hurt and me a lot of paperwork."

Mrs. Ottoboni's porch light gleamed brightly, as it had for more than two years—since she saved my life by calling the police when a pair of hoods jumped me as I came home in the dark. I'd offered to pay part of her electric bill—it was for my security, after all—but she refused, claiming she did it for her own peace of mind.

The familiar smells and sounds of my half of the Victorian two-story welcomed me, and I swigged down a Bellehaven ale as I stuffed a frozen dinner into the microwave. While it was electrocuted, I stood under the hot shower to steam out some of the weariness of the evening's adventures. Then, as I ate from the cramped plastic dish, I listened to the messages on my machine. The only one that caught my undivided attention was a muffled voice that called me by name and said he was going to stomp the shit out of me.

Bunch got to the office first in the morning and was listening to a similar threat on that machine.

"You know who this is, don't you?"

I picked the mail out of its drop. "I don't recognize the voice but the message is familiar."

"What are we going to do about it?"

"You want to start a war?" Bunch didn't answer. "I don't. I think they're trying to scare us off. They're up to something on that farm, and they don't want anybody snooping around. They don't know we're after Taylor; they think we're after whatever they're trying to hide, and they're not sure how much we know. Let's just let things cool off for a couple weeks and then see what we can do."

"Think Security will go for that?"

Schute had wanted the case closed as soon as possible. "I'll give him a call in a bit and explain things to him." Most things, anyway.

Two of the envelopes held letters I'd been waiting for. One was a reply from TRW, the commercial credit bureau we subscribed to: Mrs. Chiquichano's name was on their files and came back clear. The other was my return envelope with the credit report on Mrs. Chiquichano from the Citizen's Bank and Trust. It gave her an A rating, sketched the method of payment on her home—monthly—and contained the list of references supplied by the applicant. The names included the address of next of kin, one Alonso Hernandes, a brother, living in Coronado, California; Morris Matheney, M.D., whose office in the Associated Medical Pavilion was over on Downing Street near Warner Memorial Hospital, and Rebecca White, an ex-employer whose address was also local.

"Want me to give them a call?" Bunch was reading over my shoulder.

"You try her brother. I'll talk to the others in person." References tended to be a bit franker that way than over the telephone, where an interviewer couldn't see their eyes.

I called and made appointments with each of the local references and then telephoned Schute in New York and explained the difficulties. "The place he's holed up is an isolated farm. We have some photographs of him, but nothing incriminating."

"You can't put a twenty-four-hour surveillance on the farm?"

"Not without being spotted—it's open prairie all around. No concealment for a longtime station. Our best bet right now is random surveillance, and even that's tough as long as he stays on that farm."

"What about luring him off?"

"We're looking at that angle, but we haven't come up with anything yet."

"I see." The line hummed and buzzed with other voices at the edge of hearing. "I'd like to get something substantial as soon as possible. As I told you, we're facing the statute of limitations on this one."

His next sentence would express regret that Security Underwriters would have to try another detective agency. I interrupted that line of thought: "We're also looking at Ace Roofing.

Taylor hasn't shown up there yet, but if he does, there's no problem with surveillance."

"I see. All right, try that. But we need results. And we need them soon."

"We'll keep you informed, Mr. Schute."

I hung up and Bunch looked at me with raised eyebrows. "We're not sitting on Ace Roofing, Dev."

"We will be." I started looking through our collection of telephone directories for the roofing company. "And we've got a dog to snatch too," I reminded him.

"I told you I was working on that!"

Bunch took his turn with the telephone. His voice was a background rumble for my search. After a while, I found the roofing company listed in the White Pages of a rural telephone book that held numbers for half a dozen small towns, including Erie. The only address listed was a familiar rural route number.

"Okay, Dev—I got the information on Mrs. Chiquichano's brother." Bunch held a notebook flipped over a forefinger. "Alonso Hernandes, naturalized American citizen originally from El Salvador. He rents at seven-three-nine G Avenue, apartment three B, Coronado, California. Is employed by the Hotel Del Coronado as a grounds keeper and maintenance man. Has worked there for the last nine years. Never declared bankruptcy, good credit rating. Recently paid off a 1984 Oldsmobile Cutlass at Weepin' Willy's Used Cars. Single with no outstanding debts or credit card accounts, and has a current savings account of fourteen hundred forty-two dollars and thirty-seven cents plus a checking account of four twenty-one eighty-eight. The car and his household goods are his total listed assets. Neighbors say he's quiet and polite."

That last bit of information told me Bunch had been talking to Retail Credit, another bureau we subscribed to; they liked to provide more personal notes, including neighborhood gossip, on the subject. "No investments in his sister's business?"

"No investments at all, according to Retail. Looks like one

of these marginal wage earners who puts a little aside each month and prays that nothing big goes wrong."

"Just like us." He certainly didn't look like the brother of a relatively well-off slumlord and labor broker. And definitely not one she could have borrowed money from to get her start.

Bunch limped for the door. "I'm on my way to Broomfield for that debugging estimate. Anything you want me to do?"

I pulled a standard contract from the drawer and handed it to him. "Try to get a signature. If you can't, be sure to tell him about our expertise in industrial security."

"I know the pitch." The door closed behind him and I heard his uneven tread go down the iron stairs.

Ace Roofing was next. I dialed the number and a woman answered with the company name. Making my voice sound older and more cautious, I told her I was interested in having some roofing work done, but wanted to see some of the outfit's work first. "They on a job now? I want to see the work, not just talk to people about how good they are."

"Yeah? Well, wait a minute—let me look at the book."

The phone clicked into silence and then the voice came back. "They're on a flat-roof job over in Lafayette right now—the Adams Machine Shop building. It's on Chester Street, the three-hundred block there."

I thanked her and left a note telling Bunch where I'd be. But my first stop was nearby in the 2700 block of California Avenue in downtown Denver: the R and W Realty offices. It was one of those old mansions that had been refurbished into business suites, and a series of ornate brass shingles were screwed beside the doorway—a couple of law offices, a graphics and design firm, an insurance agency, and R and W Realty. A receptionist smiled hello as I introduced myself and asked for Rebecca White.

"Just a moment, please."

It wasn't even that long. The young woman set down the phone and smiled again. "Upstairs to your left, please."

The stairs, illuminated by a multicolored skylight over the well, provided a major architectural effect. A series of short landings rose past the law offices and turned to face the realtor's door. A smaller brass sign said PLEASE COME IN.

There was only one person in the office, which had a large desk and filing cabinets at one end, and at the other a living room set cozily arranged around a large coffee table near sunny windows. "Miss White?"

"Mrs. What can I do for you, Mr. Kirk?"

She was a tall, intense brunette with that wiry thinness that comes from a combination of genes and ceaseless activity. I wasn't surprised to see, framed in random patterns on the wall, photographs of Mrs. White and a bicycle standing against various backdrops of mountains, European villages, famous landmarks. On the desk was a chrome trophy sporting another bicycle and the legend "Amateur Time Trials Second Place Winner." "Mrs. Camelia Chiquichano cited you as a reference on a loan application, and I wonder if I could ask you a few questions about her."

"This is a bit unusual, isn't it? Aren't these verifications usually done with a phone call?"

"I happened to be in the neighborhood. Are you the R in R and W Realty?"

"The R and the W—it's a bit more impressive if clients think a realtor doesn't work alone. Especially a woman."

"She listed you as her employer on a recent home loan application."

"Yes. She cleans all the offices in this building." She added, "Which I own."

"Has she worked with you a long time?"

"Six, perhaps seven years. She's put together an apparently very successful janitorial business, and I've been happy to recommend her services to acquaintances. In fact, the last person I referred to her said she couldn't take him—she has too much business now. It's a real success story."

"The cleaning crew are women? Spanish-speaking women?"

"Yes, and they're very hardworking. I get the impression that Mrs. Chiquichano is a demanding employer."

Something of a slave driver, in fact. "And," I guessed, "you also helped her in a real estate transaction?"

"Why, yes, I did. I specialize in urban properties, particularly sleepers—those that are undervalued and can be enhanced with a little sweat equity. Mrs. Chiquichano mentioned several times that she was looking for a suitable investment property, and when this deal came up, I brought it to her attention."

That was the kind of opening I'd been looking for. I told her about my adventures with my half of Mrs. Ottoboni's duplex; she told me about the tribulations and triumphs—especially the triumphs—of what she called her "urban pioneers": young couples, usually childless, who moved from the suburbs back into the city to buy and spruce up cheap older homes in run-down neighborhoods. We ended up talking over coffee around the low table spread with copies of *Better Homes and Gardens* and *Denver Real Estate*. Her motions were quick and nervous, but not random, and I suspected she had won the battle against cigarettes through a tremendous effort.

"So you found Mrs. Chiquichano's home for her too?"

"No. Only the investment property—an apartment building over in Swansea. It was a good deal all around; the sellers were thinking of tearing down the building because it had deteriorated so much, and Mrs. Chiquichano was looking for a property she could improve and still profit from. Fortunately, I was able to put the deal together. It's so difficult to find low-income rentals anymore, that things worked out quite well."

"She had no trouble with the loan approval?"

"None at all—she put one third down in cash."

"That much?"

Mrs. White smiled slightly. "Not all women are helpless and impoverished, Mr. Kirk."

"And many women are very good business people, I agree.

I'm just surprised that someone who immigrated ten or fifteen years ago, with no apparent marketable skills, would have saved up enough capital to invest in an apartment house."

"Well, apparently she was very frugal for a number of years. And frankly, it wasn't all that much—twenty thousand. As I said, the property was very run-down and the neighborhood is almost totally zoned for industry now. In fact, I think that was the last R-two zoning left in that block."

"Wasn't the land worth more than the building?"

"It could have been, except no one was interested in buying a lot that small, and the owners were tired of paying taxes. Plus, they faced a condemnation order on the building."

"What did she put up for collateral?"

"It wasn't needed. There's a city program of loan guarantees for investors willing to develop low-income housing. I helped her qualify for the program."

"When was this?"

"About four years ago."

"Do the rentals have price ceilings?"

"Of course. One seventy-five a month for a single, up to a maximum of two fifty a month for large families. I understand there are no vacancies."

"Do you know who handled her home purchase?"

"That was an owner-sold property. We talked it over and I gave her some advice on how to arrange the financing, but essentially it went through the lending company and that was it."

"Did she put down one third on that, too?"

"I advised against that—the interest there is tax deductible. I told her she would come out ahead with a low down payment on a thirty-year fixed rate. I don't know whether she took my advice or not."

"How much did the house cost?"

"Somewhere in the one nineties; I can't remember exactly."

"She was able to afford that?"

"She said she could handle the payments, and as far as I know, she has. You'll have to verify that with the loan company, not with me."

I thanked Mrs. White and headed for my next stop, the Associated Medical Pavilion on Downing Street. The name had echoed familiarly, and I stood a minute or two staring at the bronze letters mounted on a heavy wooden sign. But the connection wouldn't come. The building showed busy Downing a windowless brick wall and some bushes, but the sidewalk leading down the front revealed brick, glass, and chrome. The main entry was halfway down the facade, recessed for shade from the summer sun and open to the low winter sun for warmth and coziness. A series of concrete benches lined the walk, separated by carefully tended grass and flowers, and I wondered if Mrs. Chiquichano had the lawn care franchise as well. A receptionist learned that I was neither patient nor drug salesman and frowned as she glanced down an appointment book crowded with names in every fifteen-minute slot.

"I called earlier and made an appointment with Dr. Matheney," I reminded her.

She looked in another book. "Oh, yes. Just a moment, please."

She lifted a phone to talk to someone, and I listened to the muted background music and tried to pick out the melody among the curlicues of tinkling notes. The scattering of patients leafed through magazines and politely ignored one another.

A series of bronze plates on the waiting room wall named the doctors and their specialties, most of which seemed to deal with allergies and internal medicine. Matheney's name was listed under Immunology and Surgery. I guessed that as in many medical groups, the doctors here had private patients and were also on call at nearby Warner Memorial. Those private cases too complex to be handled at the clinic were transferred to the hospital and its more extensive care facilities. It was a familiar symbiotic arrangement and one that seemed very profitable as well. The building itself had been designed for its purpose as a clinic, with—I found out shortly—smaller waiting areas near the office of each specialist, looked after by each doctor's nurse. Examining rooms emphasized comfort and privacy, hallways stressed womblike security and warmth, and the doctors' offices, if they were all like Matheney's, breathed a sigh of order, competence, and wealth. The patient knew he was getting the best.

"Mr. Kirk! How may I help you today?"

Morris Matheney was very tall, with an Abe Lincoln beard and large horn-rimmed glasses that magnified eyes as brown and soft as a collie's. His hair swept back from brow and temples in a billowing gray puff that increased his height. His hand, when he shook mine, was strong and hairless and so polished by scrubbing that its skin looked like a taut surgical glove. I explained about Mrs. Chiquichano while he listened with fingers laced and thumbs against his lips.

"Yes. I remember her. She provided janitorial services for the clinic."

"Did? She doesn't work here anymore?"

"We recently found it more economical to share the hospital's janitorial crew. The use of beds has declined enough so the hospital subcontracts some of its routine services to various nearby clinics. The janitorial service is one."

"But you were willing to be a reference on her home loan application?"

"Of course. And would be again. She and her workers did a fine job, and I was quite sorry not to renew her contract. Unfortunately, the hospital had certain union obligations with its staff, and it was just easier all around to make the change. I think Mrs. Chiquichano will be an excellent credit risk. I found her to be very meticulous and thorough."

"I see. How long did she work for you, doctor?"

"I believe it was two years. I don't remember the exact dates."

"Do you know who her other customers are?"

"No. I had no reason to ask."

"Not even for references when you hired her?"

"I'd rather judge a person's worth by their work for me, not by what someone else—who may be far less demanding—says about them. If her work had not been highly satisfactory, I would have fired her."

Hire and fire—now I remembered where I'd heard of the Associated Medical Pavilion. "You do the health tests on Mrs. Chiquichano's employees too?"

"I beg pardon?"

"TB tests—blood tests. Felix Frentanes . . . and Nestor Calamaro. Doesn't your group provide the screening tests for the people who work at the Apple Valley Turkeys plant?"

Matheney's fingers tugged at his chin whiskers. "Our lab does a lot of industrial screenings. Immunology is one of our areas of specialty, after all."

"And Mrs. Chiquichano brought them here for the tests?"

"I don't know, Mr. Kirk. She may have—especially if she was working here at the time. But that kind of scheduling is taken care of by one of the secretaries, so I couldn't tell you if Mrs. Chiquichano arranged it or not."

That was it: straight answers to straight questions, and nothing more to ask. I thanked the good doctor and wound my way back through color-coded halls with a sense of letdown. Whatever I had expected to discover, it wasn't here.

The drive up to Lafayette took about thirty minutes, but with the top down and the September sun cooled by the wind, it was a pleasant ride. The Healey enjoyed the curving country roads that branched off the freeways, and so did I. Lafayette was one of the faster-growing towns in the area, serving as a bedroom community for both Boulder and Denver, and support businesses had begun bringing people and money into what had been a village as small as Erie. Surrounding housing developments rose and fell with the prairie and looked naked and sunbaked on the grassy ridges, but the old part of town had settled under tall trees.

That's where the machine shop was, on a street that was still predominantly residential but unzoned. A familiar blue pickup truck with a tar-bucket trailer sat in front of the cinder-block building, and a pair of tar-stained ladders leaned against the walls. At the foot of one, a deeply tanned and shirtless man ladled melted tar from a portable heater into a bucket and hauled it up to the roof by a pulley at the ladder's top. On the flat roof, another bronzed man, heavier, carried the buckets away. Neither was Taylor, but noise and gestures indicated more workers out of sight somewhere in the center of the roof's expanse.

I drove past slowly and then circled the block to get a good look at the building. Through my telephoto lens, the bearded faces zoomed close, and I shot a couple of stills, hoping that the men hidden beyond the eave would come forward into focus. But they didn't, and I drove to another angle, cruising along a rutted dirt alley crowded with rusty oil drums used as trash cans. From this spot I could make out another shape busy on the roof, but couldn't get a clear picture of it through the heavy leaves. Parking, I walked down the alley and tried half a dozen shots. Maybe dark room magic could bring out what I couldn't see. And maybe if I swung around to come down the other end of the alley, I'd have a clearer view of the workman.

I was back in the Healey and turning around when they spotted me. The one catching buckets at the edge of the roof pointed my way and said something to the one on the ground. He wheeled and squinted in my direction, and I kept my face averted and my rearview mirror focused as I quietly pulled the Healey away. So much for the day's surveillance. The last glimpse I had was of the two men still in that tableau, staring after me.

6

Erie was in Weld County, and the Weld County Sheriff's Office was in Greeley, another forty miles north on U.S. 85. The sheriff himself wasn't available, but I managed to corner an undersheriff who heard what I wanted and shrugged. "Yeah, we know a lot about that bunch, Mr. Kirk, but there's not much we can do about them unless somebody swears out a complaint. And so far, nobody's wanted to." He added, scrubbing the inside of a nostril with his thumbnail, "Can't blame them, either. That's a rough bunch."

"Can you tell me what they're suspected of being involved in?"

"It ain't official. Just hearsay."

"I won't quote you."

"You name it: drugs, prostitution, extortion, murder, organized crime . . . They're tied in with another local motorcycle gang, Sons of Silence. And that bunch, I hear, is tied in with the Hell's Angels to supply drugs and what-all to this area."

And all I wanted was a picture of one William Taylor doing push-ups or chopping wood. "Does the Colorado Bureau of Investigation have a jacket on them?"

He shrugged again and shifted the thumb to the other nostril. "Doubt it. They don't do much with organized crime. Forensics is their big thing."

Which meant that the only central police agency that might have something on this gang would be the Denver Police Department, and that I'd wasted an afternoon touring the northern Colorado plains. I thanked the sheriff's officer and headed south, making the most of the trip by letting the old girl find a sweetly resonant rpm and settle into the sway of the highway.

By the time I reached Denver, Bunch had returned to the office and left for his afternoon workout; he'd be back in a couple hours. A note on the desk beside the blank contract said, "Guy wants to think about it," and I had a pretty good idea what that meant. Well, he might find people who would do the debugging job cheaper, but no one who could do it better—for all the good pride did our checking account. I was refiling the form when the telephone rang and a woman's voice I didn't recognize said, "Mr. Kirk? I have some information to sell."

I flipped on the recorder. "About what?"

"Something you're working on. Something that will help you."

A lot of tips came with a price tag, but usually the seller wasn't quite so open about it. "How much?"

"A thousand dollars. Cash."

"That's a lot of money." And more than I was going to give for some vague promise. "What's this about?"

"I don't want to talk over the phone. You meet me somewhere."

"Come to my office."

"No! I just want to get the money and leave the state—you meet me somewhere safe. Do you know Clear Creek Canyon? You ever go up that canyon?"

"I know it."

"Meet me at the west end of Tunnel Three. There's a pullout there. You know where it is?"

"I can find it. When?"

"One hour. Alone."

The line clicked into silence and I glanced at my watch. An hour wasn't much leeway for that distance, but if the traffic was light—and if the Healey wasn't feeling temperamental after her drive up to Greeley—I could get there in forty-five minutes. Early enough to survey that corner of the steep canyon before making a target of myself, in case the tip was more than it promised to be. I left a note for Bunch and swung through the snarl of delivery trucks on Wazee and out toward the Valley Highway.

For a time a hundred years ago, Clear Creek was one of the richest gold lodes in the world. High up its canyon, the town of Central City still mined tourists with its Victorian buildings and Old West gift shoppes. In the old days, when the road was for wagons, it clung like a painted stripe to the twists and angles of the rock walls above the foaming plunge of the creek. The newer road, U.S. 6, is a bit straighter, thanks to the series of tunnels cut through massive shoulders of rock; but the two lanes still swing and wriggle as they follow the creek, and I liked the chance to feel the car do what it was built to do. I went through the gears and we flashed past craggy bluffs, oases of cottonwood and mountain willow, and an occasional car or pickup truck pulled over in a wide spot near the stream.

Tunnel One is just outside Golden; Tunnels Two and Three, a couple miles farther up, are close together and pierce through the mountains where the creek makes a large loop around abrupt faces of almost treeless gray rock. I slowed as I came out of the west portal and saw why the caller wanted this spot. In addition to its being remote and cut off by steep cliffs, on the south side of the highway the remnant of the wagon road—now blocked by carefully placed boulders—formed a pull-off wide enough for three or four cars to park. A worn path led along the old stony roadbed and down toward the water to disappear beyond the ridge's shoulder.

I was ten minutes early and drove slowly up to the next spot wide enough for me to swing the Healey around and then coasted back toward the tunnel's black entrance. No other cars were at the pull-off, nor did the whine of an engine signal a vehicle coming down canyon behind me. I eased the low Healey across the eroded shoulder, set the hand brake, killed the motor. Then, loosening the old .38 Police Special I'd grabbed from the office safe, I got out. Without the throaty rumble of the Healey's pipes, only the rush and clatter of water tumbling against boulders echoed along the canyon walls. My watch said two minutes before the hour. At two after, a diesel thundered out of the tunnel with a push of air and a streamer of black smoke and whined up the lanes and out of sight around the next bend. At five after, my feelings about the whole cheery adventure began to slip toward uneasiness, and at six after, my feelings proved right.

The first shot missed. I heard it hum like a large, angry insect past my scalp and I knew what it was. But before that knowledge could translate into running legs, the second round, coming with the crack of a heavy rifle, yanked at my coat sleeve and thudded solidly into the Healey's rear deck. Another smacked into the windshield, snowing chips of glass across the cowling and into my hair and splintering a web of cracks from one brace to the other. By the time the sound of that shot reached me from a saddle in the ridge above, I had sprinted for the tunnel's overhang to wedge myself against the cold, blasted stone. Perched on the six-inch ledge that formed a curb leading into the dim shaft, I waited. The tunnel wind fluttered louder than the creek through the chimney of concrete. But no further shots came from the spine of mountain that the tunnel cut through. A sudden blare of sound and a semitruck thundered past, a road-grimed streak of wind and blatted exhaust and the startled shriek of air horns as the driver's eye caught me pressed against the jutting rock. Then it was gone, leaving the odor of smoke and my own icy sweat.

The truck—a high, swaying rectangle of grimy doors—faded up the canyon, and I counted ten and then dashed for the Healey, dodging from side to side like a rabbit under a hawk's claws. Rolling beneath the steering wheel, I crouched low to crank the starter. I didn't think there was another shot, but I couldn't tell for certain because all I could hear was the pulse of blood in my ears and the grinding of an engine that had chosen this moment to be coy.

"Come on, you son of a bitch!"

It coughed, died, cranked.

"I'm sorry—for God's sake, I'm sorry!"

It coughed again and fired, missed, caught.

"Good girl—attagirl—knew you could do it!"

I had the car in motion, spinning dirt and gravel in a rush back onto the highway to plunge toward the shelter of the tunnel's mouth. It's usually hard for me to hunker down in the cramped cockpit, but I managed, letting the fishtailing car almost steer itself while I kept an eye on the ridge above.

The shots had come from somewhere along the ridge that crested between the east and west portals. I figured the assailant had followed me up the canyon, parked at the east portal, then worked up the trail to find a rest that would overlook the west pullout. Using a scope, he—or was it she?—waited until I came back and got out of the Healey. It was a good maneuver, a nicely laid trap, and I had stood there admiring the scenery while the would-be killer zeroed in. But as with a lot of people unused to firing downhill at a steep angle, that first round was high, and that was what had saved me. From the sound of the slug, it had been aimed at my head; and from the speed with which he got off his rounds, the shooter knew how to handle his weapon. But the high round had been his first mistake. The second was letting me reach the Healey.

The tunnel was maybe a quarter of a mile long, and I could already see the pale arch of the other end and the road leading out toward the second tunnel. I might be able to reach the east portal by the time he scrambled back to his car and took off. I wasn't sure what I'd do if I caught him—his weapon was a lot heavier than the four-inch barrel of the .38. But he might not know that. Besides, I was angry enough to rely on inspiration.

Jamming down the accelerator, I leapt the Healey toward

the tunnel mouth and saw the empty highway beyond the opening as I shifted up into fourth. Few other cars would be able to hold the curves of the canyon as well as the old girl, and all I needed was a glimpse of a fleeing bumper and I would have him. I had just dropped into gear when the pale semicircle began to dim with a heavy shadow. Just ahead of me, something was being moved across the entrance. I slammed on the brakes and pushed back against the seat away from the splintered windshield, but there was nowhere to turn. Like a bullet rifled down a barrel, the Healey bounded from one rock wall to the other and shrieked into the side of the still-moving pickup truck, and that was the last I remembered.

The smell was familiar: the clinical sharpness of a laboratory and a kind of empty, odorless tang that reminded me of one of the gas jets in a high school chemistry class. The oxygen jet. That's what it smelled like, and I blinked against the glare, half expecting to see the long, waist-high tables and the zinc-lined sinks with their superstructures of glass retorts and tubing. But all I saw was a curtain, and I felt under my nose the thin plastic hose that pumped a little more oxygen into my lungs. Hospital. I was in a hospital and injured, and I didn't know how bad.

Starting with my toes, I began to take inventory, half fearful that something I tried to move wouldn't be there and too afraid to look down my sheeted body until I had felt everything answer. My head hurt and I could feel bandages pressing lightly across my scalp, so there was some damage there. Which, Bunch would grin, was the safest place for me to be hurt. Bunch. Looking around the drawn curtain, I saw the electronic paraphernalia of beeping monitors and a network of tubes running into various parts of my anatomy. No chair for visitors. No bed table with plastic pitcher of water and house telephone. I was in intensive care, and though it was a relief to know that my brain could recognize where I was, it was no relief at all to find out. Slowly, wincing against a sudden pain somewhere deep in my right shoulder, I groped for the call button that should be at the head of the bed. Almost as soon as I touched it, a nurse came through the curtain.

"Awake at last! How do you feel? Can you tell me your name?"

I answered her.

"What?" She leaned closer and I realized that what had sounded clear to me had come out as a faint mumble.

"Kirk. Devlin Kirk."

"Good—that's right. I want you to lie still and rest. The doctor will be right down."

"Call Bunchcroft."

"Please lie still, Mr. Kirk. You're not supposed to move."

"Call Bunchcroft."

"You want me to call someone? You want me to let someone know you're here?"

"My office. Call Bunchcroft."

She finally understood and, fumbling through my wallet in the personal effects tray under the bed, found a business card and asked if that was the number. It was, and out she went, and I did too.

I woke again to a light burning into my pupil and a thumb peeling my eyelid back.

"Just lie still, Mr. Kirk. You have a slight concussion."

The doctor's hands went out of sight and I felt his fingers probe here and there with firm but gentle curiosity. While he was busily checking this and that, he asked me what year it was and the name of the president of the United States. Then the bearded face came back.

"You're really a very lucky man, Mr. Kirk. I think the concussion's the worst of it. Do you feel discomfort anywhere?"

"Shoulder."

"Um hum." The fingers began poking again and found where it hurt most. "That hurt?"

"Goddamn!"

"Um hum." The fingers focused on the sorest spot and bore in for a moment. "We'll take an X ray later, but I think you separated your shoulder briefly during the impact. I don't feel anything out of place now, but the picture can tell us more."

"Okay."

"There are a couple people waiting who need to ask you some questions. I'll check back in a while."

The first and most important was a businesslike woman with a clipboard. She wanted to know who was paying for all this.

"Health insurance. Card's in wallet."

She fished it out, being careful to let me see everything she took from the wallet, and that she put it all back. When she was satisfied and her admissions form completed, my next interrogator came in.

"Mr. Kirk, how you doing? Want to tell me what all happened?" The highway patrol officer also wanted to see my driver's license and insurance verification.

I told him about the truck pulling across the tunnel exit. "Did you find out who it's registered to?"

"We found the truck down the canyon a ways. It was pretty beat up. Somebody drove it as far as it would go, looks like, and then walked, I guess. The owner claims it was stolen—he didn't know it was gone until he started to go home after work." The sergeant stuck a thumbnail between two crooked front teeth and thought a moment. "Did you see anybody in the truck at all before you hit?"

I closed my eyes and tried to bring back the moment, the rock walls that seemed to collapse around me, the truck swelling with nightmare swiftness as the Healey shrieked and tried to stop. "No. I can't remember much except the truck. But I didn't see anybody in the driver's seat. . . . I'm sure I would have seen anyone there." I ran the scene through memory once more: The driver's window was empty. "Someone must have pushed it across the tunnel mouth."

The officer nodded. "I see. Well, Mr. Kirk, we estimate your speed at around seventy miles per hour at the time of the accident. That about right?"

"I don't know. I wasn't looking at the speedometer."

"Well, your skid marks show you were going at least seventy miles per hour, and the speed limit there in that tunnel is forty. I'm going to have to cite you, Mr. Kirk."

"Me? What about the guy who pushed the truck across the road? Doesn't he get a ticket?"

He handed me a yellow copy of a speeding ticket that explained where I had to be and when, and what it might cost me in money and points. "If we catch him, sure. But tell you the truth, I don't think that's very likely. I'm inclined to think it was kids trying to do something funny. Except the truck was wiped clean—no prints at all where you'd look for them. That doesn't sound exactly like kids, does it?" He waited but I said nothing. "Well, everybody nowadays knows about fingerprints, don't they?" It wasn't a question and I didn't volunteer a nod. "You don't have any idea who might have done it, do you?"

"No."

"Kids. Some of them get pretty destructive, anymore." He handed me some more forms. "You'll have to fill out an accident report, and be sure and list your insurance carrier. Mail them or bring them by your nearest highway patrol office within the week, Mr. Kirk." He started out and then came back. "Almost forgot to give you this, too." It was another ticket for failure to wear a seat belt. "Have a good day."

"What about my car? How bad?"

"Totaled."

A good day indeed.

Sometime during the night I was moved from intensive care into a semiprivate room. That's what my insurance allowed for, though the businesslike lady did suggest that for a few dollars extra I could have the luxury of private accommodations. The health care business might have been overbuilt, but it wasn't going to surrender profits without a struggle. Neither was I. My roommate, who had the window bed, lay silent behind drawn curtains with his television flickering and only occasionally shuffled past the foot of my bed to the bathroom, where he spent a long time. I lay and watched the half-open door to the hallway and waited for Bunch. Just after the nurse brought breakfast on a plastic tray holding tiny portions of equally plastic food, Uncle Wyn, leaning heavily on his cane, tapped on the door and was followed in by Bunch.

"Jesus, Dev, you eat this crap?" Bunch asked.

"Not because I want to. At least there's not much of it. What have you found out?"

"I found out you got a concussion and a few bruises, and you might get out later today if the doc figures everything's okay."

"I already knew that much."

Uncle Wyn lowered himself gently into one of the two chairs, his arthritic knee supported by the cane. "We also learned that the Healey's in worse shape than you are, and I learned that it probably wasn't no accident. Want to let your old uncle know what the hell's going on?"

"What did Bunch tell you?"

"Not damn much."

Uncle Wyn was my closest family—all of it, in fact—and he had given me the capital to get Kirk and Associates started soon after my father's death. But the interest on the loan hadn't been the real reason he backed us. It was for something to fill empty-nest days as well as for an echo of the competitiveness and excitement that had been the routine pace of life during his professional baseball years. Though I often discussed cases with him, I tried to avoid the ones that might hint of danger to the only son of his deceased only brother. But there was no avoiding what the man could see plainly, so I told him as much as he needed to know.

"The motorcycle gang? You think they did it?"

"Somebody set me up. Who else?"

Bunch wandered restlessly along the curtain separating me from my cellmate. "We're going to have to square things, Dev. If we don't, they'll just keep coming at us."

"I thought you were planning to snatch their dog?"

Uncle Wyn shook his head. "It's not good, Dev. First assault, now you're talking escalation. Preventive strikes. Whatever. I wouldn't've given you the money to start this business if I knew it was going to lead to World War Three. You're goddamn lucky. You know how goddamn lucky you are? You could have been dead twice over—shot at, booby-trapped in a goddamn tunnel. It was damn dumb you went out there alone in the first place!"

There was no answer to the question or to his anger. Bunch finally asked, "What'd the cop say about the bullet hole in the Healey, Dev?"

"He wasn't looking for it and I didn't help him find it. As far as I know, he never noticed it."

"That's good. I had the car towed to Archer's."

Archy didn't report bullet holes to the police. "What the hey," he told me once, "they don't pay no repair bills." I asked, "Did Archy say anything about her?"

Bunch shook his head. "Just a long, sad whistle."

Which could have been the car's dirge. I hoped not. There were only a few of the Austin-Healey 3000s still around. You saw them every now and then taken out of storage for a *cours d'élégance* or an old-timers' rally on a sunny day in summer. But there weren't many, and none for sale at a price I could afford. So a lot depended on what wizardry Archy could do with the pieces that were left. "I hope he can do something. She's a good car—the only one I could fit in."

"If he can't, I don't know who will."

We talked over the variables of the attack until Bunch's restlessness drove him to the doorway. "I'm going out and around, Dev. These places . . ." His hand included all the life-support equipment. "If you're not sick when you come in, you get sick looking at it."

Uncle Wyn listened to the heavy tread of Bunch's shoes fade down the corridor. "I knew a lot of guys like that—big guys, afraid of nothing except catching a bug."

"I think the hospital reminds him of Susan."

"Yeah, probably. It's hard to get over something like that." Uncle Wyn, too, stood and braced himself with the cane. "First he gets his goddamn leg nearly chewed off, now you get busted up. This line of work you guys are in, Bunch better get used to hospitals. Listen, that offer's still open. You know—going into business with me. I'd really like that."

"Thanks, Uncle Wyn. It may sound funny from a hospital bed, but I'm doing what I want to."

"It'll sound even funnier on your tombstone."

7

Even a short stay in the hospital is one of those intense and all-encompassing changes of environment that leave one's sense of time distorted. Coming back to the familiar office late in the afternoon, I felt . . . not distant, exactly, but placed at a slightly different angle to the routine life that had gone on without me. The accumulated mail was an indication of that routine, and I spent the rest of the afternoon winnowing advertisements and bills, many of which I had finally caught up on, while I telephoned here and there for leasing information on a car to replace the Healey. "Replace" wasn't the word and I felt a pang of disloyalty for even thinking it. But either necessity overrode or I would walk. To make up for the pang, I called Archer's Garage to check on the victim.

"This is Devlin Kirk, Archy. How's my girl?"

"She ain't no virgin no more. Ain't much of nothing else, neither."

"Can you put her together again?"

"Jeez, I don't know. Even if I can find the parts, it'll cost like hey. Why don't you get yourself a Hyundai or a Yugo? You waste one of them, you ain't out so much."

"How about seeing what parts you can find, and let me know what it'll cost?"

"All right. It'll take some time, but I'll put it on the wire. You want I should look for another Healey in case this one's kaput?"

Talk about fickleness! But with a sigh I fell victim to the temptation. "See what you can find."

"Probably be cheaper to do that. Oh, yeah, I found the bullet. It was in the fire wall on the rider's side. Son of a gun just missed the gas tank. Went through the deck lid, the rider's seat back, and halfway through the fire wall. That dude must of been firing a cannon at you."

"Bunch or I'll be by to pick it up. Thanks, Archy."

One of the envelopes tucked away between mail order catalogs for electronics gear was from Warner Memorial Hospital, a response to the inquiry from Kirk and Associates Medical Underwriters about the treatment of services provided one Nestor Calamaro. The statement of account was accompanied by photocopies of the health insurance claim form and a standard-treatment form with its list of services and their diagnostic and procedure code numbers. The block for "Med. Emergency, Office" was checked with a dollar amount following; "Immunizations and Injections" noted a tetanus shot and its fee; a scribble under the "Sutures" section indicated that Nestor was sewn up. Farther down, columns of code numbers without labels had checks and amounts marked here and there. I matched them against the procedure code in the Blue Cross/Blue Shield physician's manual and put together an impressive list of diagnostic tests. Nestor's treatment involved an extensive battery of blood tests that seemed far beyond the needs of a simple cut. Apparently the hospital's billing office was sensitive to the requirements for those services too, because a photocopy of the doctor's order asking for them was appended. The doctor was Morris Matheney.

"Dev—you should have called me! I could have picked you up at the hospital."

"That's okay, Bunch. Uncle Wyn gave me a ride."

"And a lecture?"

"The one about 'consider the future.' "

"I've always liked that one. You all right? Head cleared up?"

"I feel a little dopey—and no comments, please. The doc said it was the result of concussion. And my shoulder's touchy. But I'm a hell of a lot better off than the Healey."

"That car's no loss, believe me. I talked to Dave Miller in vice and narcotics. He didn't know anything about the Wilcox farm people, but he said he'd ask around DPD." He added, "Your uncle was right, you know—you really were dumb to get suckered that way."

"Naw, I figured it for a setup, Bunch. That's why I went out there early."

"Well, that's one way to check it out—stick your head up and see if they shoot. That the way the Secret Service taught you to do it?"

" 'If all else fails . . .' By the way, Archy found the bullet. It went through half the car before lodging in the fire wall."

"Yeah. That figures. It was a high-velocity weapon they used on us at the farm, too. You know that hard crack they make?"

"Believe me, I do know." Another envelope held something of interest to Bunch and I handed it to him. "You'd better see this."

"What is it?" He read and then looked up. "They can't do this—it's my goddamn leg and my goddamn dog bite!"

The letter was from the city and county health department. It warned Bunch that unless the dog that bit him was located and tested, he could be subject to rabies shots. If he had established a religious exemption from inoculation, he was to call a certain number. If not, he was to call either the referring physician whose name appeared below or the health service, number supplied, and make arrangements to start the inoculations.

"They can't do this!"

"It's a public health issue. Rabies is a contagious disease."

"I don't have rabies!"

"The first sign is unreasonable anger and irritability."

Bunch forced up the corners of his mouth "Then *you've* got

fucking rabies. Look—I'm smiling. I'm talking very calmly and rationally. I do not have rabies. They cannot make me take those shots."

"It doesn't say you have to. It just says you might."

"Goddamn dogs. Goddamn shots. I hate them both!" He pulled up his pants leg to show a scabby but smooth patch of flesh surrounded by the yellow of old bruise. "Look, it's almost cleared up. No infection, no bleeding, no goddamn rabies."

"No dog either."

"I said I'm working on that." His voice emphasized sweetness and light. "But if I steal that dog, Dev, it'll be because I want to and not because some fucking bureaucrat tells me to. I'm not going to do one thing I damn well don't want to do." Tossing the crumpled letter into the trash, he added, "And while you've been laying around in the hospital pissing and moaning about that lousy car, I've been working. You know what today is?"

"The day before tomorrow."

"An anniversary. The third week to the day that Nestor disappeared."

I waited for him to tell me why that was important.

"I went back over his route home. I figured maybe other people were on schedules too. That they touched his route the same time every Tuesday, maybe, or worked in the area and started home about the same time. People we missed when we went out to knock on doors."

"And?"

"Well, if you're not all that interested . . ."

I was interested; Bunch had a good idea. But he didn't need me stroking him—he was doing well enough on his own. "Out with it."

"An ice cream vendor. You know these people that pedal ice cream carts around town? The three wheelers?"

"A tricycle cart? He saw something?"

"She. Got legs on her like a linebacker. Face like one, too. She remembered seeing Nestor get picked up by a van."

"How'd she know it was him?"

"His picture. She says she crosses Williams Street every afternoon, all summer long, just about five-fifteen. Two or three times a week, she'd see Nestor coming down Forty-seventh Avenue, and he'd usually buy something from her—Popsicle, snow cone, something cheap like that. He always walked by himself, but he was friendly, like he didn't have many people to talk to. In fact, she thought that's mostly why he bought something—to practice his English, and maybe because she was somebody he kind of knew. So she was surprised when this van pulled to the curb and Nestor went over to see what they wanted. Then he got in, and off they went."

"He just got in? Didn't argue with them or try to run?"

"That's how she described it. They talked for a few seconds and then he got in."

"Description?"

"Plain white van. No side or back windows. Colorado plates, but she didn't get a number."

"She see anybody?"

"She thinks it was a man driving, but she's not sure. A man in the rider's seat talked to Nestor. White. She didn't think he had a beard or mustache, but she won't swear to it after this long. By the time she crossed the street, they were already pulling away."

It wasn't much and it didn't seem to lead anywhere. But so far, it was the last glimpse of a missing person. "If it had Colorado plates, it probably wasn't the immigration people. Federal plates are white."

"That's what I figure. I checked with missing persons again, too. Nothing on either Nestor or Serafina. But I found out where Mrs. Chiquichano's cleaning crews will be working tonight."

"How'd you do that?"

"The usual, Watson: ratiocination and inductive reasoning. Besides, she had the work schedule posted on her office wall."

"You went by?"

"After hours."

Bunch told me what else he'd found in the office of Olympia Janitorial Services, and it didn't come to much—a small desk, an answering machine on the telephone, a work schedule for the crew, and a file drawer with a few employee records. "She could run the business out of her home. All she really needs is a phone. But she's got this dinky one-room office in a house over on Twenty-third."

"Who owns the house?"

"Good point. I'll check with the tax people." He heaved off the desk. "Let's get some dinner and then see what the cleaning crew has to say."

Bunch drove his Bronco and we headed for the southwest corner of the city, an area of shopping malls and office complexes surrounded by restaurants that did good business with the singles and working couples who populated the area. Health spas, mom-and-pop franchises, and large, high-rise apartment buildings filled up the rolling hills and promised luxury living close to downtown.

"How many employees?"

"The books say ten. But her schedule only lists about fifty jobs. There's no need for ten workers to clean that few offices once a week."

"Shadow employees? A tax dodge?"

"She's doing it on her apartment house. Why not on the cleaning business, too? On the books, she has a small business with ten independent contractors who work part-time—no FICA, no mandatory medical to pay. In fact, she runs four or five illegals who work their butts off for nothing. She writes off a little overhead, pays a little tax, pockets a lot of wages. Anybody needs to know, that's how she struggles along to make a living. Meanwhile, she's got a sockful of thousand-dollar bills tucked away somewhere."

"You think she launders the money somehow?"

"Why should she, Dev? Is IRS after her? No. Is she living beyond her means of support? No. What she can't do is invest the money—not legally, anyway. My guess is she's hiding it outside the country. El Salvador, maybe. Cayman Islands. Hell, maybe she just stuffs it in a trunk under the bed. She wouldn't be the first one to bury a coffee can full of dollars in the backyard."

True enough. The people who had to worry about laundering money were those who wanted to spend a lot of it in this country and whom the IRS had under a microscope. The Bronco edged to the curb in front of a line of tan brick shops and parked behind a battered carryall. Through the plate-glass window of a friendly neighborhood loan company, we could see bustling figures vacuuming, wiping, dumping trash cans into large plastic garbage bags. A man leaned against one wall and smoked as he watched the women work quickly. Bunch rapped on the glass door and the man looked up, puzzled. Then he came over to open it slightly.

"Yes?"

"Are you with Olympia Janitorial Services?"

"Yes."

Behind him, the women had stopped to stare. I recognized the one on the vacuum cleaner as the woman who had been washing Mrs. Chiquichano's car. Her eyes recognized me too, but her face was a mask.

Bunch flicked his ID card and leaned against the wavering door. "We'd like to ask you people a couple questions."

The man's pockmarked face turned a sick gray and his lips sucked up somewhere under his full mustache. Sudden tension rang like a bell through the room, and for a moment they looked like birds poised to leap into the air.

"We're private detectives," I said in Spanish. "We're looking for two missing people." I held up the photographs of Nestor and Serafina. "Do any of you know these people?"

The man, breathing again, shook his head. "No."

Bunch easily pushed the door open against his weight and stepped in. "You haven't even looked at the picture, my man. Here."

He stared first at Bunch, growing aware of his size, then

carefully studied the photographs. "No sir. We don't know these ones."

"Show them to the ladies, Dev." He smiled at the man. "What's your job on the crew?"

"Me? Supervisor. And I drive the truck."

"Mrs. Chiquichano pay you well for that?"

Behind me, I heard the supervisor mutter uncomfortably and Bunch ask something else. The first woman looked carefully at the photographs and then, mute, shook her head and turned quickly back to her mop and pail. The next shrugged and said, "No." The woman on the vacuum cleaner looked hard at me before she gazed at the photographs. "No, sir," she whispered, her eyes snagging mine again. Without moving her head, she rolled her eyes toward the back door and then handed the picture to me. We thanked them, and the man watched us pull away into the night. I told Bunch to go around the block and let me off at the alley.

"What for?"

"One of the women wants to tell me something."

"Jesus, Dev, don't you ever learn? It could be another setup."

I pulled my cap tighter over the bandage that still gripped my scalp. "These people have no reason. The bikers are the only ones to pull crap like that."

"I'll follow along anyway."

"Suit yourself."

But halfway down the silent and dark alley, I was relieved to think of Bunch at my back. The only light came from the main street, over the wall of stores—a thin glow reflected off the low clouds that had started to fill Denver's shallow valley as the day's air cooled. The far end of the lane was marked by a fainter gray, and glass chips grated beneath my shoes as I picked my way past garbage cans and Dumpsters whose doors hung blackly open. The sudden rush of a dog behind a fence on the other side brought a prickle of quick sweat down my back, and I paused a moment to let the deep growls die out.

It was hard to make out the shop names on the doors, but I glimpsed light falling from a rear window and peered through the dirty glass. One of the women scrubbed rapidly at the washroom mirror. I leaned beside the closed door and waited.

A few minutes later, the door opened and a pale plastic sack of trash thumped onto the pavement. Another followed, and a female shape stepped into the darkness and dragged one of the bags toward a Dumpster at the corner of the building. The shape wrestled it in and turned and saw me against the wall.

"Aiii!"

"Shhhh—*cuidado! La otra mujer quiere hablar conmigo.*"

"*¡Dios mío, señor! ¡Usted me asustó!*"

She went inside quickly, and a moment later, the other woman came out, carrying a half-empty bag of trash.

"You've seen those people in the photographs?" I whispered in Spanish.

"No, senor. I'm sorry. I don't even know them. But you're looking for them to help them, yes?"

"Yes. Their relatives hired me to find them."

"Hired you? Ah . . ."

"What's wrong?"

"I have no money."

"Does that mean you want me to find someone?"

She spoke quickly before I might say I wouldn't help. "Felicidad de Silva. My friend. She's gone—disappeared."

"When?"

"Three months ago."

"What happened?"

"I don't know." The woman stopped suddenly and listened. From inside the shop the man's voice called "*¡Catalina!*"

"*¡Momentito!*" she called back. "Here." She fumbled inside her brassiere and handed me a folded piece of paper, warm from her flesh. "This is Felicidad's boyfriend's name. Can you help me? I don't have any money now, but I will pay when I can—I promise!"

"*¡Catalina—vamos ahora!*" the voice called again.

"Go on in—I'll toss the trash." I shoved the paper into a pocket and hoisted the last bag over to the Dumpster. The door shut behind her, and the silhouette of a man's head filled the small wire-glass window as he peered suspiciously into the dark. I waited, motionless against the bulk of shadow that was the Dumpster, until the silhouette disappeared and the light clicked off.

Bunch was leaning against the Bronco's fender when I reached the end of the alley. "I thought you were going to back me up."

"You told me to suit myself, Dev. It suited me to wait here." He slammed the door and started the car. "I sure as hell don't want to be where I'm not wanted, old buddy, and as bitchy as you've been these last few days, I'm not sure I want to be anywhere around you."

I had heard my own words on occasion lately and noted the irritability behind them. What's worse, I'd even been aware of a carelessness about how my words hit people. It was as if I were trying to provoke and anger all those around me, and I didn't seem to mind that I did. Some of it might have been the soreness in my shoulder and head. A lot of it, I decided, was because neither case seemed to be going anywhere. But none of it was because of Bunch. "I'm sorry, Bunch. I guess I'm stewing about the business. And that call from Costello—it still hasn't come through."

"Hey, no problem. Just give me a raise and all is forgiven." I lifted a middle finger. "Here it is."

"I take it that's a no?"

"And screw Senora Gutierrez and her cousin Nestor, too."

"Uh-oh. Another lead gone sour."

"Worse." I pulled the slip of paper from my pocket. "There's another illegal missing: Felicidad de Silva. She's a friend of one of those women. She asked me to look for her."

"Another one? Holy shit! This keeps up, INS won't have to worry about illegals at all."

I read the name on the paper—Rafael Garcia—and a telephone number. "This is her boyfriend. I told the woman I'd look into it for her."

"For free?"

"Why not? That's our going rate." I added, "She said she'd pay later."

"And you believed that? An old moneygrubber like you?"

"That promise is more than we got from the other two."

Bunch pulled onto the apron of a gas station and coasted to the phone hood. "We're building up points in heaven, Dev. Think of it that way."

"Yeah. No good deed goes unpunished."

The man's worried voice gave me directions. His apartment was in one of those brick boxes that nestle between private homes over on the east side, the kind called "garden level" because the shrubbery comes in the windows.

"Rafael Garcia?"

He was a thin, nervous man, around thirty, with a trimmed mustache that emphasized the width of his mouth and its narrow lips, and reminded me vaguely of some Hispanic movie star who always smoked thin cigars. "I don't know what happened to Felicidad. One day she just didn't show up no more. We had it all set for a date, you know? She and Catalina and Maria Linda, they were all going to the movies. Only Felicidad was coming over here, you know? That's the way we had to do it because of the old bat."

"Mrs. Chiquichano?"

"Yeah. Her. She didn't want any of the girls to make friends with nobody up here. Not until they worked their—" He stopped suddenly. "You guys with immigration? If you are, I got my green card. I'm legal, man."

"We're not with immigration. We're looking for some illegals who have disappeared."

"Some?"

"Felicidad is the third, so far." I showed him Nestor's picture. "You ever see this man?"

He looked at it and shook his head. "It happens all the time, man—they get picked up, you know? Pffft, they're gone, like that."

"We don't think immigration got them."

He scratched under his bony chin, long, ragged fingernails loud against the whiskers, and his eyebrows pinched together in a frown. "Immigration didn't get them?"

"You weren't surprised when your girlfriend disappeared?"

"Well, sure. But I thought *la migra* grabbed her. I figured one day she'd show up again when she came back across." He shrugged, his plaid shirt bagging loosely on his frame. "It's not like I could do nothing about it, you know? Who am I supposed to ask, immigration? The *rinches?* Who?"

"What's *'rinches'?"* asked Bunch.

"Cops," I said. "Border slang. Are you Mexican?"

He nodded. "From B.C. Sur—near Las Cruces."

"You met Felicidad here in Denver?"

"Yeah. At the movies."

"How long ago was that?" asked Bunch.

"A year, I guess. A little more, maybe. Why?" He edged away from a hovering Bunch.

"You seem a bit nervous, Rafael," I said. "Are you nervous?"

"No! Well, a little, maybe. I don't know who you are, do I?"

"All we're doing is asking some questions," Bunch said, smiling. "Don't you want your girlfriend found?"

"Sure—yeah."

"Then why don't you tell us everything you remember about Felicidad—when you met her, what she told you about herself, the last time you saw her. Everything."

He did, slowly at first and then filling in the details when he saw that it really was Felicidad we were interested in. And that we weren't in much of a hurry to leave until he was through talking. He first sat beside Maria Linda in the movie—"She's really hot-looking, you know? Big *chichis, muy culona,* a real *buenota"*—but Maria Linda wouldn't even look at him, let alone talk. She was too scared—Mrs. Chiquichano had them all too scared to talk to anybody. He didn't know that at the time; he just thought they were stuck up, which was kind of funny because he knew they were country types—real *bembas*—who wouldn't know what to do with a real man if they had one between their legs. He saw them again next week and, just for a joke and because he thought they were stuck up, zeroed in on Felicidad. By the end of the movie, he had her eating out of his hand—literally: he was feeding her popcorn, which none of them had ever tasted because they only had enough money for the movie. Felicidad started telling him a little about herself, and they would meet once a week at the movies. Pretty soon the other two would go in to the film, and Felicidad would go with Rafael to his apartment. "That woman she works for, that *zoquete,* she owns Felicidad, man. And all the others, too. Brought them up from the south and owns them like slaves, man!"

"What do you know about Mrs. Chiquichano's apartment house?"

"Her what?"

Bunch leaned toward him. "Her apartment house. And the people who live there."

"Nothing, man! I never heard of it. We never talked about nothing like that."

"Did Felicidad tell you much about Mrs. Chiquichano?" I asked.

"Said she's a real bitch. Was real nice to her when she met her in El Sal, but once she had Felicidad up here, man, she turned." The thin shoulders rose and fell. "I told Felicidad she was stupid to be a slave like that. She should move out, I told her."

"Do you think that's what happened?"

The fingernails rasped again. "Maybe. But I don't think so. I mean, she would let me know." He shrugged. "I mean, she's hot for me, you know? She would tell me if she had her own place now."

"Why didn't she move out?"

"Scared. Scared if she did, the old bat would turn her in. And the others, too. That's what she told them—they were all responsible for each other. If one of them screwed up, she'd turn in the whole bunch to *la* fucking *migra.*"

"Did she say where Mrs. Chiquichano got her money?"

"She didn't have to, man—five years Felicidad promised to work for nothing. Room and board and that's it. That's where that *coda* gets her money."

"Did Felicidad talk about moving in with you when her time was up?"

He looked uncomfortable and then shrugged again. "I'm married, man. I got a wife and kids in Las Cruces."

"Felicidad knew about this?" Bunch asked.

"Yeah. I told her. After a while."

"Just before she disappeared?"

"Naw. Nothing like that. Maybe six months ago. I had to go home for a while, so I told her."

"She didn't mind?"

"Sure she did. Cried like hell. But she came back, you know?" The mustache stretched a bit. "Women are like that with me."

"Was she acting worried or afraid or in any way different before she disappeared?"

He didn't answer, and I settled back in the fake leather chair to wait. Finally, he heaved a sigh. "A little, yeah."

"What about?"

"She got herself pregnant, man." He went on quickly, "I told her I'd pay for an abortion, but she didn't want one. She said it was too far along."

"What was she going to do?"

"I don't know—she didn't know. I told her I'd give her money—she could go somewhere else—whatever." He looked up at Bunch. "Hell, man, I couldn't do much for her, could I? All I got's a green card. Immigration finds out I'm helping some illegal, I'm shit out of luck, right?"

"She was what, three months, four months, when she disappeared?"

"Almost six."

"And," said Bunch, "you were glad to see her go."

"What the hell could I do, man? I offered to pay for an abortion—I even started looking for *un matasanos.*"

"But," repeated Bunch, "you were glad to see Felicidad go."

"What you mean, man?"

"Maybe you were so glad to see her go, you helped her along."

"No, man! No way! She just stopped showing up, that's all! Ask Maria Linda—ask Catalina. She just wasn't there one morning. I mean, I asked, you know? I looked for her—hell, I was worried about her. I still am! I asked Maria Linda and she said Felicidad was just gone one morning. They came down for breakfast in *la puta's* house and Felicidad wasn't there. She wasn't in her bed, she wasn't anywhere. Just gone!"

8

"Dev, somebody would find something. Unless you're a god-damn undertaker and can handle bodies wholesale, somebody is going to find something."

We sat in the quiet office discussing the difficulties of making corpses disappear, even those that had no official existence or relatives to ask embarrassing questions.

"And why the hell would anybody kill them? What's the motive?"

We'd gone over that, too: They had nothing to steal, they made no enemies, they were too frightened to be a threat to anyone. And alive, they were a good source of income for the Mother Superior, as Bunch began to call Mrs. Chiquichano. Alive, they were the ideal citizens of the republic; dead, they weren't worth anything. There was no reason for them to be dead, but there was no place they seemed to disappear to. Agent Roybal of USINS said he had absolutely no records for any of the three—and he was very curious as to why we should be asking and how much we might know about other illegals. The hospitals, morgues, jails, and sheriff's departments responded negatively to Denver police inquiries made by Bunch's friend Sergeant Llewellen. Since the three didn't vote or own property or buy anything on credit, there were no leads from those sources, and since they were born out of the country and used fictitious Social Security numbers and home addresses, those avenues were closed too. And Mrs. Chiquichano refused to

answer our telephone calls or to reply to questions when we
went by her house or office. Three disappearances, all linked
to a woman who didn't want to admit anything about them.

"She'd have to say she was harboring and exploiting illegals,
Bunch. That's a real good reason for not wanting to be tied to
them."

"She knows we're not INS or the police."

"Maybe she doesn't believe us."

"Sure. That's why she threatened to call the cops if we went
to her office one more time." He shook his head. "She just
doesn't want anybody looking for them. Why?"

We had an answer for that question: because she had something to hide. But no answers to what she had to hide. So we
turned to things we might get answers for.

"Lou got a lab report on that slug Archy found in the Healey,
Dev. He says it's a .357-caliber rifle round, probably an H and
H Magnum. Son of a bitch can stop an elephant with one round.
No wonder it went through almost the whole damned car."

"A Magnum rifle load? That's a pro's weapon."

"Not your average squirrel shooter's rifle."

"It has to be the bikers."

"Yeah. What we figured. But he fired high on the first shot,
and that's an amateur's mistake."

"For which I'm grateful."

"I don't know," said Bunch. "I hate to see incompetence in
anything."

"Thanks. Speaking of incompetence, I don't suppose you've
found out who owns the house that Mrs. Chiquichano's office
is in?"

"Armoor Investments." Bunch cranked open the vent panel
in the office's arched window for the cool night breeze, and a
whiff of chemical fumes tinged the air. "Christ, I don't know
which is worse, the piano player that used to be up there or
the painter."

"She's a sculptor. She makes epoxy creations."

"She breathes that crap much longer, she'll be an epoxy

creation. And, no, I haven't found out who Armoor Investments is. The licensing bureau lists an S. Evangelou as the president, and they're licensed to do any legal business, which doesn't tell us dink."

"Anything on Mr. Evangelou?"

"Mrs. No record, no Better Business Bureau complaints, no licensing problems. A four-square citizen."

"There's something in all this, Bunch. Damn it, I feel it—there has to be something we're looking right at and not seeing."

"We'll have to keep looking until we do, then." Bunch yawned mightily and said it was time to head for the barn.

"How's your leg?"

"Fine. Muscles're still a little sore, but it's fine."

"Tomorrow's the day."

"For what?"

"For when your rabies start to pop out."

"I don't have rabies."

"I don't want you to bite me, Bunch."

"I said I don't have fucking rabies!"

"I'd feel safer if we had the dog."

"And I told you I'm working on it, all right? I'm working on it—I got a dog trainer I'm talking to and she's come up with an idea, all right?" He swung the door shut behind us and clumped down the stairs. "Jesus, you get something in your skull and you just keep after it, don't you?"

"I don't want you biting the customers either. It's bad press for the business. Look what happened to Count Dracula."

"Maybe that explains my sudden hunger for raw hamburger. Good night, Dev."

I had a hunger too, but it wasn't sudden. It was the continual gnawing that I should see something about Nestor and Chiquichano and the others. On the way home, I swung through the north end of the city and stopped at the sagging apartment house to knock on a few doors and ask a few more questions.

But it was no good; none of them would say anything about Nestor or the Frentaneses or de Silva. Even Senor Medina, who, according to Mrs. Gutierrez, sometimes played cards with Nestor, only shook his head.

"I know nothing, senor. *Lo siento.*"

"You've heard about Felix Frentanes being picked up?"

A worried silence that answered the question.

"*La patrona* made sure that everybody in the apartment's heard about it, right?"

"Senor—"

"Okay, okay." I should have known it would be a waste of time; you could feel the terror in the chill air of the dim hallways, in the tense silences behind each door. "There are people disappearing from this place and nobody knows what's happening to them. You should at least try to look after each other."

Medina, cropped hair showing a mix of black and silver, stared down at the strip of thin carpeting just inside the door. His lips were a tight line against his feelings as I pulled the door closed.

At home, my feet up on the cold fireplace and a mug of ale at my elbow, I thought of one more thing to try if it wasn't too late for a phone call. Jerry Kagan, one of my classmates who elected medical school rather than law school after graduation, was setting up as a pediatrician; he was used to calls at night.

His wife answered and seemed relieved to hear my voice. I gossiped with her for a few seconds about her kids and the tribulations of setting up a business, before she put Jerry on the line. It had been a lot of months since we talked, and we told each other familiar stories of our days on the Stanford crew and remembered names that made us laugh together.

"Dev, you're after something."

"It's that obvious?"

"Yeah. And you better get to it before my answering service does—I'm on call tonight."

"Okay—I've got a man who cut himself enough to need

stitches. The doctor he went to is an immunologist and surgeon. He sent the patient through a series of tests—let me read them to you." I went down the list from Nestor's medical claim. "My question is why. Why so many tests?"

"I'm a long way from immunology, Dev—"

"But can you give me a guess?"

"That's all it would be. Obviously, he wanted the test panel to learn about the man's blood and tissue types. What's his blood type?"

"I don't know. Is it important?"

"It could be. Or possibly the doctor thought the man might be hemophiliac, if the bleeding was hard to stop. But that's still an excessive number of tests—even for an immunologist."

"What's that mean?"

"Aw, nothing. Just a little professional cattiness. Immunologists generally don't take much interest in patient care; they tend to be research doctors."

"The patient is an illegal alien, probably with a history of poor medical care. Would there be something special the doctor might be looking for?"

"Parasites, perhaps. Lymph problems . . . There's a variety of things he could look for. But the question, like you said, is why. Unless there was some difficulty with care for the wound, I'm not sure why all those tests would be called for."

"AIDS?"

"Well, yes, screening for HIV is becoming routine, especially by health care personnel who deal with emergencies. But again, that's just one test, initially."

"Why would he go to a surgeon rather than the emergency room of a hospital?"

"Hell, Dev, you're the detective. You'd have to ask the patient that."

"Do you know a Dr. Morris Matheney?"

"I've heard of him but I don't know him. Not my field."

It wasn't mine either, and the only other avenues I had into the hermetic world of professional medicine were the official ones, whose purpose was to protect doctors rather than inform nosy investigators. It looked like another expense of time, effort, and money that would lead nowhere, and despite the hard workout before a late meal and the dram or two of heavy, rich Bellehaven ale after, I slept restlessly enough to hear the thud of the milk box and the crackle of the newspaper man's tires as he cruised leaf-strewn curbs.

My first trip in the morning was to public records, where I learned not much more about Armoor Investments than I already knew. It was a private corporation whose stock was held by unnamed principal investors, and whose chief executive officer was Sophia Evangelou. Her address was the corporation office in South Denver. I photocopied the page and headed for my office, still foggy from lack of sleep.

The phone answerer held a message from Archy. He'd located some parts for the Healey, but was having trouble with suspension and steering units. Nobody anywhere in the country had answered his inquiry on the parts wire. "But I got a lead on two Healey three thousands—one in L.A. and one up in Portland. I can put you in touch with the sellers if you want. Let me know soon."

I called back and got the information. I didn't have to use it—there was still a chance Archy could locate the parts he needed through the Austin-Healey club. But as the mechanic said, it would be the same car in name only, anyway.

A second voice on the answerer, one I didn't recognize, asked that Mr. Bunchcroft call her and left a number, which I copied on a memo for him. The few other calls were offers I could refuse, and I had just settled with a cup of coffee to stare at the scant information on Armoor Investments when Uncle Wyn came in.

"What, a funeral?"

"Hi, Uncle Wyn. No—just I've got a couple cases that aren't going anywhere. And I'm not sure what to kick to make them move."

"Midseason slump, is it?" He limped over to the window and

gazed at the Front Range, with its remnants of snow glowing in the morning sun. "I think the Dodgers are going to take it. The Dodgers and the Yankees. Just like the old days—except it's not like the old days. The old days never come back. The Los Angeles Dodgers, for God's sake."

He was one of the few left who still remembered, let alone bemoaned, the Big Sellout. "I'll put my money on Boston."

"And I'll take it. What are you giving me?"

"You give me odds— What's the matter?"

He had grunted a sharp, involuntary sound. "Knee—damned arthritis. If I wasn't so old, I think I'd get a new one."

"A new what, Mr. Kirk?" Bunch closed the door behind him.

"A new knee. One of those plastic things you can't feel."

"Hey, why not a whole new leg while you're at it? They're transplanting everything else."

"You're right, Bunch. New leg, new heart, new lungs. I need a complete body job."

"Yeah—just like Dev's car." He glanced into his in-box. "What's this?" He held up the memo with the telephone number to call.

"Another missing Salvadoran," I lied. "Found it on the tape when I came in."

He grunted and dialed the number. Uncle Wyn and I talked baseball until Bunch hung up. I suspected it was Uncle Wyn's way of pulling me out of the mopes, and it worked.

"That was a lady with a dog," said Bunch. "Things are all set."

"Ah." Then, "Tonight?"

"Tonight." He looked uncomfortable. "She says she's coming along."

"Wait a minute—"

"I already told her it's not a good idea. She says she's the only one who can handle her dog."

"Bunch, you know what those people are like out there!"

"Yeah. I know. But she says she's coming along anyway."

With a twinge of pain, Uncle Wyn heaved himself to his feet. "And something tells me you boys got work to do. See you later."

"Hey, Mr. Kirk, don't run off—"

"I won't run, that's for sure. But I got work to do too."

"Bunch, we're not taking anyone else out to that farm."

"We'll talk about it. Hell, you talk about it—you tell her that tonight."

A few minutes after Uncle Wyn left, Bunch and I followed. The landlord for Olympia Janitorial Services had her offices in a small suite of rooms on the eighth floor of a tower that overlooked the Denver Technological Center. From the large windows, we could see various glass and concrete buildings loom as widely scattered modernistic shapes across the rolling prairie south of the city. If Ms. Evangelou felt dwarfed by the room and its spacious view, she did not show it. She was a small woman, with long, slightly wild hair that spiraled out from her head. Her movements were quick and decisive, and she told us as we came in the door that she didn't have time to waste.

"We appreciate your giving us a few minutes," said Bunch. "It's a routine security clearance and shouldn't take long." He had called to tell the woman that Mrs. Chiquichano's firm had bid on a janitorial contract for a company that did restricted work for the government, and that we were employed by the company to run a clearance on the applicant. "How long have you known Mrs. Chiquichano?"

"A little over three years. Three years and three months, to be exact."

"And how did you meet her?"

"We advertised office space for rent. She answered the ad."

"Has she been good about paying her rent?"

"Every month." A slight smile that showed two lines etched at the corners of her mouth. "We give one month's grace—and only one."

I asked, "Have you had any dealings with her other than the usual business contacts?"

Ms. Evangelou's dark eyes traced my outline from face to shoes and back again, slowly. "No, Mr. Kirk. I'm very selective about who I contact in my private life."

"Meaning you don't like her?"

"Meaning I have no reason to meet her except on business."

"Have you heard of anything that might disqualify her or her company from working around classified information?" Bunch asked.

The woman shook her head, lips pressed in thought. "No. But she is a recent citizen, I understand."

"From El Salvador?"

"I think so. I don't know if that's good or bad. Most of the traitors one reads about are born and raised in Boston or some such."

"Does she do a lot of business out of her office?"

"I don't know. Enough to pay the rent, at least."

"How much is that?" Bunch asked.

She flipped through a Rolodex file. "Four twenty-five. It's one of the smaller units."

"Does she really need an office to run this kind of business?" I asked. "It seems she could do it by working out of her home."

"She chooses to have an office, Mr. Kirk. Perhaps for prestige—perhaps it's a tax advantage. I do know that she uses her garage space there to park her company van."

"What kind of van?"

"A Dodge carryall, I think. Is that kind of information really vital to national security?" She began to busy herself with papers.

"You're the manager of the building where Mrs. Chiquichano's office is?"

"Among other time-consuming duties, yes."

"It's owned by Armoor Investments, and you're the president of that firm as well?"

She looked up, surprised. "Yes. Why?"

Bunch said apologetically, "There's a section on the form for evaluating respondents—it's all routine. Can you tell us who the principals are in the investment firm?"

"I could, but I don't know why I should. I'm the one answering questions—not them."

"Yes ma'am. It just helps us do our job a little better—looks more complete on the form. You know how the government likes things. And it might help Mrs. Chiquichano's application."

"It seems rather silly . . . It's your fairly standard real estate investment company. I'm one of the partners, and the others are doctors. I used to be a nurse; they hired me to run the company when I got fed up with nursing."

I nodded. "We've run across a number of businesses like that. Can you just give us some names to jot down on the form?"

"Blomquist, Butler, Fletcher, Matheney, and Zales."

"That's Morris Matheney?"

"Yes, and if you need their addresses, you can find them in the physicians' section of the Yellow Pages. Now I'm quite busy, gentlemen . . ."

Both of us were quiet on the way down. Finally Bunch said what I was thinking. "That guy Matheney—his name's beginning to come up a lot of times."

"And usually in connection with Mrs. Chiquichano. Maybe it's just coincidence."

"Right. And we both believe in coincidence. What time is it?"

"Close to four. Why?"

"It's not Wednesday, so he's not playing golf. I think we should talk to him again." Bunch pushed open the building's glass door and we stepped into the heat outside. "You know what Spinoza says: Accident is the name we give to an event whose causes we don't understand."

"I didn't know Spinoza said that."

"Well, if he didn't, he should have." Bunch turned up the air conditioner as I pulled the rented Subaru into traffic. "You literary types—no imagination."

Dr. Matheney's receptionist looked doubtful when I admitted we didn't have an appointment.

"It'll only take a couple seconds, miss. Less time than a drug salesman takes. Tell him it's about Nestor Calamaro—one of his ex-patients."

She came back with her worry relieved. "He's with a patient right now. He can see you in about ten minutes."

We were moved from the general reception room to Matheney's private waiting area, where the magazines were newer. The doctor himself came to lead us into his comfortable office. The soft brown eyes, magnified by their glasses, studied each of us for a long moment. "You were here a few days ago," he said to me. "It was about . . . ?"

"Mrs. Chiquichano. You gave me some information about her."

"Ah, yes. I remember now. What can I help you with this time?"

I showed him a copy of Calamaro's medical form. "I understand you requested these tests?"

"May I ask how you got this?"

"Through the medical insurance underwriters, doctor. There was some question about the necessity of the tests."

"Question? What question?" Something leapt and hardened in the man's eyes, and his smooth, strong fingers began to stroke the fringe of chin whiskers. "There is no question—it was my judgment that he needed those tests. That's all there is to it."

"We understand that, doctor. We only need a little information about the basis for that judgment."

"The basis of that judgment, Mr. Kirk, was the lab report of his blood samples. Samples which I routinely order before any type of surgery."

"Yes sir. The lab report said . . . ?"

"Obviously, there were some abnormalities in his blood."

"Yes sir. Can you amplify on that?"

The doctor smiled slightly. "Not without the patient's permission. Do you have permission to access his medical records, Mr. Kirk?"

"No. He disappeared three weeks ago."

"Then, without his permission—or a court order—I cannot discuss his case. Now, if you gentlemen will excuse me, I have patients waiting."

"Perhaps your information can help us find him, doctor."

"Didn't you hear what I just said?"

Bunch spoke up. "How serious was his surgery?"

"What do you mean?"

"He came to you for a cut—an industrial accident. Not pre-planned surgery. Why didn't he go to the emergency room at Warner or Denver General?"

The fingers again stroked the glossy black beard. "Perhaps because he was familiar with us. I believe, Mr. Kirk, you pointed out that we did his TB screening, right?"

"Yes. But this was an emergency."

"Since you insist: Mrs. Chiquichano telephoned me to say a friend of hers was hurt and to ask if I would take a look at him. Naturally, as she was an acquaintance . . ."

"But why you? Why not an emergency room that could handle it quickly?"

"Because he was an illegal alien, Mr. Kirk! Because he was afraid to go to a hospital—afraid they would turn him in. I helped him. And, I might add, I helped him pro bono. I am not with the immigration authorities, I am not an employer of illegal aliens, and I do happen to believe that people who need medical help should receive it. In fact, I've taken an oath to provide it." He stood and opened his office door. "One of the stupidities of the immigration authorities is to force into hiding people who could well have contagious diseases. That endangers public welfare far more than the presence of a few low-paid immigrants. Now if you have no other questions, I am in a hurry."

"Have you seen or talked to Mrs. Chiquichano since her people stopped cleaning your offices?"

"No."

"She didn't bring in Mr. Calamaro?"

"No. I believe he came by cab or bus. And left the same way. Why?"

"One of her workers, Felicidad de Silva, needed medical treatment. She was an illegal too. I wondered if Mrs. Chiqui-chano brought her to you."

The man's brown eyes behind the heavy glasses stared levelly back. "No. I never heard of that woman."

9

"That guy lies like a rug." Bunch geared the Bronco down and turned off the paved highway onto a graded dirt road that wound upward between two steep outcroppings. We were in Coal Creek Canyon, about fifteen miles west of downtown Denver, looking for a dirt driveway and the name Fairbaugh. "Matheney's a liar, Dev. You know it and I know it."

An aura of deceit had clung to the man's words, and I was as certain as Bunch that the good physician knew more about Calamaro than he admitted—and perhaps even something of Felicidad. "How do we prove it?"

"We go in and take a look around his office."

"Bunch, you can bet any files on Calamaro have been cleaned up. And if he did see any other illegals, their files have been destroyed by now."

"Yeah, probably. If Matheney even made any to start with." He slowed at a Y in the road. A dozen or so name signs were nailed to a fencepost, their letters fuzzy in the twilight. Some pointed up one branch of the road, some pointed to the other route. "There it is." He turned left and we lurched over a spine of rock that erupted through the grit and sand. "But then again, he might have overlooked something. We ought to check it out, Dev."

If a PI got caught breaking the law, he'd lose his freedom as quickly as the next burglar. "It's a bad risk." Contrary to television, PIs didn't just break and enter on a whim. Not many good burglars did, either. It took at least a bit of planning: reconnaissance, logistics for the right equipment, a tight schedule that accommodated any security patrols, and concealment of some kind. It took the kind of preparation Bunch and I were doing right now in advance of our little raid on the Wilcox farm.

"I looked his office over this afternoon, Dev. It has a two-bit security system tied into the phone lines. A quick clip and it's dead."

"It's not worth the gamble."

"I'm trying to tell you there is no gamble. It's a walk-through. Think about it: ground floor, dead security, plenty of shrubbery around the windows. I told you I checked it out."

"Well, let's worry about one caper at a time, okay? If we get through this in one piece, then we'll think about Matheney."

" 'Caper'?"

"That's detective talk. All the literate-type detectives talk about capers."

Another sign for Fairbaugh pointed us up a two-rut road that led between tall pines and a scattering of shorter aspen. "You literary types really impress me. I'd no idea how much I was missing from my life."

"Admitting ignorance is the first step to wisdom, Bunch. Even on a journey as long as yours. Is that the place?"

The track twisted among the pale, smooth trunks of aspen. Just beyond the grove, at the edge of a meadow, stood a dark A-frame. Its porches and eaves were trimmed with freshly painted flowers and scrollwork like something from Switzerland. A large retriever heaved to its feet and watched our approach, tail wagging hesitantly. A woman came onto the porch to wait for us. She wore jeans and a plaid shirt against the chill of the mountain evening, and her hair was pulled back into a long ponytail. Bunch turned off the engine, and we sat a second or two enjoying the almost total silence of the mountains.

"Come on in—the coffee's on."

"Hi, Anita. This is Devlin Kirk—Anita Fairbaugh." She

shook hands with a strong grip and a wide, white smile that lightened a pair of pale blue eyes all the more surprising against her dark and tanned skin. We followed her into the A-frame's small but tidy living room, where a standing metal fireplace fit under the steep slope of roof. A long wall of bookshelves jammed with titles divided that room from the rest of the cabin. Bunch had told me a little about the woman on the way up: She had been married to a Denver cop killed during a routine traffic stop. Now she lived alone at the edge of Roosevelt National Forest and apparently liked it. She also trained dogs, and that's why we were here.

"Is Matilda ready to do her thing?" Bunch handed a cup of coffee to me and dumped some milk into his.

"She's ready to go. She's in the run out back."

"This could be a tricky operation tonight," said Bunch.

"You've already told me. I'm still going."

Bunch shook his head. "It's not a good idea. Tell her, Dev."

"You shouldn't—"

"Matilda's not going alone, Mr. Kirk. She's in heat—she'll be nervous enough as it is, and with a new handler, she might not work at all. Besides, if I'm not around, she could run, and I have no intention of losing a good dog."

"If something happens," I said, "we're all going to run. We'd be damn fools not to, and this is no place—"

"For a woman? Is that what you were about to say?" This time the smile did not reach her eyes.

"For anyone who doesn't know what they're getting into. And especially for someone who doesn't have to be there. If there were another way to do this, believe me, I wouldn't be going."

"Come on, Anita. I told you they shot at us already. These are bad dudes—they came close to killing Dev, here. Would have, too, if he wasn't as lucky as he is dumb."

"I know what you told me. And I know what my dog is like." She drained her cup and said in a reasonable tone, "It's either both of us or neither of us. Which do you want?"

We rode down the canyon in silence, the dog carriers in the rear of the Bronco and Anita in the backseat. In the distance, glimpsed between the shifting walls of rock, we could see the lights of Denver glowing against the dark of the prairies, and above them, in long, silent glides, running lights of airplanes stacked up in the holding pattern over Stapleton Airport. Ahead of us lay the flatlands, and in vague darkness to the north, the Wilcox farm. It took about forty minutes to reach Erie, and by the time we got there, night had fully arrived. Bunch drove slowly down the now-familiar county lane, and we pulled off in the shadow of a ridge and turned off the headlights to let our eyes adjust.

"Is it far from here?" Anita had let Matilda out of the carrier and was stroking the dog's ears.

"Half a mile, a little more. The farm's just over that rise." Bunch and I zipped up the dark nylon windbreakers that we called our ninja outfits. We had on dark trousers, too, but boots rather than the tennis shoes we usually wore. The prairie was full of cactus and yucca spears that canvas wouldn't daunt. "You stay close to us, Anita. Like I say, these guys don't mess around—they'll start shooting."

"I understand."

She tried not to show her nervousness, but it was in her voice and I didn't blame her. I was nervous too: I'd been here before. We got out of the truck and stepped carefully between the strands of barbed wire and started up the slope. Behind me, Matilda's panting made a steady rhythm as I followed Bunch's shadow and, occasionally, looked back to see if Anita was still with us. This time, instead of camera and night scope, I lugged a dog carrier whose plastic sides scraped loudly against the weeds. It was empty now. If things went the way they were supposed to, it would be full coming back.

"There it is."

Bunch's whisper was more felt than heard through the dark, and Anita and I edged forward to look down the slope at the farm, with its steel-blue yard light and its low windows glowing.

The breeze rose upslope, floating the sound of heavy steel guitars twanging and wavering discordantly.

"Sounds like a party going on," said Bunch. "We'll go down this way and come up behind the barn where the shadows are."

Matilda whined once, but Anita's sharp whisper hushed the dog and we crouched and eased our way downslope. The faint glow from the yard light seemed to pick us out as if we were on stage, and I welcomed the heavier shadows of the cottonwoods that waited at the foot of the hill. We paused there to study the farmyard. The smell of gasoline and oil came strong from the crowd of motorcycles lumped together in the darkness. The guitars screamed to a long, high note that stretched and repeated maniacally and then cut off to a startling silence. The faint cry of a child came across the yard and died out a few minutes later.

"Better let Matilda do her thing so we can get out of here," I muttered to Bunch.

"Yeah. Anita?"

She whispered to the dog, "Matilda—round 'em up, girl, round 'em up."

The dog whined once and then padded out into the light and began sniffing in wide circles as she drifted toward the open space in front of the barn.

A sudden deep bark erupted from under the porch and the German shepherd lunged toward Matilda, who cowered and rolled over, tail tucked between her legs and wagging eagerly. A figure came to the front door and flicked on the porch light. Its strong glare stabbed into the darkness around us, and we hid in the fragments of black cast by the motorcycles.

"Is that the one?" whispered Anita.

"The dog? Naw. It was a pit bull." Bunch gestured her into silence.

The man on the porch stared through the glow of the yard light, and another silhouette joined him.

"What's the matter?" The voice carried across the farmyard clearly.

"Lothar was barking at something."

"See anything?"

"Another dog, it looks like. Stray."

"Want to shoot it?"

I felt Anita stir and gripped her arm.

"Naw. Lothar can take care of it." They went back inside. The screen door slapped.

Anita made a chirping noise with her lips and Matilda, followed closely by the German shepherd's nose, trotted toward us. Bunch waited until they were within ten feet, the prancing German shepherd too interested in Matilda's strut to notice us. The soft thump of the air pistol said Bunch had fired the tranquilizer dart. The shepherd yelped once and bit at his hip and then slowly turned in a circle and, with a puzzled whine, flopped over. The porch light flicked on again.

"Lothar? Hey, Lothar!" The bearded man whistled shrilly. "Lothar—here, boy!"

"Matilda—round 'em up, girl, round 'em up."

Matilda trotted back into the yard and wagged her tail at the man.

"What's the matter, John?" The voice came from the living room.

"I thought I heard Lothar yelp."

"He's probably after some coon."

The man on the porch didn't answer. Instead, he crouched down and tried to call Matilda forward. The dog sat and watched him, panting happily. He came slowly down the steps toward her. "Here, dog. Nice dog. What's your name, fella?"

Matilda backed toward us, tail wagging. The man followed a few steps and then looked around and whistled for Lothar again.

"I thought she only rounded up other dogs," I whispered.

"With that guy, she can't tell the difference," mumbled Bunch. We crouched, ready to jump the man when he came close.

"Lothar! Here, boy—here, Lothar!"

We watched him stand and listen to the night, head cocked to hear the German shepherd's bark somewhere. Finally he said, "Shit," and went back to the house, walking more quickly. The screen door slammed but the porch light didn't go out. Instead, the man came out with another dog on a leash and unsnapped it. "Go, Sid—go find Lothar."

The pit bull trotted down the steps, its heavy-jawed head out of proportion to the rest of its stubby body.

"Matilda—round 'em up, girl."

She whined and pranced back out. The pit bull growled and ran hard toward her and, as Matilda rolled over, began to sniff an interesting scent. Crouching, Matilda walked our way, looking over her shoulder at the pit bull and the man watching from the porch. "Sid—go find Lothar, boy. Go find Lothar!"

Matilda whined, and Sid had things other than Lothar on his mind.

"Sid! Sid Vicious—come back here, Sid!"

Bunch aimed, the barrel of the air pistol following the stiff-legged walk of the pit bull.

"Goddamn dumb dog!" The man came forward to reach for the bull's collar, close enough for us to smell his fragrance of sweat and tobacco. The pistol popped and the man said, "What the fuck." He slapped a hand at his neck and swayed for a long moment before falling heavily in the dust. The pit bull, ears up, stared at him in surprise, then at us, and then snarled. Matilda was forsaken.

"Shoot him, Bunch—get him."

"I'm loading the damn thing!"

With a growl the dog charged, a dim white shape streaking through broken shadows toward us. I shoved Anita onto a tree limb and swung up myself as Bunch kicked out to keep the dog away. But it snapped onto his leg and began to twist sideways, trying to gouge out a mouthful of Bunch's flesh. He shoved the dart gun against the dog's chest and fired, and we swung out of the tree and pulled back into the shadows as another man came out onto the porch, drawn by the bull's snarls.

"John? What the hell's going on? Johnny?"

"Come on, Anita. Time to go."

"What about Bunch?"

"He's coming. Let's go."

We kept to the shadow of the barn, moving as quickly as silence would allow toward the ridge. Behind us, I heard Bunch whisper curses as he tried to pry the limp and dragging dog from his leg. "Wait up, Dev, goddamn it—wait a minute!"

"Use the pistol barrel—pry his jaw off with the pistol barrel!"

He wrestled with the clamped mouth.

"Goddamn dog!"

"Is it the same leg?"

"Yes."

"Count your blessings."

"Matilda—come, girl. Come!"

I dumped the unconscious pit bull into the carrier and crouched as I followed Anita and Matilda to the edge of the barn's long shadow. Behind it, on the other side of the tall building, we heard the same voice calling John and moving closer.

"Let's get the hell out of here," muttered Bunch.

We managed to crest the high ground before John was found. A voice shouted for people in the house to come out, and the four of us ran as hard as we could down to the Bronco. I drove this time, letting Bunch swab at his latest dog bite with the hydrogen peroxide we'd brought just in case.

"Look at that stuff bubble up, Bunch—it's rabies, for sure."

"Just drive!" He shone the flashlight up and down his wet calf. "It's not as bad as the first time." Two pairs of heavy, knee-length wool socks contributed to that. "He bruised the hell out of it, but he didn't break the skin."

In the backseat, Anita patted Matilda and fed her bits of dog biscuit. "Do you people do this often?"

"More than we need to. All Bunch had to do was take a few little shots—but no, he had to choose the hard way." I lurched the Bronco onto the paved road and we sped up I-25 and took a roundabout loop back to Anita's cabin.

It was after midnight when we reached Denver again. I asked Bunch how his leg felt, and he said fine. "I've had worse scratches in the sack with a broad." Then he added, "I think we should make one more stop, Dev, while we're dressed for the occasion."

"You want to go by Matheney's clinic. That it?"

"Hey, the night is young and we're so beautiful. Besides, like I told you, it'll be a walk-through."

It might have been except for the banks of glaring lights that surrounded the building and left no shadow for an avenue of approach to its doors and windows.

"Well, he didn't have the damn things on during the day, did he?"

"Bunch, anybody looking out a window from one of these apartments will see us. The place looks like a goddamn car lot."

"Guy's electric bill must be a bitch. Why you think he spends that much on lights?"

"Because he doesn't want people like you and me breaking in."

Medical offices were favorite targets for dopeheads; many doctors were careless with drug storage. They found safes to be too cumbersome for the day's business and relied on building security to protect their medicines and samples.

"Let's try the alley. There's bound to be a way."

We cruised down the crowded, narrow lane that ran behind the office and neighboring apartments. A high board fence blocked off the rear of Matheney's building from access, but a latched door led from the trash bin through the fence. Bunch coasted out the other end of the alley and turned onto a side street and parked. "We go in the back door."

"There's an apartment with two hundred windows looking right down on it."

"It's the only way. Besides, I got a gimmick."

I followed him down the shadowy side of the alley and he opened the gate. We stepped through, pressing ourselves against the half-lit boards of the fence. In front of us, a pool of glaring light spotted the rear door like center stage on opening night. Bunch pulled the dart pistol from his shirt and aimed carefully aloft.

"What are you doing?"

"Shhhh."

The long barrel made its soft, muffled pop. A metallic clatter bounced from the hood protecting the bulb.

"See how quiet that is? Nothing to worry about."

"I'd be less worried if you were a better shot."

He aimed again, and the pop was followed by a louder pop and the tinkle of sprayed glass, first against the metal hood and then on the asphalt below. The bright circle of light on the back door faded to gray.

"Let's give it a couple minutes," said Bunch.

We listened for footsteps coming to investigate. The only sounds were traffic passing on surrounding streets and the distant, fading wail of an emergency vehicle headed for Warner Memorial. Bunch told me to wait, and he strolled toward the dimness and paused a moment at the corner where the telephone line dropped from a pole and snaked down the wall into the building. Then he bent over the brass lock in the door, both hands busy. I scanned the alley and the windows of the tall apartment building behind the clinic. Finally Bunch whispered, "Okay," and stepped inside.

Beyond the small delivery and storage area, the hallway led past a series of doors, most of which were open. The light reflecting through uncurtained windows was enough so we didn't have to use the penlights; Bunch opened one of the shut doors and hissed for me.

It was a treatment room, complete with operating table, lights, anesthesia tanks, equipment trays, monitors. A small compressor in the corner of the room ran with a steady, muffled shudder.

"Matheney's a surgeon," I said. "Maybe he does the small stuff here."

"Looks like a MASH unit to me."

"Come on, Bunch—his office is down this way."

The color-coded hallway led around a couple bends to Matheney's dark waiting room. The pale ghosts of my hands, gloved in latex, pressed open the office door. I closed the blinds across the outside window. Bunch began rifling through the filing cabinets beside the nurse's desk. I started on the drawers of Matheney's desk.

They held what desks should hold: papers and forms of various kinds, clips and rubber bands and stickers, notepads, memo pads, stamps, the usual paraphernalia of offices everywhere. In the side drawers I found a few thin folders with his personal correspondence and flipped through the typed sheets: letters about professional meetings, unanswered inquiries from young doctors wanting positions, copies of letters from Matheney to other physicians about patients. A second, thinner file held correspondence with Cryogenic Biological Laboratories and dealt with technical descriptions of blood and tissue types and the physical environment necessary to transport them. The third file simply said "Personal" and held letters to friends.

Using the small Nikon Tele-Touch, I photographed any files that seemed even remotely promising, then turned to the remaining drawers. They held drug samples and fliers from pharmaceutical companies touting their wares and—in much smaller print—outlining risk factors. The pictures showed smiling doctors administering dosages to even happier patients—usually young and pretty women, or blue-eyed children who smacked their lips over the latest wonder drug. In prints of striking color, stern sentences warned against substituting cheaper generic drugs. Patients, the reader was assured, appreciated the best of care and the best of pharmacology. In one drawer was a ready supply of tongue depressors, cotton, pads, and tape. The bottom drawer held a lint brush, a shoeshine rag, and a wad of dust.

"You find anything?"

Bunch, a looming shadow vaguely lit by the tiny light, sighed. "Nothing that we're looking for." He turned off the computer screen with its menu of files and started thumbing through the manila folders in another cabinet. "He's got a decent practice, but nothing big."

"Charges twice as much to make up the difference." I went to the nurse's desk. On it were displayed a series of children's pictures and an awkwardly fashioned clay mug for pencils with "To Mom with Love" baked into the enamel. The drawers held a larger number of forms, a wider variety of medical supplies, the lists of often-called telephone numbers, and no drug samples. I shot a couple pictures of the telephone numbers, the white flash of the tiny strobe followed by the whine of the camera's automatic advance.

"Can I use that?" asked Bunch.

"Got something?"

"Calamaro's jacket." He bent over the open folder and the flash winked once. "It's not much."

I looked over his shoulder. The printout, a single cryptic sheet, listed a history of services rendered: periodic health tests and dates, and, more recently, stitches and a reference to Warner for the blood panel. It was marked paid. Felix Frentanes had a file too; it listed two years' worth of routine health tests only. Felix's wife didn't have a file, nor did de Silva.

"We'd better split." Bunch glanced through the blinds. "The door rattlers will be coming by soon."

"Private security? You didn't tell me anything about private security!"

"Didn't want you to worry." He led the way back and we glanced quickly into each of the closed rooms as we went. Desks and examining tables, an occasional coffee room. Workroom with copy machines and storage shelves. Supplies of a variety of items ranging from surgical masks to stainless steel operating tools. Small laboratory crammed with electronic analyzers that my partner lingered over.

"Come on, Bunch."

Finally, the back entrance.

A row of waist-high cylinders stood darkly against a shadowed wall, and Bunch ran his penlight across their barrels. Oxygen, liquid nitrogen, nitrous oxide. "The oxygen for operations, the nitrous oxide for anesthetics. What would he use the liquid nitrogen for?"

"Freezing tissue, probably—a local anesthetic. Warts, small incisions, biopsies."

Bunch counted the tanks and rapped them with his knuckles. "Three tanks of liquid nitrogen, two of them empty. That's a hell of a lot of warts. Whoa . . . I almost forgot." He turned and trotted down the hall. I heard drawers carelessly flung open and the flutter of a mess being made. A few seconds later, he came back with a dangling plastic bag. "Drug samples—the phone lines are cut and they'll know someone broke in. Might as well let them think it was for this crap."

We threw the pills into a garbage can down the next alley, and Bunch guided the van slowly toward my house as we compared notes on what little we'd found. It was obvious that the files, if they ever existed, had been dumped. The folders on Nestor and Felix were there only because other records tied the men to Matheney.

"Maybe he's telling the truth, Dev. What reason would he have for seeing Felicidad?"

"She was pregnant."

"She needed a doctor to tell her that?"

"And we both think he was lying about something."

"Yeah." He pulled the van to the curb in front of my duplex. Mrs. Ottoboni had left her porch light on as always. "There is that. What time is it?"

"A little after three."

From the back of the vehicle came a scuffling, snorting sound and the low growl of the pit bull.

"Sid's coming out if it," said Bunch. "Right on schedule."

"Sounds like he has a hangover."

Bunch rubbed his chewed leg. "No sympathy from me. See you in the morning, Dev."

"Make it the afternoon."

It was midafternoon before I reached the office. I don't like those tossing, dream-plagued times when you try to force sleep long past its usual reveille. I always feel wearier, perhaps, than if I'd stayed awake and started the new day without going to bed at all. A long workout helped, and a gentle pummeling in the Jacuzzi at the fitness center, so that when I finally reached the office and its unopened mail, I felt nearly human.

Two notes from Bunch sat in my box. The first said that Sid Vicious hadn't shown any rabies symptoms yet. The second said that Bunch was at the photo lab developing the pictures from last night. The mail was the usual and I did the usual with it. The phone recorder held a variety of voices. Allen Schute of Security Underwriters urged me to expedite the Taylor case. He didn't say "or else"; it was in the tone of his voice. Bob Costello finally called to tell me he would not be needing the services of Kirk and Associates after all, thanks anyway, and he'd be in touch as soon as something else came up that we could help him with. You're welcome, Bob. The Hally Corporation was inclined the same way, and I was beginning to suspect the unwelcome consequences of halitosis on career and social life. The stack of bills seemed to grow taller as I stared at them. Several blank spaces on the tape indicated callers who didn't want to leave messages, and an unidentified voice said simply, "You can run, you son of a bitch, but you can't hide." I was mulling over that aphoristic bit of wisdom when Bunch came in and tossed a large envelope on the desk.

"Here's a blowup of Calamaro's sheet. The one we found in Matheney's office."

I tilted the glossy out onto the blotter. "Bob Costello called; he doesn't need us."

"Too bad."

"Hally Corporation doesn't either."

"Uh-oh."

"Allen Schute wants us, though. He wants us to do something on Taylor. Soon."

"Do something? You want I should send him a picture of my dog bites?"

"I don't think that's a good idea. But we'd better have more surveillance."

"They're looking for us."

"You have anything better to offer?"

He shook his head and sighed, thinking of the cramped hours ahead. "No." He tapped the photograph. "Take a look."

It was a crisp color shot that made the file page starkly visible. I read with closer attention than I had been able to the night before, but aside from the factual information of Nestor's physical description and blood type, there wasn't much new.

Bunch, looking over my shoulder, rubbed a finger across the photographic print. "I hope that's not a flaw in the glass."

"What's not?"

"That blurry spot—it looks like the camera lens has a scratch."

I peered closely at the photograph. A trace of oil from Bunch's finger dragged across the shiny surface where the letters on the form seemed hazy and ill-defined. "It doesn't seem to be the photo. It looks like the paper was scraped—like somebody erased something." Using a magnifying glass, I examined the section. "See? That's not the photograph. It's the paper itself."

"Somebody changed his blood type?"

"That's what it looks like." Something had blurred the

printed line to be filled in as well as the print on each side of the gap. Then a crisp new letter had been typed in over the careful erasure: "A."

"You're right, Dev—it's a different typeface, even." Bunch moved the magnifying glass back and forth over the rest of the photograph. "The other type's one kind—look at this 'A.' Now, that's a different typewriter."

I dialed the records office at Warner Memorial and read from Nestor's health insurance claim form. "This is Dr. Simpson. I understand you did a series of blood tests on a new patient of mine, Nestor Calamaro." I cited his patient number, which gave my name all the authority it needed, and asked for his blood type. The woman's voice asked if I would like to wait or if she should call me back. "I'll wait."

A minute or two later, her voice came back and she said with slight hesitancy, "It's Rh null, doctor."

"It's what?"

"Yes sir. I've never heard of it, but he's had a lot of blood work done and that's what it says: Rh null."

I thanked her and hung up.

"Why would Matheney want to change the man's blood type?" asked Bunch.

I didn't have an answer, but we did have a suspicious act. Also we had a question. And as one of my old profs who was fond of John Dewey used to say, the question entails the answer.

Bunch went out to the Ace Roofing construction site, driving a rental van and armed with the camcorder and a telephoto lens. We had no proof Taylor was working that job, but it was a place to start and I could call Schute and tell him with clear conscience that we were actively pursuing the case even while I spoke to him. That done, I tried to call Jerry Kagan, but his nurse said he wasn't available and would I like to leave a message. I put it off until later that evening, and when I finally reached him, I offered a dinner for him and Judy by way of apology for bothering him again.

"It sounds good, Dev, but we'll have to take a rain check; Judy and I are going to a medical conference in Hawaii." The phone was silent for a moment, and I wondered why they never had conferences in places like East St. Louis or Detroit. "You know, I don't understand why anyone would want to change the blood type on a chart. That could be damned dangerous."

"You mean if someone gave him a transfusion of the wrong blood?"

"Among other things, yes. It could be fatal. And with that blood, the chances are extremely good he'd get the wrong type."

"Why's that?"

"Rh null is extremely rare. I've never run across it. Statistically, only one person in, maybe, two hundred thousand has it."

"Two hundred thousand?"

"Yeah. Compare that to AB, which is considered pretty uncommon. The statistics there are one in two hundred." He added, "My guess is it must have been a clerical error. But as I say, it's a damned dangerous error."

"Thanks, Jerry—kiss a wahine for me." He said he would if Judy let him, and we set a vague dinner date for sometime after he returned from his neonatal conference. I leaned back in front of the cold fireplace to think. Matheney. Billy Taylor. Chiquichano. The Wilcox farm. The pregnant women. The shooting in the tunnel. Names and events drifted back and forth through my thoughts as I tinkered first with one case, then the other. And came up with nothing.

Bunch had the same kind of luck, and then it was my turn to keep an eye on the roofers. The machine shop owner told me where they had gone for their next job—a residence in south Boulder—and I drove the surveillance van along winding streets until I spotted the familiar pickup truck and tar wagon. This job was a flat-roofed home nestled in a small valley at the edge of the city's open space.

144 · REX BURNS

A section of mountains formed the striking backdrop for the town. A pull-off at the top of a hill overlooking the house and pool gave a good view, and a squint through the binoculars told me Taylor wasn't among the men swabbing tar across the new felt. But he might be nearby or they might talk about the man, and that hope kept us on watch with binoculars and parabolic microphone. The surveillance site, on a ridge higher than the house's roof, was excellent for listening to the workmen's chatter; their voices rose on the warm air toward the parked car and the barrel of the microphone resting on the window ledge and aimed in their direction. Unfortunately, they didn't say much except to ask for more tar, and what they did say had nothing to do with Billy Taylor. I did find out where they would be working after this job, and that saved a little detecting time.

The farm was too hot to approach right now, but while one of us watched Ace Roofing, the other did tour the county roads near the farm in an effort to catch Taylor riding his bike. The wasted time was irritating to me as well as to Schute, though he had to admit we were doing all anyone could. But a more fundamental irritation came from my sense of something just beyond vision in the Calamaro case—something I should be grasping. Something . . . But exactly what remained vague, worrisome, and it contributed to the restlessness that filled me with tension even when I sprawled in front of my fireplace in the evening with a glass of ale at my elbow. It was like knowing that the phone was about to ring or a knock to rattle the door, and I couldn't just stretch out and forget that sense of something waiting to happen. Finally I gave up, drained the mug, and shoved to my feet. Better to waste the time doing something, even if it was pointless, instead of staring at the back of a dark fireplace.

Exactly what I wanted, I didn't know. But after a day sitting in the van, I did know I wouldn't spend the whole evening sitting at home. I let the Subaru decide, and it turned south to drive slowly past the unlit windows of Mrs. Chiquichano's home. The house, with its steep roofs and ivy, was totally dark, and I cruised the alley behind to verify that everyone there seemed asleep. Not that I expected anything different, but finding out that much brought a tiny—if irrational—feeling of satisfaction.

From my notes on Matheney, I knew his home address in the Pinehurst area, and the Subaru turned in that direction through the empty streets. The house was on the boundary between Denver and Jefferson counties, in one of those enclaves that sprawl at the edge of golf courses. Mansfield Avenue was a fashionably dim lane that wound past deep lawns and barely glimpsed roofs. A mailbox sported the house number on the upright, and an enameled hunting scene decorated the box itself. Matheney's name wasn't on the box. Instead, a wrought-iron arch over the drive featured an *M* in a circle of tracery, and the drive curved away into darkness toward a spread of spruce trees and elms. I corroborated that Dr. Matheney's practice paid well, but there wasn't much else to poke around for, and I swung east on Hampden and headed back to I-25 and my office.

Denver still has the heart of a small town, even if its body has sprawled widely. It's most evident in those chill hours after two in the morning, when even the police head back to the barn because the bars are closed and the dark streets are draining of hunters and hunted alike. In cities like New York or Chicago, life may change pace throughout the night, but it steps along nevertheless. And Los Angeles, for all its pockets of suburban emptiness, has its arteries of rushing freeway lights and ceaseless swirling cars every hour of the night. But Denver goes to sleep. Altitude, maybe, or the cold air that closes around the tall office buildings and drives the wanderer home and the homeless into boxes or under bridges to wait for the warming sun. You can see them if you look hard enough, scattered out from the remnants of a skid row that lingers on upper Larimer Street. The loading docks in alleys behind Wazee and Blake are favorite places, and many of the owners have nailed heavy wire mesh all the way down to the ground to keep out the bums and winos who crawl under to sleep and sometimes to die. Occasional trash piles give some warmth and concealment as well as stray bits of free paper that serve life's little necessities. Sometimes the down-and-out find protection in doorways. When it's coldest, they crowd into lines waiting for a mattress and blanket on the floors of shelter houses and soup kitchens. But not all can fit in—a small town's heart isn't necessarily a soft one.

The streets around our office were convenient to the railroad yards—the jumping-on and -off places where trains made up for California, Texas, Minnesota, and points east. So it wasn't unusual to pull into our parking lot behind the refurbished warehouse and have the headlights pick out bundles huddled against the lingering warmth of brick walls. As I shut off the engine, one of three dark shapes lifted to a sitting position and stared my way.

"Hey!" The figure struggled to its feet, hoarse voice carrying softly through the night. "Hey, wait a minute."

"What do you need?" I was already feeling for loose change.

"You got a office here? Up on the second floor?"

"Why?"

The gaunt figure came closer, clutching a ratty shred of canvas about its shoulders. "If you do, there's something I can tell you." Beneath the shadow of whiskers and grime, the man's bright red lips rolled away in a gaping grin to show the glimmer of a few lonesome teeth. "Cost you, though. Gimme five dollars and I'll tell you."

"Tell me what?"

"Five dollars is all. That ain't too much for you, is it?"

I pulled a bill from my wallet. The man's eyes followed my hands like a dog watching a bone. "Here."

He tilted it briefly to the light to read the number, a waft of dirty clothes and unwashed skin riding on the crisp air. The bill disappeared and he backed off a step or two. "Fella give me some money to warn him if anybody come. Said to throw some pebbles against that window up on the second floor."

I looked where the thin arm pointed. No light showed, but it was the window to my office. "What man? When?"

"Don't know what man. Maybe ten minutes ago. Said to throw a handful of—"

"He still there?"

"Ain't come out yet."

I sprinted for the door, yanking against the lock and cursing softly as my key fumbled at the hole. Then, on tiptoe, I ran up the spiral of iron stairs, feet loud despite my efforts. I reached the landing and heard a clatter of broken glass as a warning rock sailed into my office. The bum was proving his integrity to both sides. The dark door swung open to show a figure hurrying into the dimness of the landing toward me, and behind it came another.

The first shape was short; the other seemed larger even than Bunch. The short one's face—as much as I could make out— looked almost chubby, with his hair pulled back under a watch cap. The big one hesitated only an instant before he aimed himself at me.

Fists high, he feinted with his right and followed with a quick left uppercut that had the full weight of his shoulder behind it. I rocked outside the punch, blocked it with a forearm, and grabbed his elbow to use his own momentum to twist his torso away from me. The heel of my hand drove hard against his kidney and spine, and I heard him grunt as my knee jabbed sharply against the side of his. His legs tangled and he sprawled across the landing and thudded into the open door of my office. The shorter one, holding back, suddenly swung a flat pry bar as a weapon and came toward me.

"You're dead—you're fucking dead!"

"Try and bury me."

He did. First he came in with a hard slashing swing across my chest that told me he meant what he said. I could hear in my mind Bunch's laughing voice telling me that's what the punching techniques were good for, and why would I persist in using judo? His next swing was a backhand sweep that drove me against the railing and left my stomach open for a quick jab with the cloven end of the shaft. He tried and I parried the side of my hand against his wrist, a test of quickness, and saw in his eyes a tiny quiver of surprise. Behind him, the big one was a shadow beginning to sit up and stare my way without the slightest sign of affection. But the sweep of the pry bar kept him behind the shorter one, and I slid along the guardrail to get a wall at my back and keep them both in sight.

The shorter shadow drove at me, shoulder dipping to get all his weight behind the swing. I let him get close and, as the shoulder dropped, swiveled aside and grasped his wrist with one hand, slamming the heel of my other hard against the back of his elbow. It gave a very satisfying pop, and the steel spun across the landing as the man doubled in agony and his legs went rubbery. He tried to fall but I didn't let him. Pulling on the awkwardly bent elbow, I levered his shoulder up and back and turned under the arm to come down hard. I heard the sucking, tearing noise of tendon and gristle just before he drowned it out with his scream.

The big one's feet warned me and I spun, ducking low with my wrists crossed to catch whatever was coming. It was a foot—quick estimate, 15 triple E—and it thudded against my forearms and almost lifted me off the floor. I scrabbled at his heel but he drew back quickly and kicked out again, a side kick that had enough grace and aim to tell me it was trained. It also had enough power to land solidly against my ribs and drive my breath out in a wheezing cough that I tried to cover with a scornful laugh. It didn't fool him and it didn't help me, but from my bouts with Bunch I guessed what was coming next, and it did—a quick spin and the other leg, gathering leverage like a rock swung at the end of a taut rope, whistled sharply at my head. I dropped beneath it to scissor my legs at his knee and felt my heel hit the soft spot and the big man dropped heavily and rolled away, twisting his neck to keep his eyes on me as he tumbled. Somewhere in the background, the sound of the other's nasal wail mingled with the clang of staggering heels on the iron stairs, and the man disappeared. I paused, waiting for the big one to push himself onto his feet, cautious about bringing my legs close to those massive hands.

"I'll be back, you son of a bitch."

"Anytime. It's been fun."

And, I thought with a bit of surprise as he backed down the dark, spiraling stairs, it was. It really was. It might have been different had I been on the short end of things, but the exhilaration, the rush of blood and adrenaline, and the sharpness and edge to life that came in the fight had been fun. The restlessness, the boredom with the cases, the lack of direction, were lost and forgotten—in their place was the deeply satisfying pleasure of using nothing but my hands to conquer another man who had wanted to kill me. There was no other word for it but fun.

10

"You sure it was the bikers?" Bunch wandered from one corner of the office to the other, stepping over scattered sheets of paper from the file drawers, strewn envelopes with their canceled stamps, detritus from desk drawers that had been tipped upside down. His concern had been first for the electronics gear stowed in the air-conditioned closet that served as his workroom, then for the rest of the office, then for me.

"I'm sure. And why the hell don't you help clean up instead of just standing around with your thumb up."

"Touchy! For one thing, you said the dudes didn't have beards. All the bikers I saw looked like bench warmers on the House of David baseball team."

"I don't think they had beards. It was dark."

"For another, if it was the bikers, they'd have whacked you. They tried once already. They would have come here with a piece and used it when you showed up."

"Maybe they want me alive to tell them where their dog is." I wrestled a metal drawer back into its slides and gathered up the folders, one emptied, that held past cases and old correspondence. Behind me, the teeth-setting scrape of steel on glass said the glazier was busy replacing the broken window. "They didn't expect me to show up. And I didn't expect two of them—the bum only mentioned one."

The burglars hadn't had time to pry open the old Mosler, where the active files were kept along with what little else we thought was confidential. Scratch marks around the hinges and lock showed they had started. But they didn't have the tools to strip the safe quickly, and most likely, the rock coming through the window interrupted them.

The exhilaration of combat had quickly ebbed the night before, and for some reason I couldn't remember, my shoulder—the one hurt in the automobile wreck—began to ache. And I didn't feel like facing a major salvage job that would last until five in the morning. I figured the cleanup could wait, and wait it did. Now we were trying to put the office back in some kind of order and come up with an idea about what the bikers were after.

"You say they didn't have anything in their hands when they came out?"

"One of them had a pry bar."

"Important stuff—papers, a folder."

"The pry bar was pretty important at the time, Bunch. But no, neither one carried anything from the office that I could see."

He ran a finger over the fresh tool marks glinting in the steel of the safe. "Then they must have thought it was in here. They looked through everything else first, found nothing, and tried to peel the safe."

"Maybe they weren't looking for anything specific. Maybe they just wanted to trash the place."

Bunch shook his head. "I don't know. If they wanted to do that, they'd have busted up the electronics gear. I mean, all they had to do was walk in and start shoving things off the shelves. But they didn't. They went for papers. And the safe," he added.

It was possible. We didn't have a thing on Billy Taylor or the bikers out at the Wilcox farm, but they didn't know that. And, like most guilty people would suspect we were after the very thing they wanted to keep secret. "Maybe they want to find out why we're poking around their farm."

"Yeah." He scraped some paper together with the tip of his

shoe. "Well, they didn't find anything because we don't have anything."

"They found me."

"Yeah, but nothing vital." Bunch stood in the doorway of his closet to inventory, for the tenth time, his electronics hoard. "If the bastards had any brains, they'd have helped themselves to this stuff when they left."

"They were in a hurry. What kind of alarm system can you rig for the office?" Like a lot of people who made their living by providing a service for others, Kirk and Associates hadn't yet gotten around to serving themselves. Plumbers had leaky faucets at home, carpenters' houses needed repairs, we needed an alarm system.

"Good thought. They might want another look." He frowned and rubbed a large thumb along his jaw. "I'll see what I can come up with."

"Keep the cost down."

"Yeah. You and Hally Corp."

It gave him something to concentrate on, so I could finish cleaning up the mess. A lot of the papers were as worthless to us as they had been to the burglars, the remains of closed cases and aimless correspondence about the trivia of business life. It was about time the drawers were cleaned anyway, and as I filled another wastebasket with folded and crumpled sheets, Uncle Wyn came in and eyed the remaining litter and the glazier squeezing putty along the window frame.

"Don't tell me, let me guess: you had a visitor."

I explained a little of what happened, leaving out the fight scene.

"They came in the window? how the hell'd they do that?"

"Somebody threw a rock in. To warn them."

"Ah." He looked down at the street and sniffed. "Didn't take much of an arm." He poked his cane against the still-locked safe. "Bunch says they were after what's in here."

"Maybe. Maybe not."

"So what's in here?"

"Active cases." I changed to the singular. "Case, anyway. Tax returns. Some correspondence that shouldn't be left around."

"Well, I been doing some detective reading, you know? What you got to do is look for the unexpected thing. The little thing you're not thinking about. It's in all the books—private eye stuff, adventure stuff like this guy Clive Cussler. I like him."

"We're not in a book, Uncle Wyn."

"Hey, it's just a thought." He rapped the safe. "But there's some truth to it. You don't assume, know what I mean? You look at everything, you figure the situation and the odds, you look for what the runner's going to do."

"We're not in a baseball game, either."

He gave the safe a last tap as if to say he could take a hint, and wandered into the storage room to talk with Bunch.

The glazier finished brushing up the shreds of putty and, wiping his mustache with a wrinkled and scarred forefinger, handed me the bill. I wrote the check, hoping it wouldn't bounce, and then tidied up the last of the mess before opening the safe to stare at the small piles of documents and photographs.

The contents remained as placed in the file separators that divided the interior space. In one slot were a few letters from prominent clients that mentioned personal and sensitive issues related to earlier, now-closed cases. I went through them and destroyed as many as practicable. Beside them were the few inconclusive photos of Taylor sitting in the living room of the Wilcox farm. Nestor's file was there too, with the photographs of Dr. Matheney's correspondence stacked on a small shelf below the separator.

I spread the Matheney collection across my now-clean desk; it was as good a time as any to go through it in detail, and a welcome change from housecleaning. A rumble of background voices came from the storage room as Bunch explained the workings of one of his toys to Uncle Wyn, and I half listened as I read.

Most of the pages cramped onto the glossy prints related to the daily life of the clinic—reports on patients, queries to insurance companies about payment, replies to insurance companies about services provided. More interesting were those letters to professional acquaintances dealing with pending seminars or in-services. Matheney was in demand as a specialist in some aspect of transplant rejection that I couldn't understand. Something to do with tissue bonding and phrased in technical shorthand that I would need Jerry Kagan's help with. But I recognized that the subject fit Matheney's expertise; he was a surgeon and immunologist, and apparently taught courses in immunology at the University Medical Center. It also explained his correspondence with the Cryogenic Biological Laboratories, another file we hadn't had time to examine completely. That stack of photos seemed to depict mostly purchase requests for parts and equipment, and letters that carried a running dialogue about some project that Matheney was helping with. A separate file of memos rather than letters gave us half of a dialogue with something called Antibodies Research, and this, too, generally involved purchase orders on a project. Whatever it was, Matheney was on a first-name basis—"Dear Morris," "Dear Mark"—and the memo file was apparently much less important than the meetings which started about a year ago and increased in frequency. In fact, no new additions had come in the last four months, and whatever was being established seemed to be running smoothly or else was finished. Other correspondence included two or three inquiries for assistance in locating donors of one kind or another. One letter, buried down a bit in the stack of glossies, was a copy of an urgent request from Empire State Hospital in New York to the Cryogenic Biological Laboratories. It asked for donors with blood type Rh null. A scrawled note said, "Morris—any possibilities?"

"Bunch—take a look at this!"

He came in to peer over my shoulder. Uncle Wyn limped behind.

"So all those blood tests weren't just for Nestor's well-being," murmured Bunch.

"You mean they stole this guy's blood?" asked Uncle Wyn.

Bunch shook his head. "They'd have a hard time stealing it. Probably talked him into donating a few pints." He looked up. "Maybe it was direct transfusion. Maybe they talked Nestor into going to the recipient in New York."

"He's been gone a couple months now, Bunch."

"A couple pints a week? It's rare blood—once you get that kind of donor, maybe you don't let him go. Just keep milking him."

"But you'd have to have equally rare recipients. How much of that blood would they need?"

Uncle Wyn grunted in satisfaction. "So maybe you got somebody who kidnaps this kid for his blood. So maybe now you got somebody else who breaks into your office to see how much you know. What do you think of that, Dev?"

I said it was an ingenious idea, that he was right all along, and that Bunch and I would be happy to make him a partner in the firm. But he shook his head no, pleading age and arthritis, and said he was content to be an occasional consultant and wouldn't charge us a dime for it. On the way up to Boulder and the Cryogenic Biological Laboratories, Bunch told me Uncle Wyn's tongue was wagging like a puppy's tail at the idea he had helped us out. "The guy's always been a hard charger, Dev—always competitive. It must be a bitch for a guy like that to be crippled up like he is."

"I think he's sorry we paid off his loan. He can't come around as much as he used to."

"He can come around anytime, as far as I'm concerned. And he's right about the break-in; it could have been somebody from this cryo-bio outfit."

"He's not as right as he'd like to be, Bunch. Think about it.

Neither they nor Matheney know we went into his office and copied his files. Matheney knows we're looking for Nestor and maybe the women. But as far as we know, he doesn't have any reason to get uptight. And he doesn't know what, if anything, we have. Why should he go to the risk of raiding our office when we might have nothing?" I turned the Subaru off the parkway onto Arapahoe and headed east toward a high ridge where prairie could be glimpsed through a scattering of homes, tiny farms, and light-industrial buildings. "Besides, the way those two went through the office was a warning. They were looking, yes—I grant you that. But they were also warning us off. It all points to the bikers."

We followed the turns of one of those industrial park roads, the kind that wind like suburban lanes but are too wide and too empty of parked cars to live up to the image. A low aggregate sign sported blue letters—CRYOGENIC BIOLOGICAL LABORATORIES—and clean curbing led a gently rounded drive toward the visitors' parking lot. It was a one-story cast-concrete building whose stucco facade faced the lot. The side walls were plain slabs of cement, and few windows punctured the sun-glared structure.

A very attractive woman glanced up from her typewriter as we came in: mid-twenties, red-blond hair piled up in a loose chignon, high cheekbones, and wide lavender eyes that accepted men's admiration as only natural. Which it was.

"Is Mr. Amaro in, please?"

She corrected me. "Dr. Amaro. Do you have an appointment?"

"We told him we'd be up. He said to just come by."

"Oh, you must be the reporters! He's expecting you." She pointed to a door. "Turn right—the first office on your left."

Bunch, his camera dangling conspicuously over one shoulder and a grimy canvas bag over the other, whispered as he followed me, "You interview Amaro, Dev. I'll interview her."

"Photographers don't talk, Bunch. They just take pictures."

Dr. Amaro was a plump, olive-skinned man with a balding head and starkly black hair raked back over his skull in painted lines. He may have been in his fifties. His handshake, a brief squeeze, was cool and soft, but he was clearly excited about his business. "You're doing a story on cryogenics and medicine?"

"Medicine and new trends in technology," I said. "Cryogenics is one of the newer areas, I understand."

"Well, somewhat, although it's the more lurid uses of the field that seem to have captured the popular imagination—freezing heads for transplant in the next century, preserving the bodies of the rich. That sort of thing."

"Do you do that here?"

"Oh goodness, no! Those kinds of things—well, I hesitate to call them the work of charlatans, because we really don't know what science will come up with in the next hundred years. But they are in the realm of science fiction, as far as I'm concerned. No, here we deal with science reality—the application of cold temperatures to already proven medical practices."

We settled into the interview, Bunch gliding around the background to study the doctor through his lens and occasionally click the camera, I writing with professional aplomb in a stenographer's notebook and asking questions that would lead the doctor through a sketch of the company and its activities.

Founded in 1975, the laboratories got their start as a subcontractor in a larger Ball Brothers space project, examining the effects of radically low temperatures on various metals, plastics, and moving parts. "We pioneered some of the basic technology for the development of ultracold environments." With the gradual decline of space exploration, the company moved into developing technology that would apply to medical purposes. "There's quite a demand for small, portable cooling units that can be used to transport donor parts and tissue for transplant."

It wasn't as simple as making a small refrigerator, even one that could maintain a constant temperature of zero degrees or one that would go down as low as minus four hundred degrees centigrade for several hours. Temperature control was just one critical aspect; preservation also required the correct oxygen tension, carbon dioxide removal, and acid-base balance. "In many cases, blood flow must be maintained even as the organ is cooled. Livers, for instance. A donor's liver is immediately placed in cold salt solution and perfused as it's rapidly cooled to around ten degrees centigrade. The liquid provides a blood substitute that keeps the organ functioning temporarily, and the cold inhibits tissue decay. The result is an ischemic period of up to thirty-six hours. We're trying to improve on that." He saw my eyebrows lift. "Ischemic? It means without blood flow. The liver can be preserved for up to thirty-six hours and—if the technology is available—be transported anywhere in the world for use."

"What about blood? Can blood be preserved like that?"

"Oh yes. But that technology is fairly well established. We're not doing much in that area.

"What kind of donors do you look for?"

"That's not my field—my doctorate's in physics, not medicine. But usually the donors are obtained through various organ recovery systems that are in contact with transplant centers across the country."

"Do you know anyone I could interview? Any names?"

"Well, they try to avoid publicity, as a rule. It's a delicate subject, as you might imagine. Donors' families are often traumatized when their loved one is killed. And then to make the decision to donate organs and tissue . . . Well, it's both necessary and generous, but publicity is the last thing a transplant coordinator usually wants."

"Just a couple names for background information. I'll assure them and you that the subject will be treated with dignity and respect."

"Well, you might call John Vogel. He's the public hospitals' coordinator for the northern Colorado sector. Or Mark Gilbert. He's transplant coordinator at a small independent firm called Antibodies Research. They're just getting started in the field, and we've done some business with them. But don't be surprised if they don't wish to be interviewed. As I say, the issue is a very sensitive one."

Dr. Amaro told us more about the advances his company was making in areas other than medicine. He was especially excited about superconductor research, and I dutifully filled pages of the steno pad. When I nudged him back to medical applications, I asked if he knew Dr. Morris Matheney.

"Morris? Certainly—a fine person and a fine physician. Very active in transplant research. In fact, he's consulting with our engineers and designers on a project."

"What kind of project?"

"Oh, that's not something I'm at liberty to divulge; it involves patents and security in a highly competitive area. I can tell you this much, however: It's a model for another transporter unit. An ingenious model, if I may say so."

"Would it have to do with transporting blood or body tissue, as opposed to organs?"

Amaro's brown eyes widened and he leaned back against his chair. "Has he talked to you about it?"

"Not in any detail, doctor. But I do know his specialty is tissue rejection, so it just makes sense."

"Oh, yes—of course!" The man's round face lost its worry in a relieved smile.

"In fact, I understand you asked him for a rare blood donor not too long ago—someone with Rh null."

"Why yes! My goodness, you're thorough in your research. Yes, but I was doing a favor for a potential customer. An emergency call went out for a very rare blood type and I volunteered to query our mailing list. I do that occasionally, since we're in contact with most of the transplant coordinators and facilities in the region. But it was a long shot and I don't think anything came of it."

"Can you tell me who you did the favor for?"

"I could, I suppose. But why?"

I smiled. "As you say, doctor, I'm thorough in my research. I won't tell him where I learned his name if that worries you."

"No, no—it's nothing like that. It just seems an odd request. It was Empire State Hospital in New York City. They specialize in the more difficult transplant operations, and I occasionally go back there to observe their activities and adapt some of our standard models to their more specific needs."

"Can you give me the name of the person who asked?"

"It just came from their transplant center. An institutional request."

Bunch took a few more photographs—Dr. Ramon Amaro frowning intently at a document on his desk, Dr. Ramon Amaro gazing with quiet pride toward his laboratory—before we thanked him for his cooperation.

"When will the article appear, Mr. Kirk?"

"That's up to the editor, sir. Probably within three weeks, though."

In the car, Bunch sighed and tossed the camera case onto the backseat. "Next time I might even put some film in. And," he added, "next time you be the photographer and I'll be the reporter."

"No, no. That's reserved for us literary types, Bunch. You just stay with the camera." I thumbed through the business volume of the Denver telephone directory for the address of Antibodies Research and then through the atlas and street guide for its location. Bunch liked to complain about riding around with telephone books and an atlas shoved under the seat, but they had saved us a lot of time on more than one occasion.

"Her name's Julie Sandberg."

"What?"

"The receptionist. Julie Sandberg." Bunch folded a slip of paper into his shirt pocket. "She's unmarried and has a telephone."

"How—?"

He shook his head. "Something you literary types will never master." Steering the car back toward the Boulder–Denver turnpike, he sighed. "Never underestimate the power of the press, Dev."

The approach to Antibodies Research wasn't along sweeping lanes through a landscaped industrial park. Instead, their offices were on the south side of Denver off Santa Fe Drive. The area was industrial, all right, but gritty, cut by the Burlington Northern tracks and strangled with large trucks trying to turn in small streets. We crossed the low, muddy banks of the South Platte, with its strip of thick brush and weeds and snagged trash, and wandered among a variety of one-story brick buildings sheltering everything from printing shops to electronics distributors to the occasional blue-collar bar that snagged homeward-bound workers.

The small office was behind a security fence and showed a closed-off brick wall that offered few entrances. In fact, the only one we found was a single door with a half-panel of glass bearing the company name. It led to a tiny reception area that had a potted ficus and no chairs. In an office opening off the entry, a woman sat clicking a computer keyboard. When she looked up, it was with some surprise to see us standing there.

"Yes? Do you need something?"

She was severe. Brown hair pulled back severely into a knot, dress severely unornamental, face severely clean of cosmetics. Her eyes, dark and large, dominated the scrubbed face, but if she was aware of any dramatic effect, she didn't show it. Rather, she seemed one of those people bent on erasing themselves with noticeable vigor.

"We'd like to speak with Mr. Gilbert." I explained that we were reporters doing a story on transplant technology.

The dark eyes stared at us for a long moment. Somewhere in the small building a man's voice called unintelligibly, and the sound echoed on tile and brick. "Just a moment, please."

She went through the door and we waited. Down the hall a stocky figure in brown coveralls, intent on balancing a box of something, walked—soft shoes squeaking on the waxed floor— toward a more distant door. The secretary came back and, with a curt nod, aimed us to a short, heavyset man with a red face and clipped, sandy hair.

He didn't invite us into his office but got right to the point. "I'd rather not be interviewed about our business. We don't seek publicity."

"The article will be in good taste, Mr. Gilbert."

"Nonetheless, we try to avoid embarrassing all parties concerned."

Right. Tell that to the doctors who described their transplant successes on national television. "Do you know or have you ever worked with a Dr. Morris Matheney?"

"Good day, Mr. Kirk."

His hand urged us through the door, and after it slammed, I heard the tiny click of the lock. "So much for the power of the press."

"Some of us have it and some don't, Dev." Bunch gazed up the solid facade of brick that faced the busy street. "Be tough to get in here."

"We don't intend to try, Bunch." But Gilbert's shyness did pique my curiosity. "Vogel's office is over at the University Medical Center. Maybe he'll be more help."

Red brick dominated there, too, but the cluster of high-rise buildings had that emphasis on horizontal lines, rows of windows, and ground-level access that spelled hospital. John Vogel's name on the directory was followed by an address that didn't tell us how to find his office in the confusing spread of hallways and connecting ramps. It took a good twenty minutes of wandering through the antiseptic-smelling corridors before we located the door, on the crowded basement level and just down a concrete tunnel from one of the cafeterias.

"Mr. Vogel?"

The single room was jammed with filing cabinets and computer ware, and the small desk littered with pamphlets, directories, and papers. A bumper sticker pasted over the terminal said, "Don't take your organs to heaven; heaven knows we need them here." Vogel, about my age, had a triangular face dominated by a large nose, and bushy, straight brown hair that fell down the sides thickly enough to hide his ears. His eyes lay deep under heavy brows that made a straight line across the top of that nose; his mouth made a parallel line beneath it.

"You're the one who called earlier? The reporter?"

The gag had worked so far. "Yes. Devlin Kirk." I smiled and shook hands. "Can you tell me a little about your business?"

Vogel was cautious. "A little, I suppose. But I don't want to sensationalize—"

"I assured Dr. Amaro I wouldn't do that, before he mentioned your name. And I promise you I won't, too." I glanced at the bumper sticker. "But it's possible that some favorable publicity might incline more people to become donors."

He considered that and nodded. "You understand I can't go into specific cases. Not without the families' consent."

"I understand. Can you sketch your role in the transplant process?"

He did, hesitantly at first, then—with the excitement of anyone fully immersed in his work—more freely. The state had perhaps ten or twelve transplant coordinators; some worked for individual hospitals, a few for private firms, but most for charitable organizations that specialized in specific types of organ transplant—the Lions eye bank, for instance, or a bone bank, or University Hospital's skin bank. To prevent families of accident victims from being hounded by several representatives, the major groups had created a consortium with one spokesman, and that's what Vogel did for his geographical area.

The way it worked, member hospitals in the coordinator's region notified his office when a suitable donor was admitted. Suitable meant young, healthy, and fatally injured. "Visiting their families is the hardest part of the job," he said. "And sometimes I wish the donors could see what wonders the organs do for people who had no other hope of living a normal life."

"The permission of the families is always required? Even if the victim signed a donor card?"

"Always. If the family doesn't consent, the donation doesn't happen, card or no. But I tell them that whatever decision they make is the right decision for them. And it is."

He illustrated with the story of a young man killed in a car wreck who gave organs to four people. The heart was flown to Baltimore where a sixteen-year-old boy was hours from death, the corneas went to a woman in Colorado who had been blind for fifteen years, one of the kidneys went to a New Mexico man who'd been on dialysis for nine years waiting for a suitable donor. The liver gave life to a father of four predicted to die within days. "He gave me a letter for the donor's parents, trying to tell them how their generosity saved his life and let him stay with his children."

"Why didn't he write them himself?"

Vogel shook his head. "We have to ensure confidentiality of all parties involved, donor and recipient. It's just better that way."

"A donor's family might take the organ back?" asked Bunch.

A slight smile. "Not exactly. But sometimes a donor's parents transfer their sense of loss to the recipient. A bit of their child is still alive, for instance. Or, even, they feel they have some claim on the person whose life was saved. Psychologically, it can get very complex, and as a rule it's just better all around that the parties don't identify each other."

After receiving a family's permission, Vogel arranged for the hospital to remove the organs as quickly as possible and then, while that was going on, started calling transplant centers across the country to find matching recipients. Hotlines, computer networks, and pager systems operated twenty-four hours a day, and occasional calls would be broadcast nationwide for especially difficult matches or critical cases. Once the organs were harvested, they had to be transported quickly and safely to the recipients' hospitals where they were already being prepped for the operations. "With the right environment, a heart has about four hours of life on its own, livers about twelve."

"The right environment is a transportation unit?"

"A cooling and perfusion unit, yes."

"Do you deliver the organs?"

"Sometimes. But not often. Usually, the hospitals—especially the big ones—have their own transplant teams that fly out and escort the item back to the hospital. Pittsburgh, Chicago, places like that." He added, "They don't say it, but they don't like to trust locals handling the item."

"It must cost a lot," said Bunch.

"Most of the centers are nonprofit. They only cover expenses."

"Yeah. Sure. But those expenses run pretty high, right? A day's pay for the doctors and nurses, their airplane, the specialists . . ."

Vogel nodded reluctantly. "It's not an inexpensive endeavor."

"How much demand do you have for organs and tissues?" I asked.

More than he could satisfy, was the answer, and he rattled off figures. "Nationwide, around thirty thousand patients are awaiting transplants at any one time. Those nearest death are highest on the list, but many have to wait too long—they never do get an organ." To help distribute items, the National Organ Transplant Act of 1984 organized the harvest and delivery system and expanded the number of donors, but suitable organs were still in critically short supply.

"It sounds as if the procedures and safeguards are pretty well established."

"Well, yes and no. Transplantation is a relatively new field and a rapidly expanding one, too." He gestured toward the coffee machine steaming in a corner of his crowded office and raised his eyebrows. Bunch and I shook our heads.

"In a lot of areas, state and federal laws are only now being considered. Generally, it's illegal to sell organs, but for example, just last year Colorado established a law that attending physicians can't participate in recovering organs and that hospitals are required to have trained transplant coordinators on their staffs."

There was a note of satisfaction there, and I guessed he had something to do with that legislation. "What's that about attending physicians?"

"To avoid any possible conflict of interest. And it also protects the attending physician from possible lawsuits by the family—charging undue influence, for example. It mandates a second opinion about the patient's state."

"Whether the guy's dead," said Bunch.

"Whether the victim has any possible chance to survive," corrected Vogel.

"You harvest the guy before he's dead?"

"Ideally."

Hospitals were now required by law to ask for donation under certain circumstances or lose their Medicare/Medicaid eligibility. Moreover, progress had been made in establishing regional clearinghouses for information about suitable donors, Vogel told us.

"You mean every young person in an accident."

"Not always." Under the organ recovery act, each hospital was responsible for setting up its own criteria as to who would make a suitable donor. But there were some general guidelines based on age: kidneys, newborn to sixty-five; livers, newborn to thirty-five; hearts, newborn to thirty-five; corneas, newborn to one hundred; bone and skin, seventeen to sixty-five.

"What about blood?"

The man paused, one finger rubbing under his jaw with a slight rasp of whiskers. "I don't deal in blood; that's usually the purview of the local hospitals and blood banks."

"Do you ever have contact with Antibodies Research, Incorporated?"

The line over Vogel's prominent nose wrinkled deeper. "Contact? No."

"Aren't they in the same business?"

"Yes. Yes, they are. But they're not members of the consortium. Though occasionally they have provided organs. Mostly, they compete with the consortium for donors."

"They what?"

"Compete." He managed to look both indignant and embarrassed at the same time. "They're a private business. For profit. I've heard that in some instances they've paid hospital personnel a finder's fee for exclusive rights to a suitable donor. Four thousand dollars, in one case."

"They buy bodies?"

"I suppose that's what it comes down to."

"I thought you said selling organs was illegal."

"Technically, they don't buy them. But they are allowed to bill for the expenses of harvesting and shipping." He shrugged. "Their expenses are above average. Far above."

"You mean, it's creative bookkeeping."

"Please don't quote me on that, Mr. Kirk. This kind of technology is very expensive, and the people—the specialists—involved in it can demand very high salaries. Especially in the private sector."

I sat back in the little space that the crowded office allowed and looked at an uncomfortable Vogel. Somewhere in the hiss of forced air and the dim mumble and clink of the nearby cafeteria, a tinny voice paged Dr. Someone. "What's a body going for?"

"I'm not certain. I've read some things, but I'm really not certain."

"I'm not going to quote you. What's a body worth in the private sector?"

"You have to remember that a healthy cadaver has a number of harvestable components, some of which are mutually exclusive, some of which aren't."

"You mean," Bunch said, "you might have to screw up one body part to get at another."

He nodded. "There are the organs, if the body can be kept alive artificially, and the corneas and skin, which can be removed shortly after death. Bone powder can be obtained even longer after death."

"Bone powder?"

"An element essential to much transplant surgery—the average male cadaver can supply nearly five pounds of powder. It currently costs around four hundred fifty dollars for a tenth of a gram, so it comes to about nine hundred thousand. And the price is going up."

"For bone dust? Who pays for all this?"

"By law, the procuring agency. In fact, it's usually medical insurance of one kind or another."

"You mean my bones are worth almost a million?" asked Bunch.

Vogel glanced at the big man and a slight humor came into the dark eyes. "I'd say you're worth considerably more."

"How about that! A millionaire and I didn't even know it!"

"Why?" I asked. "Why so much?"

"There are more transplants being done, for one thing, so demand is up. But the real cost is in extraction. In pieces, select bones from a male cadaver can be sold for almost seventy thousand dollars. But to properly procure and process the bones into dust, with the quality and technical standards required for surgical use, costs a tremendous amount. It's the processed dust, not just the bones themselves, that accounts for that."

"Isn't this done by hospital laboratories?"

"Some. But the laws governing it and a number of for-profit groups are vague or not even drafted yet. These for-profits promise tremendous returns to investors and pay fantastic salaries to their medical staffs."

"Like Antibodies Research."

"Yes. Like them. In fact, there's no way a for-profit group can generate an income like that without cutting a lot of corners in quality of procurement and processing."

I gave that some thought. "Have you ever met Mark Gilbert?"

"I've met him."

"Obviously, you don't like him."

"As I said, we compete."

"He finds donors?"

"Usually at small private hospitals in Colorado and elsewhere—those whose operating margins are slim. The county hospitals—public hospitals that I visit—are required by law to notify the nonprofit agencies if they have a donor. Private hospitals can accept finders' fees, and some do."

Bunch leaned forward. "Is he snatching enough bodies to make a good living?"

Vogel's eyebrows raised until he decided Bunch was making a joke. Then his lips lifted in a polite smile. "Body snatching—that's very funny. Gilbert does quite well, I understand, by procuring donors from other areas of the country. Atlanta, Houston, Albuquerque, New Orleans—states and areas where the regulations and laws haven't yet been implemented as well as they have here."

"Have you ever worked with Dr. Morris Matheney?"

"Yes. He's one of our real experts in antigens. He's made some major contributions to allograft research."

"Allograft?"

"Transplants between two individuals of the same species. If you transplant between identical twins, that's isograft. Autograft is moving tissue about within the same host. Xenograft is transplantation between different species. Research is going on there, too, though it's been slowed a lot by animal rights activists."

"You have high regard for Dr. Matheney."

"Certainly! In fact, I've often thought he'd be my choice for a physician if I had to undergo transplant."

11

On the way back to the office, Bunch heaved a long sigh. "I got a good idea where Nestor disappeared to, Dev."

"It sounds possible. But it's damned hard to believe. And let's face it, it's not all that easy. There must be regulations for a paper trail on parts of human bodies delivered for transplant."

"Vogel said the laws haven't even been drafted yet."

And Vogel emphasized the confidentiality surrounding donors and recipients, a secrecy which, no matter how necessary, could lead to exploitation. "It has to be damned expensive, too. Think of the cost of setting up an operating room and the—what did Vogel call it?—the harvesting process." Still the devil's advocate, I added, "And there would be parts left over to get rid of."

"So? The facilities are already set up, Dev. Remember, Matheney has an operating room right in his clinic. And he has the skills."

As well as an interest in developing technology for transporting human organs. "There would be records, Bunch. Even in a clinic. No, the operating room would have to be someplace secret, and you're talking big money to set that up with all its monitoring equipment, life-support equipment, quality control stuff. Big money."

"Think about it, Dev. Hospitals and clinics charge plenty—enough to cover all that overhead. A private company could too. Figure it out: You sell the organs at 'cost,' the skin, the bones, the tissues . . . Christ, if you work it right, anything you don't make money off you can flush down the toilet. It sounds like the greatest thing since chrome hamburgers."

"It's also dangerous. You don't just grab somebody off the street, Bunch."

"Illegal aliens?"

Alone and invisible to official eyes . . . The supply side of an economic equation that would be even more favorable: cheap raw material with fewer rights than someone's pet dog. And no antivivisection groups picketing for them. "Nestor was, what, twenty-two? Twenty-three?"

"Nice, healthy young lad," said Bunch.

"With very rare blood."

When we got back to the office, I ignored the red message light on the answering machine and made a quick call back to Vogel.

"Don't blood types have to be similar for successful transplants? Doesn't the donor have to be the same blood type as the recipient?"

"Generally, that's the first prerequisite, especially for allografts: histocompatibility of blood and tissue."

"And it takes a lot of tests to determine this compatibility?"

"It can. You certainly don't want to make a mistake at an early stage and waste all the subsequent effort and expense."

"Have you had any special requests in the last couple of months for donors with Rh null blood?"

A brief silence that might have been surprise. "Why, yes! There was one. An extremely rare type of blood. In fact, I'd never heard of it before."

"Who was the requesting party?"

"That's confidential information, Mr. Kirk."

"Did you find an Rh null donor?"

"No."

"Is the transplant center still asking for an Rh null?"

"No. They dropped off the computer."

"Meaning they found one?"

"More likely, the patient died. As I said, it's a very rare blood type. The chances of a match would be quite small."

"Who has access to the organ procurement lists?"

"If you mean the computer, only those hospitals in the Colorado Organ Recovery System. But as I told you earlier, much of the search is done by telephone—personal contact. I get on the phone and call hospitals." He added, "In small hospitals particularly, when an accident victim comes in, things are pretty frenetic and often they don't have time to file a notice until too late."

"How does a private firm do it? Such as Antibodies Research?"

"Telephone. And finders' fees."

"Can you remember when the request for Rh null came in?"

Another pause. "Three weeks ago? A month? I'm not certain. It could have been over a month ago."

"Did it come from Empire State Hospital in New York?" A longer pause, and before he could say "No comment" or hang up, I went on, "Obviously, Mr. Vogel, I've talked to other sources. I'm merely trying to verify their reliability so I can write the most accurate—and sympathetic—story I can. Did it come from Empire State? Your reply is entirely confidential."

"Well, yes, it did. They do a lot of the more difficult cases."

"Can you tell me who from that hospital requested it?"

"No. I've revealed too much already. If you want that, you'll have to talk to the hospital yourself."

I thanked Vogel again and hung up and stared for a long time out the window at the mountains. Strange how in the afternoon light they seemed to hunker down and look less steep and jagged as their shadows softened the rock faces above timberline. They weren't any different, of course. The cliffs and tumbled scree were the same, and it was just as much labor to walk the long, steep switchbacks up their faces toward the wind-scoured tundra. In a way it was good to know they were the same, regardless of how they looked from this distance or at different times of day. It was good to know there were those clean and unchanging spots left.

"Dev? Oh, Dev!" Bunch rapped his knuckles on the desk to pull me back to the office. "Check out the messages, my man." He turned the rewind switch to run the tape through garbled voices and replay it for me. Among the sales pitches and blank spots was a statement to the effect that someone knew fucking-a well who stole their dog, and Kirk and Associates better start looking over their shoulders. Because the unnamed someone was coming after their asses.

Another voice, more familiar, asked me to call Security Underwriters as soon as possible. And finally, the last message was from Archy Archer to let me know he'd found another wrecked Austin-Healey in Port Arthur, Texas, and for a fee could have it trucked up to Denver to cannibalize the parts.

Schute was paying for his information. I called him first.

"What have you found out, Kirk?"

"We still don't have the kind of evidence that will stand up in court. But we're getting close—I hope to have something useful in the next few days."

"I certainly hope so. I've had to tell our lawyers to reserve a court date so we can come in under the statute of limitations. We'll delay notice of filing as long as possible, but Taylor will have to be notified then. Or we'll have to drop the case."

"How soon?"

"My guess is a week or so. But that's cutting it damned thin."

"We're working on it, Mr. Schute."

"And I'm counting on you."

He didn't say anything else; he didn't have to. No firm would rehire or recommend somebody they couldn't count on, especially when a lot of other agencies were willing to take their money.

I looked at Bunch, who had listened to the conversation over the phone speaker. "Any ideas?"

"Figure some way to lure Taylor out dancing?"

"Sounds great."

"Hey, like you told Schute, I'm working on it."

"And in the meantime, we keep looking over our shoulders."

"Yeah. About that, Dev, they've got you picked out. What say I sort of trail around behind you just in case?"

"I don't need a bodyguard, Bunch."

"I didn't say you did. I'm thinking trap—next time they try to jump you, I jump them."

I shook my head. "Ties us both up too much. We'll just keep our eyes open."

He shrugged. "Just don't meet anybody alone, okay?"

I promised, and we divided up the rest of the afternoon. Bunch would learn what he could about Antibodies Research, using newspaper files, the telephone, friends, and, most especially, friends of friends. I'd see what a trip to Warner Memorial could tell us before swinging by the new Ace Roofing job and following the workmen home; our angle this time was to see if they might meet Taylor after work.

The trip to Warner led me on a trail of diamond patterns and circle patterns in the floor tiles of institutional hallways. Wall arrows directed me along the large building's maze toward the office I had been referred to by the receptionist. There, the hospital's public relations spokeswoman assured me she could provide a press package that would answer most of my questions about Warner's famous transplant activities. I took it and then, like a true newshound, told her I wanted to get a different angle—something personal and up close was the phrase—especially about the wonder docs who made these miracles happen. But, I found out, most of them weren't available, and those who were had little time for the press. In fact, Dr. Gold was downright hostile: "I appreciate the fact that you're a reporter, but the answer is no. If a call comes, I may have a hundred minutes to scrub up, get the patient prepped, operate, and have him in post-op. There's no time for you. Good-bye."

Public relations, however, is public relations; the hospital spokeswoman, apologizing for the doctor's abruptness—

"They're under tremendous pressure, you understand"—gave me a list of stations that I could visit: The patient preparation area, where the recipient, called from home as soon as word on a donor arrived, would come in breathless and more than a little frightened, yet hopeful and excited nonetheless. The operating room itself, not nearly so filled with space-age technology as the television shows reported. In fact, compared to the hospital's bare, starkly lit room, where everything was on wheels, the surgery in Matheney's suite of offices a block or so away seemed cheerfully luxurious. Finally, the computer with its twenty-four-hour monitor and a backup sheet prominently posted that listed the types of recipients waiting.

"We have a program that automatically places calls to the transplant team when a suitable donor comes on the screen." The nurse's aide pointed to the bank of machines that filled one wall of a cramped and windowless room. "But just in case, the backup list is on the wall and I'm supposed to answer when the alert beep calls our control number."

"So all the doctors are rousted when a donor shows up?"

"No, only our specialty team and its surgeon. We don't do hearts, for example, so our beepers don't sound for those donors. St. Luke's gets them."

"What specialty does Warner have?"

"Kidney. We currently have two kidney surgeons, and we're negotiating with a surgeon in Baltimore to come and open a liver transplant center. The kidney transplant's really more difficult than a heart transplant," she sniffed. "But of course, hearts get all the attention."

"Why is it more difficult?"

"The organ. A kidney's just a mass of blood vessels that are extremely difficult to work with."

"Dr. Matheney's one of your surgeons?"

"Yes. And Dr. Gold is the other. Both are very good."

"Does Dr. Matheney ever do transplants in his own clinic?"

"Oh, no! Those facilities wouldn't do. Our operating rooms are especially placed in the hospital not only for access to patient care but also to decrease vibrations. I can't imagine doing that type of delicate transplant surgery in a clinic's operating room."

"But other kinds of transplants?"

"Perhaps in an extreme emergency. But I really can't imagine it."

I asked a few more questions, but the main thing I discovered was Matheney's access to the computer. He would know when a donor somewhere in the country was suitable for one of the hospital's waiting patients. And he would know what the hospitals were waiting for, even if it had nothing to do with kidneys.

"Dr. Matheney drops in quite often to look over the printouts of requests. He's really dedicated." She showed me the sheets, with their lines of abbreviations and numbers that outlined pertinent histological information and the assigned number of the requesting center. "A lot of this is superfluous—any donor's going to find someone somewhere with a need. But the urgent ones come on line; it's sort of a final hope." She amplified: "If we have a donor, for instance, we input the blood and tissue types into the computer, and the program searches for a matching request. It's all done at a computer bank in Philadelphia, and in a couple minutes, back comes an answer. A hospital in Florida or California might be looking for an organ with just those specifications. I'm sorry we don't have a donor now in the hospital so you could see how it works."

I told her I was, too, and thanked her for all the information.

Ace Roofing's familiar truck and tar trailer sat in the parking lot surrounding a long apartment building. Its roof was a shingled mansard topped by tar and pea gravel. Beneath the mansard, which formed the third tier of apartments, whose windows protruded past the slope of shingles, the building was a mixture of brick and plaster designed to look old-fashioned and match the name: Camelot West. It looked like the biggest job Ace had landed yet, and I was disappointed that the work force was the same size and had the same faces.

When I arrived, pulling the van into position at the far end of the parking lot, the crew was just finishing for the day. The boss, heavyset with a skin tanned boot dark, gestured where to leave the equipment for the next day's work, and I watched as they meticulously stored the stiff mops and spreaders near a series of vent pipes on the roof, and telescoped the long aluminum ladders and shoved them into the truck bed. Then they caravaned out, leaving the tar trailer parked at a far edge— first the pickup, then a Chevrolet Camaro spotted with primer and rumbling deeply. I pulled in behind, giving them plenty of room in the heavy traffic of late afternoon.

Knowing pretty much where they were headed, I could afford to drop back out of sight and move up only for periodic checks. The quickest route was Wadsworth north, and that's what they took, avoiding the tangle of downtown traffic that always clogged the I-70–I-25 mousetrap at rush hour. By the time we crossed over the Boulder turnpike, traffic thinned enough for me to stay far behind and still keep them in sight. They made the expected turn onto U.S. 287 North, but instead of turning off east toward Erie and the Wilcox farm, they passed one road after another and headed for Longmont. At the southern edge of the town and before they reached the city limits, where car dealers and fast-food restaurants crowded the frontage, they pulled into the graveled lot of a small, nondescript box of a building with two high windows on each side of a single door. Above the door a painted sign read CACTUS LOUNGE. In one of the windows was a red Coors sign; another said TOPLESS DANCING EVERY WEEKEND. A clutch of gleaming Harley choppers had been backed against the grimy brown of the bar's stucco.

Cruising past, I watched the roofing crew, now wearing muscle shirts or sweats, climb out of the cars and go in, their boots swinging stiffly through the dust of the parking area.

It took about five minutes to find a place to turn around and get back into the traffic on 287. Then I pulled the van into a dirt lane and parked, just able to see the front and side of the Cactus. If I was lucky, Taylor had ridden one of those hogs, and whenever they were through with whatever brought the gang together, he would come out and climb on and ride off into the sunset, my videocam recording him. But I wasn't lucky. Instead, another pickup truck wheeled into the parking lot after about ten minutes, and Taylor, grinning at something the driver said, climbed out of the rider's seat and followed the man through the narrow door.

I filmed it anyway, the telephoto lens bringing the bearded face close enough to read his lips. They said something like, "Shit, man, not me," and then they were in the doorway. It wasn't enough for a case, and it would help the defense more than the plaintiff because it didn't rule out any handicap. But it was the best I was going to do this day, and wearily I headed back to Denver.

Bunch reached the office about the same time I did. He'd managed to learn a little more about Antibodies Research and a lot more about their possibilities for profits.

"That's better than I did."

"Still no Taylor?"

"Not what we need. I found him out at a local bikers' bar, but he was just riding in a truck."

"Party time?"

"I'm not sure. Looked like a meet of some kind—a lot of choppers and cars, no women. Maybe fun, maybe business, maybe both."

Bunch wagged his head. "I'd like to finish that one up soon."

"We'd better finish it soon. And the right way, if we ever want to work for Schute again."

"Maybe we could trade: Taylor for the dog. Hell, the dog's worth more—they might do it."

"Right." I poured a cup of acidic coffee. "What'd you get on Antibodies?"

"Not too much. But I did find out there's more money in bits and pieces, even, than organs."

"Better spell that out for me, Bunch."

"Cells. There's a whole market for human cells and no laws

governing it. What they do is take the living leftovers from surgery and turn them into something called 'cell lines.' That's a culture that can live for a while. Like a mold, maybe. They grow enough to make panels for diagnostic kits, then use the kits to test the effects of hormones or drugs or cosmetics on human skin cells. It was a six-hundred-million-dollar business last year, Dev."

"Where'd you find this out?"

"There's a place up in Boulder I heard about, so I drove up and asked. What they do is sell human skin-cell cultures to cosmetics companies for research. The lady I talked to said they get a lot of their material from babies' foreskins, for God's sake."

"They sell the foreskins?"

"No—they buy them and extract the cells from the foreskins. Then they make clones of the cells and turn them into test kits for researchers who want to find out how a cosmetic's going to react on human skin. You can only use a kit one time for one chemical compound, and each kit costs about two fifty. That's two hundred and fifty. They did over a million dollars' worth of business last year."

"Did they buy anything from Antibodies Research?"

"No. But she says she's heard of them." Bunch shook his head. "You know some outfits even use appendixes and tonsils and tumors? Tumors are really important for testing cancer drugs. Not this company but other ones. She said there's more than three hundred and fifty companies working with these things." He added, "They're going into artificial skin."

"What?"

"Artificial skin. Skin replacement for burns and abrasions. Human skin's so hard to get and so expensive that this Boulder company's trying to develop a skin substitute. Says they'll do it too." He sniffed something from his sinuses and spit it out the window. "There went fifty bucks, I'll bet. You want to know what the big thing is I found out?"

"Well, yes, Bunch. I do."

"Tissue from aborted fetuses. I talked to one of the researchers over at University Hospital. The guy's a real hysteric about the virtues of fetal tissue implants. Diabetes, sickle cell anemia, stroke, spinal cord injuries, some cancers, and kinds of blindness—to hear the guy, fetal tissue can cure just about anything." Bunch told me why that tissue was better than other kinds of transplants. "It doesn't get rejected by the patient so easily. What they do is take a little bit of fetal tissue and graft it into a patient's body where it's needed. Tissue from a fetal pancreas, for instance—they'll graft it onto an adult diabetic's pancreas where it grows into what they call an islet. Pretty soon, the patient's pancreas is making the sugar and hormones or whatever it didn't used to produce. Bingo—no more insulin shots. For a while, anyway, but they still haven't found a way to make the islet permanently effective. He told me about experiments with bone marrow implants for leukemia, brain implants for Parkinson's disease, a lot of stuff, Dev. It's really amazing!"

"Where do they get the fetuses?"

"From clearinghouses. But he's really worried. The government's banned experiments using aborted fetuses in the National Institutes of Health. The ban doesn't apply directly to private research laboratories, but he says nobody's going to continue experiments that the federal government calls unethical." He popped his knuckles in the way he had when he was feeling agitated. "Somebody with leukemia, like this buddy of mine who got it in college—played football his freshman year, and you should have seen him six months later—I mean somebody like that, they've come close to getting a cure for. And now the government says it's unethical. It's playing politics with people's lives, Dev. That's the shitty thing about it—they call it unethical not for medical reasons but for political reasons. The antiabortion people."

I wanted to get a point clear before moving into philosophical areas. "They have a clearinghouse for fetuses?"

"Aborted ones. This guy said it's cadaverous tissue. No different from a dead adult. And the collector gets the consent of the mother to use the fetus and to make it available only to researchers sanctioned by NIH—who can't do those kinds of experiments anymore."

"These are fetuses already aborted."

"Yeah. The abortion procedure tears up a fetus anyway, he said, and they take the parts that would be cremated and turn them into tissue for research and transplant surgery. They don't get tissue from intact fetuses, he said."

"Serafina and Felicidad were pregnant. Very pregnant."

Bunch nodded. "I asked him about that. He said it's not the same thing. He said intact fetuses could be really useful, but 'harvesting' intact fetuses for their organs . . . Well"—Bunch leaned against the window railing—"he did tell me that anencephalic babies are sometimes used for organs with the parents' permission. They're the ones born with just a brain stem— they're alive, but the poor kids have no brains and they'll die in a few hours anyway. He said there's maybe two or three thousand a year born that way who could be kept alive on life support long enough to get their organs. A hospital out in California—Cerro Lindo—already used the heart from one. In fact, there's a proposed law in California to declare anencephalics dead at birth so their organs can be taken while they're still breathing."

A living organ bank. "So there's money to be made from intact fetuses."

"He said baby organs are really rare because a lot of parents just don't want to donate—I guess that means high demand and low supply: classic profit situation, right? But even aborted fetal tissue is a gold mine. There's this private lab out in Alameda, California, purifies insulin-producing cells from aborted fetuses and makes a onetime treatment for diabetics. Dev, the treatment alone costs five thousand dollars, plus doctors' fees and hospital time. This outfit's projecting revenues of four hundred million dollars within the next five years. And that's only the beginning."

Vaguely, I recalled reading somewhere about a diabetic woman in Minnesota who wanted to get pregnant and abort so the fetus's pancreas could be grafted to hers. "Where do people get intact fetuses?"

"My man didn't know. Or said he didn't, anyway. He only works with the aborted ones. I asked him about the clearinghouses but he got pretty vague. Only thing he said was that biological experiments and research were government-regulated. I got the feeling, in fact, that he didn't want to talk about that part of it." He pushed off the rail and walked restlessly back and forth between the desk and the door. "My guess is that clearinghouses get their fetus supply from abortion clinics. I mean, where else could they get a steady supply? Some states require abortionists to get the mother's permission to dispose of the fetus. But there's not much said about how it's disposed of, and I can't figure anybody wanting to take it home with her. Hell, suppose a clearinghouse opened a chain of abortion mills and got its tissue that way? God knows, they'd be making a fortune at both ends." He thought a minute. "Maybe it's a good thing the government's pulling NIH out of it—competition drives the price up, some company might start paying women to have abortions." Then he shook his head, remembering. "But I keep seeing my buddy in college—the one with leukemia. If he'd just had a chance . . ."

To get whole organs—baby organs—instead of just the tissue, you needed a whole child, not just the bits and pieces vacuumed out during an abortion. A seven- or eight-month-old fetus, alive in the womb, organs already formed and working, heart a rapid thump through the stethoscope, and then a cesarean, a quick cut for the desired organ—transport it to the waiting patient, and everybody's happy. Except the mother, but then her organs and bones and flesh could turn a tidy profit, too. You only needed a pregnant woman that no one would miss.

"How do we get inside the Antibodies building, Bunch?"

"Uh huh. I figured you might want to do that." We both

thought of what we had seen: a compact building whose windowless brick wall faced the street through the heavy chain-link fence that guarded the grounds. "Right now, I'd say we go in through the roof. But you can bet your Aunt Hetty's long johns they've got some humongous protection around that place."

12

Percy Ahern was an ex–Secret Service agent. I had been assigned to work with him when I finished up at Bellesville, and that year's tour had been the best of the lot. After serving his twenty, he—like a lot of ex-agents—set up his own investigation business; but his was in New York, where business was considerably better. We kept in touch—he did favors for us there; we did favors for him in the Rocky Mountain region. We both liked the arrangement better than going through the World Association of Detectives directory. For one thing, we trusted each other's work; for another, if the favor didn't involve a lot of time or overhead, it was done for free—a consideration more important some times than others. This was not one of the others. I called him and left a message on his tape recorder for any information on Empire State Hospital and their request for an Rh null donor. Please expedite if possible.

Bunch, too, had a telephone call to make and I listened while he asked the health service if Sid Vicious had shown any signs of rabies. Hanging up, he smiled. "We can pick him up. He's clean as a hound's tooth!"

"It's a relief to me, too, Bunch. I wouldn't want you chewing my shin."

"I wouldn't chew that soup bone if I did have rabies. Nobody else would, either." He patted his thigh. "It was my leg the dog went after: quality and quantity in massive portions."

I gave him advice on what to do with his massive portions,

and we spent an hour or so getting the gear organized for the evening's excursion. When I locked the office for the day, I swung downtown to the Denver Public Library and wandered through the medical section to do a little light reading. The University Medical Center library would have more texts, I knew, but they would probably be both too technical and too narrowly focused. What I wanted was an overview in layman's language of the transplant technology and especially its business side.

I found almost nothing on the business aspect, but was luckier with the medical. One tome let me know that the total number of organ transplants rose to a hundred thousand in 1988 while the estimated number of new people awaiting transplant each year hovered around thirty-three thousand, and that only about 10 percent of the year's cadavers provided organs. A more technical book pointed out that the success rate on liver transplants from cadavers was 80 percent in the late 1980s, while the success rate on liver transplants from living donors was 95 percent. One text testified that the two principal aims in transplant surgery were to minimize the genetic distance between recipient and donor and to suppress the recipient's immune rejection mechanism. The first area was one of genetic classification and matching rather than modification: select the best donor (a young healthy twin, if you were lucky), then compare the tissues of donor and recipient to find the closest match. The chapter went into greater detail about the methods and codes used to classify various kinds of tissue, and the several ways to type blood. It offered tables of probability of success based on various combinations. Rh null didn't show up on any of the tables.

In the area of immune rejection, the history of the development of various chemicals to overcome the body's rejection of foreign objects was detailed and buttressed with panels of statistics. In recent years, the discovery of cyclosporin A increased organ transplant success dramatically. However, no one agent seemed to be totally effective. So combinations of prednisone, Imuran, antilymph serum, monoclonal antibodies, and cyclosporin A provided a pharmacology that approached 90 percent effectiveness even in using cadaver grafts. The rate went up when the donor was alive. Unfortunately, the cost of medications was quite high, adding to the expense of already costly operations. It had reached a point, in fact, where economics was superseding medical considerations as the determinant of who would or would not receive a transplant.

The article ended in a plea for more research, recently cut back by government belt-tightening, and that led to the next book, one which focused on areas of medical exploration. One dramatic area was the transplantation of cells from a normal brain to brains that had lost the capacity to generate certain chemicals, and I recalled what Bunch had told me from his interview. Such diseases as Parkinson's, Alzheimer's, and Huntington's showed short-term favorable reaction when chemical-producing cells were transplanted as islets; however, the long-term results tended to be negligible as the diseased brain gradually killed off the new cells and the disease reasserted itself. Research on why the transplanted cells died had been slowed by the government prohibition on using fetal tissue. Other similar research also affected by the prohibition included islet-cell transplant for certain types of diabetes and even some forms of trauma effects. Areas in which exploration was only in the beginning stages were the search for the chemical causes and cures of such psychological disorders as schizophrenia and severe depression, and the use of animal organs for xenograft transplant to human recipients. Recently, a genetically engineered protein was discovered to kill transplant-attacking cells in mice, offering hope of a cheaper, more effective way to overcome the body's rejection system.

I didn't find much on fetal tissue transplants or on the clearinghouse business. But the information I did find supported what Bunch had reported, and led to the same conclusion about the possibilities for major profit by private scientific laboratories, especially those who might ignore the NIH prohibition.

What it boiled down to was a tremendous industry of research, application, and development that promised unimaginable benefits for tens of thousands of diseased people. It also showed a very expensive and often ill-governed process involving many, many people in public and private institutions, not all of whom would be in it for purely altruistic reasons. In fact, several major drug manufacturers here and abroad were investing millions in the chemical areas of transplant research, in the hopes of making billions in return. Reputations for the researchers and vast profits for the sponsors were there to be won, and because of this there was a temptation not to look too closely at the means of achievement.

The hours hunched over the library table had made me stiff, and I stopped at the health club to stretch and work up a sweat on the lifting machines and to jog around the track until the manager flicked the lights to tell the few remaining clients it was closing time. Then I drove over to an Italian restaurant in the Highlands neighborhood where Bunch would be waiting.

Little Pepina's was one of the few restaurants in Denver that always gathered a late-night crowd, and I had to search among the talking, eating faces for Bunch. Finally, he raised an arm from across the room and I worked my way over.

"Calamari to start with." He dished a spoonful onto my waiting plate from the hot crockery bowl. "Then the pasta." Between mouthfuls he told me that we were set for our visit to Antibodies. "Everything's in the van. Got your stuff?"

I nodded, mouth full.

"Something else I figure we should do too."

"What's that?"

"Put the squeeze on Mrs. Chiquichano."

"Why? And how?"

" 'Why,' because I figure she's the lead to Matheney. Think about it, Dev. She provides the raw material, Matheney buys it. But he's sitting on a cushion; he's a respected surgeon, lives in a nice house, pays a lot of taxes, has important friends, and so on. He's not going to spill a thing, not unless we've got a clear case against him. Chiquichano's the weak link."

"She might not know what Matheney wanted those people for. Hell, even we don't know that for certain—we're just guessing."

"I'll put money on our guesses, Dev. I want her to tell us she took money for those people—and who she took it from."

"Right. What we do is go up and ask her, she says yes, then we start to squeeze. Come on, Bunch!"

"Maybe it'll take a late-night chat. Just the three of us in a cozy, secluded spot."

"You want to break her kneecaps, that it?"

"It might not hurt if she thinks that."

I shook my head and drained my wineglass. "She'd laugh at us while we did it and sue us for assault afterward. No, if we want to threaten that woman, we've got to have some ammunition to do it with. And to make it worth her while to cooperate."

A string of spaghetti snaked into Bunch's pursed lips with a slight sizzle, and he nodded and mopped his plate with a wad of bread. "Yeah. She's a tough old buzzard, that's for sure."

Later, after we'd changed into our ninja outfits of dark clothes and tennis shoes, Bunch eased the van across the jolt of railroad tracks and into a shadow cast by the corner of one of the warehouses that dotted the manufacturing district. Across a ribbon of black that was the bed of the South Platte River, South Denver's lights formed a curtain of glare against the eastern sky. Only occasional street bulbs gleamed dully among the buildings surrounding Antibodies Research, and here and there the splash of security lights illuminated walls and doorways. We had driven slowly past the small building three or four times from different directions, and now we'd walk around the perimeter fencing before we attempted to get in.

Bunch, a carefully muffled tool kit in a belt pack around his waist, led the way through the shadows. I carried the small satchel and followed. We located the gates and, watching for the stray patrol car that might cruise the neighborhood, traced out the tall fence with its strands of gleaming razor wire spiraling along the top. Bunch looked for any electronic sensors that could make the fence hot, but Antibodies apparently believed in wire alone. A heavy brass padlock held the small gate shut, and Bunch worked the tumblers in the dark, feeling his way with the pick and spring. When it clicked open, we eased through and listened for the sound of night watchmen. Only the steady whisper of distant cars speeding along elevated I-25 and, in the warm darkness, a motorcycle winding up through the gears a block or two away. Bunch led me to a corner of the building where the shadows were deepest, and I fished the grapple and line from the satchel. It took two tosses, both achingly loud despite the electric tape wrapped around the metal shafts, before the hooks caught firmly on the edge of the flat roof.

"You think they have a night guard?" I asked.

"Naw. Place this small, maybe part of a large security patrol—check the fences, rattle the doors, respond to alarms. That should be it." He tugged hard on the line. "You ready?"

"Go ahead."

I held the line taut while he walked up the side of the building, pulling himself hand over hand up the rope. His large shadow slid out of sight and I heard the tiny crackle of pea gravel against the sky. In a couple minutes, he was back to wave me up. I followed, feeling the ache of my shoulder start again under the strain of the climb. At the top, I paused a minute to work my shoulder around and ease the tightness; then I pulled the line up and coiled it ready at the roof's edge.

The top of the building was a small plateau in the dimness, broken here and there by vent pipes and, near the middle, by a block that should house the stairway. Two or three skylights lifted like small glass tents, and one of them glowed faintly.

"Somebody's inside, Bunch."

He tiptoed over to peer through the glass, pulling on his rubber gloves. Then he crept back. "It's from the lobby. Maybe they do have a security team."

"Goddamn it, Bunch—"

"Hey, maybe they don't, too. Relax, it's in man's nature to take chances."

"Man's nature can be behind bars, too."

" 'When a spider plunges from a fixed point to its consequences, it always sees before it an empty space where it can never set foot, no matter how it wriggles.' "

"What the hell are you talking about?"

"Kierkegaard, literary type. Kierkegaard in the middle of the night on an empty roof. And we're about to take the leap of faith."

"Christ, Bunch, just do it. Don't try to think—just go ahead and do it."

"That's what Kierkegaard says."

We walked as lightly as possible to the roof door. From there we could see the back of the building and the delivery and storage compound sheltered by its walls. Near the rear entry, pale in the gloom, a closed white van sat nosed against the landing.

"Bunch, what kind of vehicle did Nestor get into?"

He looked over the edge where I pointed. "Yeah. A white van. With Colorado plates and no windows. Just like that one."

"I think we've detected something."

"It's about goddamn time."

The roof door was locked. Using his penlight, Bunch traced along the crack of the door and spotted, at the top, the coppery glint of a contact that would register an alarm if the door opened. He threaded a piece of aluminum foil around it and completed the circuit by taping it to the door's metal frame. Then gingerly he picked the lock and the door swung out stiffly, its hinges making a muted groan despite the penetrating oil I'd squirted into them. We left it open and groped down black stairs into the chemical-smelling breeze that lifted from the building's interior.

We were after records, primarily, but we also wanted pictures of equipment that might support our suspicions and provide evidence for a warrant if needed. Exactly what we would do if it was needed, I wasn't sure. But that was one of those bridges that could wait. Right now, we had several thousand square feet of unfamiliar building to search in the dark, and with a possible security guard lurking somewhere. Bunch, a gliding shadow of thicker darkness ahead, pressed open a fire door at the end of the stairs, and we were in a long hallway that stretched into gloom. Wordless, we turned toward the front of the building and the offices.

Cautiously we opened doors along the way, our tiny lights playing quickly over their interiors. Storage rooms held a glitter of chromed medical equipment, tanks of oxygen and nitrogen, a series of cooling units, all portable and one as large as a walk-in freezer but ornamented with an impressive array of monitoring gauges. One large room housed a collection of wire cages and the musty smell of animal. The scurry of tiny feet and an occasional squeak punctuated the darkness.

"Lab rats, Dev. They're running some kind of experiments." Bunch's light slid along the identification tags on the cages and gleamed back at us from a hundred blinking sparks. I eased open the drawer of a filing cabinet and studied the headings of the dividers. Most of the index was made up of dates and chemical formulas, and a glance at the contents showed careful recordings of variations in weight, food and water intake, temperatures and behaviors, and finally the chemical analysis of the rats' organs and fluids. It made little sense to me, but it was clear the experiments were long-running and extensive. The camera's flash winked and set the animals scurrying nervously, and we closed the door behind us.

Next was a well-appointed operating room that rivaled the one in Warner Memorial. Windowless, it had an efficient arrangement of tables, lights, life-support equipment, and monitors. The space was cramped but suitable, and a rack of surgical gowns, masks, and bootees hung ready in a small adjoining room with a scrub basin and covered racks of sterilizing equipment and instruments. I took half a dozen photographs, the flash blinding us for a few seconds, and we waited until the red blossoms of reflected glare faded from our eyes before moving again.

Bunch, poking around beyond a concrete-block partition, hissed for me to join him. Tucked away and glowing pale blue through a line of ventilation ports, the gas pilot light of a large and well-insulated incinerator hissed comfortably. The black jets, visible in the glow, were large and numerous and focused to create extremely high temperatures.

"Here's where they get rid of dead lab rats and other bits of flesh," said Bunch.

Ceramic containers of various sizes were stored in antiseptic cabinets along one wall. "I think these are for powdering bones, Bunch." Another sterilized glass rack held portable perfusion units at the ready. I photographed the setup.

"It's a factory, Dev. A goddamn 'harvesting' factory."

I nodded and finished up that roll of film and reloaded. Antibodies had improved on the Nazis' technology as well as their economy of production.

Back in the hallway, we followed its turn left and were partway down the short leg when Bunch's large hand pressed hard against my shoulder to halt me.

"Guard."

I heard the creak of crepe soles on the waxed floor and an instant later a jingle of keys. A circle of light swung up the wall and down again, and Bunch and I slipped through an open doorway as the light swung up once more. It angled around the corner of the hallway, its reflection catching the leather and brass of a quasi-military uniform and the features of a face, whistling softly between its teeth, turning toward us. I closed the door softly and we froze, waiting as the shoes squeaked down the hallway. The vague tune floated above them. A couple minutes later, the sounds came back, punctuated by the jingling keys as the guard completed his round and headed back to the television set. Opening the door a crack, I watched the bobbing glow of the flashlight fade and finally wink out.

"Well, we know there's at least one guard," whispered Bunch.

I grunted yes and turned the light to survey this room. One wall was filled with computer equipment and another with a library of disks and three screens for reading and printing.

"Jesus, Dev—look at all this crap. It looks like they've got their own mainframe."

It sure wasn't your basic home computer, and the cost of the equipment probably rivaled that of the entire building. Quickly I photographed this room, too, careful to get shots of the filing system for disks, and we slipped back into the hallway.

The offices were around another corner and next to the main entry. We could hear the mechanical noises of the television from somewhere near the tiny lobby. The offices consisted of two rooms, the outer one for the severe secretary whose nameplate on a small desk caught the light: Phyllis Whortley. A large table held most of the work space as well as a telefax machine, filing cabinets, and another computer terminal. The inner office was filled with expensive modern furniture—a desk almost as large as Phyllis's worktable, a swivel chair almost as large as the desk, and a visitor's chair whose leather upholstery made up for its diminished size. Another computer terminal, a calendar, a telephone with memory buttons, and a matching pen set rested on the desktop. I photographed the telephone index.

"Look up there, Dev."

Bunch's light rose up the wall to show a pair of golden eyes glaring down at us. Behind the eyes, spreading like a dark cloud, a set of wide antlers loomed. On another wall glinted the ivory teeth of a snarling, hairy lion's head. Other, smaller trophies decorated different walls.

"Looks like he's transplanting heads, too," said Bunch. He

went to the door and stood guard while I rifled through the filing cabinets and drawers, delayed briefly by a locked cabinet.

"Anything?"

"No. Invoices. Bills for supplies. Telephone records." I took pictures of those sheets with their columns of numbers and times and costs, then eyed the computer's black screen.

"Bunch—you check the computer files. See if the records are there."

He did, and I took his place near the door and listened to the friendly beep and rattle of the keyboard as Bunch turned the machine on and played through the menu and coded file names. We had to halt once, tense in the blackness as the computer motor wound down to a dying wheeze and the guard took another tour down the hall. The same flashlight beam swung carelessly in the dark; the same half-whistled tune echoed from the walls. Then Bunch clicked the machine on again, its beep greeting us loudly.

After a while, he whispered, "Dev—look here."

The pale orange letters read DONOR C-3 (IBRAHIM HASSAN RH NULL), followed by a list of dates and coded references and figures.

"Look at the dates, Bunch."

The file had been opened on the seventeenth of last month. On the nineteenth occurred P & D with a notation ROSENBERG. On the twenty-second, a large figure with many zeros.

"That's Nestor," whispered Bunch. "It's got to be!"

"Yeah. C-three: Chiquichano, three? Can you find C-one and C-two?"

"Hell yes, I can find them."

He did, and gradually more of the code began to make sense. The figures were amounts of money received for the tissue or organs the donors supplied, the dates were the dates of removal and transfer, the initials indicated disbursement. "P & D" could mean almost anything, but the dates were important there— they coincided with the disappearances. Antibodies Research (AR) received most of the income, and my guess was that someone like Matheney would get his pay from Antibodies' cut as a dividend or consulting fee. That would be recorded somewhere else in the system, and with enough time Bunch would be able to find it. Prominent in this series of C donors was AC, who received five thousand dollars for C-1 and C-2, and ten thousand for C-3. I photographed the screen and Bunch rummaged through the secretary's drawer for a blank floppy disk. Then he began punching keys.

"What're you doing?"

"Copying the disk. Take a couple minutes."

It did, the hum and twitter of the machine startlingly loud in the silence of the building. I checked my watch—we'd been in for almost three hours—and guessed that the guard would be coming along the hallway in another twenty or so minutes.

"How much longer?"

"Just finishing up."

He replaced the disks in their sleeves and inserted the original, and we eased into the hallway. Three minutes later, we were sliding down the rope. We flipped the hook free and it clattered dully to the gravel drive. We even relocked the gate on our way out.

Through the open window over the kitchen sink, I heard the faint music of Mrs. Ottoboni's stereo. A tenor rose to an achingly pure note and held it for a long count before giving way to the matching melody of a soprano. The two distant voices chased each other like butterflies in the hazy late-morning sunshine, which washed a golden mist over the clumps and swirls of color that were Mrs. O.'s flower beds. Beyond them, the answering call of birds told me there was a whole world of beings that never fretted about human greed or missing people or murder. It was good to wake up rested and remember that.

But flowers and song were only temporary respites from a too-insistent world, and after breakfast I played back the messages that had collected on my home answering machine. The only one of interest was a voice I recognized, "Dev, lad, it's your old mentor Perce. I've got something you'll be wanting to hear, so give me a jingle when you can."

I made the call from the office where I could tape the conversation. Percy was away from his telephone, his mechanical voice told me, and as per instruction I left my name, number, and the time I called. It always puzzled me how, in detective stories, the hero picked up the telephone and got right through to the person he was calling, including the chief of detectives or even the governor. I figured I called people who were a hell of a lot busier; certainly Percy was, but he managed to get back to me within the hour.

"You know, Devlin, I had a time of it to make somebody at that hospital open up his soul to me. Suspicious they were, and downright shy of strangers asking even stranger questions. Blushingly mortified, in fact."

"They're hiding something?"

"Oh, you've been in this nasty business too long, laddie. You've grown a mean and sneaky mind. Corrupt. Far different from the naive young lad with pink cheeks who nestled under my wing so many years past. Now your eye is on the evils men do, and you've no thought for the sweetness that dwells therein."

"You're telling me they're hiding something."

"Of course! But they swear their skeletons are the legal sort found in every doctor's abode, and they cite the rights of patient confidentiality, professional ethics, government regulations. The more I'd ask, the quicker they'd deny, damn their eyes, which of course made me persevere the more. At any rate, I was able—through my legendary Irish charm and Jesuitical machinations—able to pierce to the heart of the matter. Percy's Pierce, I call it, and indeed demonstrate occasionally to the awe and delight of the female population."

Percy had always been his own best audience. I let his laughter subside before prodding him back to the subject. "Did they ask for an Rh null donor?"

"They did. They did indeed. It seems there was this very rich

Arab sheik whose fifteen-year-old son by one of his wives—I never did get it straight which one—needed a kidney transplant. But the lad had extremely rare blood, so no one offered much hope to the poor kid. It's hard enough, they say, to find your run-of-the-mill kidney, since not everyone wants to part with theirs. But to match this Rh null blood, well, Dev, it's statistically awkward, to say the least. But the dialysis machine wasn't doing the job anymore; the lad was drifting toward that final rest that awaits us all, sinner and saint. So his father, desperate and sorrowful but by no means destitute, came to the famous Empire State Hospital in search of wonders. He offered a million petrodollars cash for an Rh null donor. That latter part is very hush-hush, you understand, since it's illegal to peddle parts, spare or otherwise. But the chap who told me was in a position to know and, after drinking an extraordinary amount of fine Irish water of life, was in a frame of mind to tell me too."

"They got it, didn't they? The donor!"

"Don't jump to conclusions. It's my nickel and my story, and I'll tell it at my own pace." I envisioned him settling back in the creak of his swivel chair to prop long legs on the desk, the way he had when he used to explain the facts of bureaucratic life to the new agent. "As I was to say before being interrupted, the sheik offered a million dollars for a donor. The best the hospital could do was try the operation with a kidney from a different blood group. But the chances were slim, Devlin, slim indeed, that either kidney or kid would survive. So to placate the distraught but wealthy father, the hospital put out a request for an Rh null kidney, asking every soul they could think of if they knew of this rare and wonderful organ. Knowing full well the chances of finding one were at best impossible and at worst sub-zero. Imagine their surprise."

"Did he say where it came from?"

"Denver, lad. Denver. You may have no blue bloods out there, but you can boast of one Rh null."

"Who was the responding doctor?"

"Wasn't a doctor but a faceless corporation: Antibodies Research, Inc. How can an antibody be *in corpore,* I wonder? A bit of a Latin pun there that would bring tears of merriment to the eyes of old Sister Boniface."

"When, Percy?"

"When she heard it, Devlin. When else?"

"No, damnit, when—"

"Ah, the impatience of youth. Not a brief instant to waste on a moment of joy. Hot-blooded, if I may safely use the term. Let me see now—I've got it written down somewhere. Oh where, oh where did my little note go . . . Ah, yes: They sent out the request on the fifteenth of last month, and two days later the miracle occurred. The seventeenth."

One day before Nestor disappeared. "You're certain? The seventeenth?"

"You impugn my reliability?"

"No. But they couldn't have gotten the organ until the eighteenth."

"The reply, Devlin. Why don't you listen? The answer came on the seventeenth. The kidney came a day or so later, after they scrambled a team to do the operation and made ready to pop it into the grateful recipient, who apparently is living happily ever after. The even more ecstatic sheik showered the premises with gratitude and lucre and departed back to Oman or Yemen or wherever."

"He paid the million?"

"More. That and more. My informant was getting a bit incoherent by this time, but I thought I heard him say ere he sank out of sight that the million was only the finder's fee— paid to Antibodies Research. He also paid the cost of the operation on top of that, and a munificent bonus for its success went to the hospital's operating fund—pun intended."

There were other questions I had which Percy couldn't answer, but he said he'd try to find out more when he could work it in. Bunch came in as I was thanking him, and when we hung up I told him all about it.

"A million dollars!"

"Plus expenses and a generous tip."

He leaned against the iron rail in front of the window. Overhead, the rumble of heavy casters across the bare floor told me the sculptress was moving one of her acrylic creations to a new angle of light to start the afternoon's work. "Matheney knew Nestor's blood type—knew how rare it was. He'd sewn up that cut a week or two earlier," I said.

"He knew about it from the health exam Nestor took for the job at Apple Valley. My guess is the bit of surgery reminded him of it."

"And he knew about the request. That guy at Cryo-Bio—Amaro—sent him a copy of it."

"But would he know of the million-dollar finder's fee?" Bunch asked.

"He could have responded to the inquiry and been told—indirectly and ever so politely, but clearly enough. Or perhaps Gilbert heard of it—it's his line of business to know stuff like that. He must have contacts all over the country who would let him know of an offer that size."

"For a percentage."

I agreed.

"Maybe," said Bunch, "Matheney thought he could convince Nestor to donate a kidney if the price was right."

"But Nestor said no?"

"Or he said yes, but the knife slipped. Or Matheney and Gilbert were greedy and old Nestor was twofers."

We listened to the casters roll back again, the muffled sound drifting across the ceiling like distant thunder.

Bunch sighed. "The rich buy, and the poor die—so what else is new?" He paced across the room. "We've got motive and opportunity, Dev. And we even have the means: that operating room in Antibodies."

I pushed back the chair and studied the mountains. As Bunch said, it wouldn't be the first time that those with money stole the lives of those without, but that fact didn't make this knowledge any easier. "This is getting pretty deep, Bunch. Maybe it's time to ask for a little help."

"You mean official?"

"As you say, we have means, motive, and opportunity. And we know of three missing people."

"They'll just laugh at us, Dev. Something like this, we need a body."

"Well, there aren't any bodies. There aren't likely to be any, either—you saw that incinerator. But we have good grounds for suspicion. If we don't report what we suspect, we could be liable."

"The hell we could—we're trying to solve the case, not protect the criminals."

"Concealing a death is a class-one misdemeanor. And accessory—a felony—includes 'to prevent the discovery' of a criminal. It's shaky, but close enough if an assistant DA wants to haul us into court."

"I wish to hell you'd never gone to law school."

I reached for the telephone. "We'd better cover ourselves."

"If that's the way you want it, fine. But take my advice: Don't start with the DA's office. Let's talk to Kiefer in homicide first."

13

I called the homicide office and made arrangements to meet Detective Kiefer at a cop hangout, the Satire Lounge on East Colfax, around five-thirty. "I'll be on duty, but you can drink a beer or two." That also gave Bunch and me time for a couple other chores. The first was another call to Jerry Kagan. He was back from his pediatrics conference, his office told me, and would return my call as soon as possible. When he did, I offered him a late lunch and he wanted to know what he was being set up for.

"I'd rather tell you in person. It might be harder for you to say no that way."

"That important?"

"I believe so. And I think you'll believe so too."

He paused to go over his schedule. "All right—let's do it now. Can you meet me in twenty minutes at that little beanery near the clinic? You know the one?"

"On the corner?"

"That's it."

He did more listening than eating, his fork full of chef's salad hovering somewhere between his open mouth and his plate as I told him about Nestor, Antibodies Research, and Matheney.

"Empire State Hospital? They do fine work, Dev! They take cases no one else will touch. I can't imagine them being linked to anything like what you're telling me. And Matheney! He's a highly reputable transplant surgeon—he's also one of the leading researchers in his field. . . ."

"My guess is, the hospital didn't know where the kidney came from or how Antibodies got it. Maybe they routinely don't ask—or maybe they were too surprised and grateful."

"Too grateful or too assuming. I mean, one assumes a certain level of professional ethics."

"Perhaps one assumes too much."

"Obviously, if what you say is true. But I have a hard time believing somebody of Matheney's stature would do this, Dev. For God's sake, I hope you're not talking this around—it's character assassination just to think of it."

"We've kept it quiet, Jerry. But something's going on. If Matheney's clean, he deserves to be warned about Antibodies before the egg hits the fan. If he's not, well, that should be known."

He chewed on his salad and thought. "What do you want me to do?"

I had a list of questions that Jerry might or might not be able to find answers for: How did the New York hospital advertise the reward? Was Matheney involved in the transplant operation? Who was the official donor, and was he dead or alive? Was there a doctor named Rosenberg involved? He jotted the questions down on a paper napkin, holding his objections until I finished. "These aren't the kinds of things people are going to be open about, Dev. Especially that million dollars. I can't promise a thing—and I'm not going to push too hard. I mean, the people I ask will want to know why I'm asking, and if you happen to be wrong about Matheney . . ."

"I'd appreciate your trying."

"I will, don't worry. If any of this is true . . ."

He promised to call a couple medical school friends in New York as soon as possible and to let me know what turned up. The rest of the hurried meal was a report on the latest in neonatal care, told with animation—and relief.

The second item of business was our visit to Mrs. Chiquichano. We found her in her office and spoiled her afternoon.

"I'm going to call the police!"

Bunch sighed heavily and settled his weight on a corner of her desk, making it creak ominously. "Here we are trying to be friendly, and you treat us like that."

"I have nothing to say to you people. You people leave me alone!"

"She has nothing to say, Dev."

"Maybe she'll think of something," I said, and placed a record of her payments from Antibodies on her desk. The copy had been neatly printed by our word processor in bulletin font, with the amounts in boldface for emphasis.

She stared at the large print for a long moment. "What's this?"

"Your finders' fees from Antibodies Research, Mrs. Chiquichano. For finding Felicidad de Silva, Serafina Frentanes, and Nestor Calamaro." I smiled. "Now you're supposed to ask where we got this."

She didn't. She only stared at me, her lips a pinched line.

"All right, I'll tell you: from Antibodies' files."

Bunch said, "They're going down, senora. Gilbert, Matheney, the whole gang. They're going to prison for a long time, and everybody with them."

"This is no proof!"

I opened the briefcase and placed photographs of the operating room, the gas oven, and other printouts on the table like a winning hand, one card at a time. "Those numbers mean a lot of money. Gilbert will have to explain to the police and to the IRS where it came from. And where it went. And for what reasons."

She stared at the photograph of Nestor's transaction. "*¡Es un millón de dólares!*"

"And you only got ten thousand. One one-hundredth."

". . . *millón* . . ."

Bunch said, "You're a fool, Chiquichano. You're no smarter than those poor peons you rip off."

"And now you're going to jail," I said. "A lot of years in jail and no chance to spend the money you've hidden away. Maybe somebody else will get to it while you're in prison. Maybe you'll die before you get out."

She looked up, black eyes staring at me and at the future.

"All that work. All that planning. All that saving. For nothing."

"Then again," said Bunch, "maybe you can work a deal. You tell what happened, the police settle for deportation. You get to keep your money—you get off free."

The face turned stiffly to Bunch, as if moving her neck were an effort. "I know what you do."

"You're right," I said. "We want you to talk. It'll help us, it'll help you."

"No!"

I gave her a few seconds and then gathered up the papers and photographs. "Suit yourself. Without your help, it'll take a little longer. But you can see we know what's going on, and you can see the game's just about over." I placed one of Kirk and Associates' business cards on her desk. "This is your chance to get on the right side, senora. Better do it before it's too late."

Neither Bunch nor I was convinced she would change her mind. More likely, she would run instead of help us; grab as much floating cash as she could lay hands on and—if it wasn't already out of the country—take her bank accounts and flee. We let her see us get into the Bronco and then drove around the block, where Bunch let me off at my car.

"If you need backup, let me know," I said.

Bunch looked down the street at the entrance to Mrs. Chiquichano's office. "I can handle it. I'll call you later."

I started across town for my meeting with the homicide detective. Kiefer was waiting in the Satire, a watering hole whose customers ranged from on-duty cops grabbing a fast dinner in the restaurant half of the building to citizens and denizens talking across the large bar on the other side of the dividing wall. As usual, he looked slightly out of place—a short, somewhat heavy man in his thirties who even in summer wore a dark blue blazer. He didn't smoke, but every time I saw him, I expected him to pull out a pipe and begin tamping it down. We'd met a few years ago over the body of an apparent suicide—a case that had generated some mutual respect—and he was the closest thing to a friend I had in the Denver Police Department.

"Hello, Dan."

He stood to shake hands formally and then lifted a finger for the waitress to bring another coffee. After a few how's-it-goings and is-that-so's, he got down to business. "So you might have something for me?"

I showed him the same photographs I'd laid out for Mrs. Chiquichano, explaining what they meant, and then told him about Felicidad and reminded him about Serafina. Like the professional interviewer he was, he didn't interrupt but quietly jotted a note or two in a small book as I talked. When he was certain I had finished, he leaned back and took a long pull on his coffee.

"Where'd you get the photographs?"

"Let's just say it's inadmissible evidence."

"I see. And you have no hard evidence about the missing people?"

"I don't have a body, no. But tell me it's not suspicious."

"Ah. I can't say that. No, I can't say that at all." A pair of uniformed policemen came in to sit at the booth in front of the plate-glass window and ordered rellenos smothered in green chili. Kiefer nodded hello to them. "But I can't get a warrant with what you've told me, either."

"I know that. I'm not asking you to. What I want you to do is see how much you can find out about Antibodies and Mark Gilbert. And Dr. Matheney."

He nodded without committing himself. "If I can do it quietly. Somebody like Matheney, I start asking questions, I'd better have a damn good reason."

"Don't forget the victims. They're reason enough."

"No—you said it yourself, Dev: They don't exist. Not legally, anyway. As far as the city and county of Denver are concerned, there never were any such people."

"Come on, Dan! A murder's a murder—illegals or not."

"I said as far as the city and county are concerned. Me, I want to hang the bastards. But I'm telling you there won't be much help from the department or from social services. Nobody wants to go looking for extra work; and if this has substance, it's going to be a hell of a lot of work."

"Yeah. Bunch told me to talk to you instead of the DA's office."

"Bunch was right. How's he doing?"

We talked for a few minutes about Bunch. "So you can help us out? You'll look into it?"

"Yeah. What the hell, it's not like I have enough to do already."

We left it at that, saying we'd get in touch with each other as soon as something turned up. It wasn't very promising, but at least Bunch and I had done our civic duty by notifying the police of our suspicions, and that should hold off any accessory charge.

The red circle on the calendar said we had one week left to get the goods on Billy Taylor. Beyond that, Schute's lawyers would have to drop the charges. They wouldn't like that; Schute's bosses wouldn't like that; Schute wouldn't like that. We wouldn't either. But how to get to the man and film him going about his normal life? That was the problem, and I was pondering some kind of gag—naming him a winner in a lottery whose prize had to be claimed in person . . . having a sexy female voice say she was a friend of his ex-wife and wanted to say hello . . . But those brilliant ideas were snuffed by the telephone. It was Jerry Kagan. "I talked to an old classmate at Empire State Hospital, Dev." A long, slow breath. "I think it's true. I really think a lot of what you told me is true."

"What'd you find out?"

"He didn't know all of it, just some rumors here and there. But apparently an Arab patient did come in for a kidney transplant." Kagan explained: "Anybody with blood that rare is hard to keep secret. Anyway, just like you said, the hospital put out a request in a dozen channels. And sure enough, they got a match. Rh null. I couldn't find out if it was from Denver, but they did get a donor."

"The million-dollar finder's fee?"

"Yeah. That's all over the hospital too. Though nobody's saying anything very loud about it. You know how these things go—somebody says something to somebody else, and nobody knows where the information came from. It's just heard. Anyway, that's the rumor. The fact is, the operation was a success. The patient checked out and was flown back to the Middle East on a medical flight a couple of weeks ago."

"Who was the surgeon?"

"Oh yeah—Rosenberg. The name you mentioned. He's one of their top kidney men. But I haven't talked to him and don't expect to."

"Do you know who brought the kidney in? Was it a transplant team from Empire?"

"All I know is it wasn't a cadavergraft."

"It wasn't?"

"The kidney came from a live donor. Better chance for success."

"Nestor was taken back there alive?"

"If it was Nestor." He added, "There was some talk of an increase in the bonus if the donor was alive."

"I see . . ." And that explained more of the numbers and cryptic entries in the file. "What happened to Nestor, Jerry?"

"I don't know."

"How can we find out?"

Another meditative silence. "Let me make some calls; maybe somebody knows somebody on the team. I'll get back to you."

But it wasn't Kagan who got to me next; it was a voice I didn't recognize right away. "Mr. Kirk? I'm glad I found you in. This is Mark Gilbert of Antibodies Research. I'd appreciate talking with you very soon."

"About what, Mr. Gilbert?"

He was in no mood for fencing. "I've heard you're making some wild and unfounded accusations about our company. Perhaps I can explain things and set your mind at ease."

I glanced at my watch. "You're at your company office?"

"Yes."

Overhead, the casters rumbled again. "I can be there in half an hour if that's all right."

"I look forward to it."

The industrial area was almost clear of workers' cars and trucks by the time I drove up through the twilight, and it seemed a bit odd to walk to the front entry as an honored guest. The door was locked, but a night bell offered itself. I pushed the botton. A minute or so later, I heard the jingle of keys and a vague tune being whistled. The guard—a young man with cropped blond hair—unlocked the door.

"Yes?"

"I'm Devlin Kirk. Mr. Gilbert's expecting me."

"Oh, sure. He's in the office. This way, please."

His crepe-soled shoes made a familiar squeak on the waxed tiles as he led me through the entry and into the hall where, the night before, Bunch and I had crouched tensely to let him pass. The outer office was empty; the guard knocked softly at Mr. Gilbert's closed door and stuck his head in. Then he stepped back and nodded me through before squeaking away.

In the light, Gilbert's office seemed larger, and the animal heads mounted on the walls receded to a stiffly polite distance. Gilbert, his florid face set in a taut smile, shook my hand and gestured toward the leather chair, which wheezed softly as I sat. "You do a little hunting?" I asked.

PARTS UNKNOWN · 213

He glanced up at the lion's glass eyes staring down at us. "Looks impressive, doesn't it? Actually, I bagged him in Texas. Haven't had time yet to go to Africa for the real thing. But I intend to. And I'll be ready when I go."

"They have lions in Texas?"

"A big game ranch." He wagged a finger at the heavy-maned trophy. "The animals are familiar with humans and have no fear of them. That means they're more dangerous than the wild animals. I find great pleasure in a challenge like that. Do you hunt?"

"Only information, Mr. Gilbert."

" 'Only information.' I see. Well, let's get to the point then, shall we? I'd like to know exactly what it is you think our company's engaged in, and what—if any—'information' you have to support your allegations."

"Obviously, Mrs. Chiquichano's talked to you. She must have told you what I showed her."

"Not in any clear detail; she was quite distraught. Apparently you frightened the poor woman."

The poor woman hadn't been afraid of me and Bunch together. "I think she—and you—know what happened to Nestor Calamaro."

Gilbert's sandy eyebrows lifted. "I have never heard that name, Mr. Kirk."

"The donor with Rh null blood. The guy with the million-dollar kidney."

Instead of answering, Gilbert gazed up at the lion, his own pale blue eyes as void of expression as the glass ones that looked back. "I'm not going to waste my breath pointing out the need for organ transplants, Mr. Kirk. Nor the benefits that such transplants bring to hundreds of otherwise crippled human beings every year—"

"Organs that come from willing donors."

Gilbert rustled in the desk drawer and pulled out a slip of paper, pinning it on the polished wood with his forefinger. It was a receipt for fifteen thousand dollars, and it had not been in his desk last night. "I knew that donor as Mr. Martinez. It's what he called himself when he made arrangements to donate one of his kidneys. As Mrs. Chiquichano perhaps told you, he was in this country illegally—a fact which I discovered only recently. However, we did make certain arrangements—financial arrangements—that could be construed as violating the law against the purchase of human organs. Mr. Martinez said he was willing to donate a kidney, but we would have to send money to his family in El Salvador."

"That's what this receipt is?"

"Yes." He held it a moment more to let me see the payee line before folding it into his vest pocket. It was made out to Raimundo Calamaro. Then he leaned back against the wide wings of the chair. "It was not a purchase, not directly, but it could cause us embarrassment. That I fully admit. However, Mr. Kirk, that kidney—that very rare kidney—saved the recipient's life and sent Mr. Martinez back home a relatively wealthy man."

"He went home?"

"As far as I know." Gilbert smiled. "The only reason he was working in America was to make enough money to buy a farm. I understand he flew directly home from New York once he recuperated."

"What about Serafina Frentanes and Felicidad de Silva? Did they fly home too?"

Gilbert's smile disappeared. "I don't know who you're talking about."

"The two women you paid Mrs. Chiquichano to provide. Two pregnant women whose babies were almost at term."

"I do not know them, and there is no evidence we ever paid Mrs. Chiquichano a single penny for anything."

There would be no evidence in the now-purged files, that was certain. And I strongly suspected that the farm Nestor bought wasn't the one Gilbert told me about. But the story was plausible enough to want checking out.

"The very nature of this kind of endeavor borders on the sensational, Mr. Kirk. That's one of the many reasons we prefer to keep a low profile. More important, of course, is the possibility that sensationalism might cause suffering to the families and loved ones of the donors." He cleared his throat. "I'm sure you can understand that. Now, I don't know who has employed you to investigate this matter"—he paused to let me fill in the blank, but I remained silent—"but you may tell them, very confidentially, that Mr. Martinez willingly donated his kidney. You may even mention the—ah—remuneration. In a sensitive way, of course, one which won't cause discomfort for your client."

"Don't you pay finders' fees to hospital employees who notify you of suitable corpses?"

"There's nothing illegal about that!"

"Perhaps not. But it does raise questions about those sensitivities you keep mentioning."

"And what about sensitivities to those whose lives can be dramatically enhanced by organ transplant? What about sensitivities to the living recipients?"

"And what about profits on this trade? Your profits?"

"All money received in excess of overhead are reinvested in the operations, Kirk! Organ transplantation is an extremely expensive endeavor. Where do you think the funds come from for those 'finders' fees' you sneer at? And—I assure you—the recipients would be willing to pay far more than we ask for the chance to lead normal lives." He stood and held out a broad hand sprinkled with red hairs. "I suspect I haven't changed your mind, have I? No? That's too bad—too bad indeed." The hand gripped mine with a tightness that wasn't friendly. "But let me assure you and whoever hired you of one more thing: Any slander you bring against us will be answered in court. Too many lives depend on what we do, Kirk, to let somebody destroy us through insinuation and innuendo. I assure you, we will fight back."

In addition to trying to pump information from me and warning me, Gilbert's purpose had been to convince me that Nestor was alive and well and living in El Salvador. He hadn't. His only evidence was a piece of paper he waved around, and his word—which was equally flimsy. But if there was no evidence that Nestor or the women were alive, there was none they were dead, either. And unless I could come up with something as definite as that, Sergeant Kiefer had little or no ammunition for his probe.

From the office, where I went to wait for Bunch, I telephoned Percy, hoping that the two-hour time difference between Denver and New York meant he would be at home. He wasn't. The answering machine asked for any message I cared to entrust. Then I tried his office and got another answering machine. So I left the same message: Very important, please call as soon as possible. But it wasn't until later in the evening that I finally talked to him about what Jerry had told me and what I needed now.

"So you want me to find out if the donor was alive, in fact?"

"If he was alive after the operation. And what happened to him—where he went."

"There should be a paper trail on something like that—there should, indeed, and old Perce will pierce through to the truth of the matter, never fear."

"I hate to tell you this, Perce, but time's important."

"When isn't it, lad? The little black mouse, the little white mouse, nibbling nibbling at the thread that holds us suspended over the void. And then one fine day . . ." Percy delighted in what he called his front-row seat at the *comédie humaine,* and if, at times, his constant laughter tended to irritate, that irritation was smoothed by the knowledge that he was genuinely interested in snooping because the more he discovered, the greater the laughter. Consequently, the jobs he did were thorough ones—even the freebies.

"As soon as you can?"

He promised an expeditious effort or double my money back. Which—given what I was paying—was a safe gamble.

It was well after ten before I heard the familiar heavy step on the iron stairs outside the office and Bunch came in.

"Don't tell me, let me guess," I said. "She didn't do anything different."

He groaned and stretched, his wide hands brushing the ceiling, "I'd rather run twenty miles than sit on surveillance. How in hell can you get so tired just sitting there?"

I knew the feeling. "What she did do was call Gilbert, and he told her to stay cool, that he could handle it."

"You know something I don't know," said Bunch.

I described my visit to Gilbert's office.

"That receipt wasn't in his desk last night, Dev."

"And he held his thumb over the date when he showed it to me. My guess is he sent the money this afternoon when he finished talking to Chiquichano."

"If he sent it."

"No, I think he did. He got Nestor's father's name and address from Chiquichano and sent it. It indicates Nestor's willingness to donate a kidney and explains his disappearance— it's central to Gilbert's alibi, so he wouldn't fake sending it. He wants me to know it's authentic."

"What about the two women?"

"Swears he never heard of them. And he's cleaned his files of any reference to them, you can count on that."

"Yeah. I figured we'd risk that. Well, you're right about Chiquichano. She didn't do anything out of the ordinary. Stayed at her office, made a few telephone calls, went home for supper, and then made a quick inspection of the cleaning crew. Now she's safely tucked away dreaming about getting richer." He yawned widely. "And I'm going home to dream too—about making that woman sit in a car for forty-eight hours without moving."

I locked the office and we went down to the parking lot behind the building. Bunch had just settled into his Bronco and I was unlocking the door of the Subaru when four hefty shapes materialized in the driveway and a voice said quietly, "Hello, assholes. We been waiting for you."

They were bearded, wore jeans and motorcycle boots and sleeveless vests with the gang colors. In their hands they carried things that glinted and clinked.

I moved to keep the car at my back. Behind me, I heard the Bronco's springs creak as Bunch got out whistling "How Much Is That Doggie in the Window?"

"You people want to party?" I asked. "Or are you just going to stand there?"

"Goddamn! You're asking for it—you really are asking for it, ain't you?"

That was the last coherent sentence. The next sounds were the grunts and gasps of bodies lunging at each other as the four of them closed against Bunch and me. I saw Bunch's arm reach out to spear the throat of one of the shadows, and then I was tangled with the greasy smell of sweaty flesh and a thudding shock as a pair of brass knuckles bounced off my hunched shoulder. Swinging back, I pulled the leather vest forward over my outstretched leg and chopped down hard at the back of the man's neck, and heard him grunt as he tumbled into darkness. Then I aimed an elbow beneath the upraised arm of the other one. A short, thick pipe hovered in the street glow and came whistling down to scrape along my forearm. The blow numbed my hand and sent prickles all the way up to my neck. My knee came up solidly into the figure's crotch, and an explosion of hot breath dampened my ear as I grabbed a wrist and twisted it up behind the man's back in a hammerlock. His cap flew off, leaving a balding patch of scalp surrounded by a fringe of long hair that offered a handy—if greasy—hold. Twisting the locks in my fingers, I thudded the man's face against the roof of the car and wrenched high on the arm to try and pop it from its socket. He was strong, and tough, and he bore down against me to keep his shoulder in place. I bounced him again, feeling something spew from his open mouth, and he tried with his free hand to whip the pipe back against my skull. It worked, cracking solidly across my scalp and sending yellow and red lights shooting through my vision.

It was enough to loosen my grip and he twisted, swinging again, and pulled away. The pipe came down on my crossed wrists this time and I shoved his arm high and stepped in with a solid, cutting thrust of knuckles under his ribs and heard the man's breath drive from his body. Something was clawing at my back, and fingernails dug into my shoulders and neck, and I swung a high elbow back to thud solidly into something and then came forward again with the blade of my hand across the bridge of the first man's nose. Before I could drive the splinter of bone up into his brain with the heel of my hand, he dropped out of sight, rolling and kicking, and scrambled somewhere.

I couldn't tell where because the one behind me wrapped an arm across my neck and began to squeeze, hammering at my face with his other fist. It was reflexive, the response good training instills: I reached behind his back and grabbed the flailing elbow and, with my right hand, yanked on the man's pants at knee height to pivot him across my hip. Stepping forward through his body, I lifted his leg and threw him over in a head-dive onto the graveled earth. A quick kick to his temple and he lay making uh-uh noises and scratching one foot in the dirt.

I looked around for Bunch in time to see his large shadow leap into the air with a flying front kick that caught his target in the chest and drove him, arms flailing a length of chain, back against the building's wall. He bounced, falling forward into a side kick from Bunch that dropped him. A skitter of flying gravel whirled me around in time to see three figures running for the street.

Bunch, breathing heavily, said with satisfaction, "God, I needed that. I hate surveillance!"

We dragged the fallen warrior up to the office. While I dabbed Merthiolate along the already swelling fingernail scratches on my neck and shoulder, Bunch closed the blinds and sat the groggy man down in a wooden chair tipped back against the wall. Like the rest, he was fully bearded and wore jeans and steel-toed motorcycle boots and a sleeveless vest—the familiar uniform that expressed his freedom from stifling convention and a dedication to colorful individuality. He also wore a swollen right eye and fresh blood and snot that glistened in the gummy hairs under his nose.

"Dev, I told you and I told you: Get away from those throws and holds. Use the punching techniques."

I winced as the medicine burned into raw flesh. "I like my way, Bunch."

"Yeah—and look what it gets you. Cut. Me, I come out clean."

"Looks like a mouse under your eye."

He touched the purpling flesh. "Well, almost clean. But you look like you tangled with a tom cat—maybe you better get some rabies shots."

The owners were dirtier than their dogs, that was certain. I buttoned my torn shirt and turned to the man in the chair, whose open eye had begun to show he was awake. "What's your name?"

"Fuck you."

Bunch smiled. "The name does fit the face. But before we have a major misunderstanding, dickhead, let me explain something." He picked up the length of chain the biker had used, and twisted it into a knot. His broad fists turned first red, then white. "It's really easy to understand. We ask you questions, you answer them." The chain snapped and Bunch dangled the broken link in front of the man's wide eye. "Or I'll unbutton your goddamn spine like this. Now what's your name?"

He ran his tongue across his lower lip and stared at the chain. "Benny."

"Benny. A fine name—I like that name, don't you, Dev? Benny. Now, Benny, who was it tried to kill my partner here in the tunnel?"

"What?"

Bunch wagged a finger close under the man's soggy nose. "I said we'd ask—you answer. One of you people tried to kill my partner up in Clear Creek Canyon, and we want to know who it was."

"I don't know. Nobody tried to kill the son of a bitch up there. When you came out sneaking around the ranch, sure. What the hell you expect, sneaking around like that?"

"Then, who was it broke into our office, Benny?"

He shook his head. "I don't know. It wasn't none of us— this is the first time we been here."

"Benny, Benny, Benny—you're not being helpful. We like you, Benny. We want to save you some hurt." The big man leaned close to Benny, who pressed back in his chair. "But I will twist your fucking arms off at the elbows if you don't start telling me the truth!"

"It is the truth! Swear to God—nobody tried to kill anybody up in Clear Creek. And we didn't come anywhere near your goddamn office except tonight. I swear to God!"

"Is this what you literary types call an inveterate liar, Dev?"

"Sad but true, Bunch." I smiled at Benny, who didn't like what he saw there. "How much do you think we can get for his bones and blood?"

"What you mean? What you people talking about?"

Bunch shook his head. "Not much. They're in pretty shitty condition."

"And they're going to get worse." I smiled again.

On the quiet street outside, a sound of motorcycle engines cruised through the darkness. Benny's eye lit up. "You fuckers better let me go. You don't let me go, they're coming back here."

"You really believe that?" asked Bunch. "Come on, Benny, you believe they're coming back for you?"

He said nothing, Adam's apple bobbing dryly.

"I wish they would. But they're not that dumb, Benny. You're here all alone with us. Just you. Now, who tried to kill my partner? I want a name."

"It wasn't us! The only time we seen you is when you came sneaking around the ranch. We want to know what the fuck you're doing that for—what the fuck you took our dog for!"

"Why didn't you just ask?"

The eye blinked. "Well, you was messing with us." He added, "You mess with us, we kick the shit out of you." It made sense to him.

"Like tonight?"

"Yeah, well, you jumped us. You was ready for us."

"Was Billy Taylor with you tonight?"

"Who?"

Bunch hooked his foot under the chair and pulled it out from under the man, who crashed hard to the floor. Then he placed a large shoe on the man's shin and pressed down. "You heard me. Yes or no?"

"Ow—goddamn, you're breaking my leg!"

"Answer, scumbag. I'm tired of playing with you."

"Yes! Goddamn, yes—get off!"

Bunch lifted him by his leather vest and stood him against the wall, hauling him off the floor high enough to be eye level. Outside, the motorcycles made another slow pass, but Benny wasn't listening. "We got your goddamn dog. You want him back, you tell Billy Taylor to come get him. Hear?"

"I hear!"

"Tell Taylor to come on his bike and come alone."

"Where?"

"We'll call you and say where and when. What's your phone number?"

He told us, voice hoarse from his weight pressing his throat against Bunch's fists.

We walked him down the stairs to the parking lot. Somewhere at the far end of Wazee Street we could hear the motorcycles. They seemed to be stationary, waiting, trying to decide what to do next.

"Benny," I said, "I don't believe that crap about you people not trying to kill me. In fact, I bet you were the one."

"No, man! It's the truth—nobody I know of did anything like that."

"Benny, if they do try again, they'd better do it right. You understand what I'm saying?"

"Yeah, I understand. But I'm not giving you no shit, man. We didn't do it. That's the truth."

"A pleasure talking to you, Benny. Give our regards to Taylor."

We watched him stumble quickly toward the sound of the motorcycle engines. A short time later, they popped and roared and faded into the night.

I asked Bunch, "What's this about giving Taylor the dog?"

"Hey, it came to me right then! All we got to do is set it up right—it's a chance, Dev."

Hell, it was the only chance. "You think Benny was lying about the shooting?"

"Sure." Bunch added, "But he was convincing, wasn't he?"

"Why not? He's had a lifetime of practice."

14

It took two or three days before Sergeant Kiefer got back to me. For one thing, I was far down on his list of chores, somewhere below "Miscellaneous," but still above "Circular File." For another, he didn't have much good to tell me. "Dev, I'm not going to be able to help you much."

"Why's that?"

"I asked a few questions here and there, trying to find out things about Antibodies Research. This morning I got a call from the DA's office. An assistant over there—he tells me to lay off."

"They're working up something?"

"No. He tells me I'm on the verge of harassing a respected businessman and causing material damage to a legitimate business that, according to all the evidence available, has broken no laws."

"The DA pulled you off it?"

"This assistant did. Art Maddox. I made a couple calls anyway, and Dev, I got to tell you, the people who own stock in Antibodies are some of the biggest names in town. They're making a potload of money and they don't want to see anything bad come down about it."

"Do they have any idea what's going on?"

"I doubt it. My guess is they don't look past the profit statements. I know for certain they don't want anybody—that is, me—asking anything that might embarrass the company and shake these profits. I've been told to stop nosing around unless I have indisputable evidence of criminal activity. Period."

I couldn't ask Dan to put his career on the line. Not yet, anyway. "Gilbert swings a big stick."

"More likely, whatever stockholders he talked to. I checked him out, by the way. No criminal record."

"I'm sorry to get you in hot water, Dan."

"Hey, I've backed off. No trouble." He went on, "But if you do get something 'indisputable,' I'd like to shove Maddox's nose in it. All the way up to his goddamn eyebrows."

"All I have is circumstantial. It won't help much."

"Well, like I say, I can't do anything more. But you keep poking around and I'll keep a quiet ear out. Somebody's sweating for some reason, and it's interesting."

It also took some time to set up our meeting with Taylor; Bunch muttered something about arranging a meet and took off. I called Schute and gave him the news that we should have something definitive on Taylor in three or four days.

"That's cutting it goddamn close, Kirk. Will it do the job for us?"

"It should," I said. The quiver in my mind didn't quite make it to my voice. "My associate's arranging the—ah—situation right now."

"I don't want to hear about that part of it. Just send me the results."

"Will do."

Jerry Kagan finally called too. "According to my friend at Empire State Hospital, the donor—a Mr. Martinez—was on life support when the transplant took place."

"He was still alive?"

Jerry paused. "Technically. Perhaps he even had some brain activity. But he wasn't expected to live and his next of kin must have signed the donor form."

"What did he die of?"

"I heard it was a drug overdose, but couldn't confirm it."

"He was flown to New York on life support?"

"Apparently so. I don't know for certain. It was an interesting operation—the blood was so rare, they had to give it to the recipient as a transfusion. Took it out while the kidney was being removed."

"What about the corpse? What did they do with it?"

"I don't know. Routine disposal, I guess. Or returned it to next of kin."

"What if there were no next of kin?"

"Then I'm not sure. Most hospitals send the cadaver to potter's field or use it for medical study." He added, "I didn't ask my friend about that. He was reluctant enough to tell me as much as he did."

"All right, Jerry. This is a big help and I owe you more than a dinner."

Bunch returned to assure me that Schute would be happy soon. "I called those scumbags, Dev. I told Taylor where to be and when."

"You talked to him?"

"Yeah." He paused. "At least he said it was him."

The location was a little-used county road in a small canyon between Golden and Boulder. "Think he'll show up?"

Bunch nodded. "He'll show up. But he won't be alone."

"Fine," I said. "This time we'll be ready."

And finally, late in the afternoon, I heard from Percy.

"I managed to talk to this Dr. Rosenberg, Devlin. If talk is the name for something so brief."

"Not much help?"

"Oh, he said he did the operation, all right. Was justifiably proud of it, in fact. But who the donor was, where he came from, and what happened to him afterward was downright irrelevant to his interest in the case. His concern was with the living recipient and only a local corner of the recipient at that. He's a specialist, you see."

"Did he know what happened to the body?"

"He didn't. But I located a nurse on the team. The remains were cremated."

"Cremated?"

"There was this generous act by the next of kin, Devlin lad, that allowed the hospital to recover what other organs they could and cremate the remainder, thereby saving the hospital the cost of shipping the corpse back for burial."

So much for any dental records or other positive proof of identity.

"The nurse said it wasn't all that unusual. Out-of-town donors are often cremated and sent home in a tin box. It's known as getting your ashes hauled."

"But he had no relatives, Perce."

"All I know is what she told me: that she saw the authorization form and saw the orderlies remove the body after the operation."

"There's a paper trail on the cremation?"

"Of course! This is New York—everything aboveboard and honest. In fact, I took the liberty of photocopying the death certificate and cremation authorization. I can fax them out if you want."

"Yes—send them on."

"Will do."

It took about twenty minutes for the documents to be processed through a system that was always crowded at the end of New York's working day, and I faxed a photograph back with one final chore for Percy. When the machine stopped chirping, there they were: a copy of the New York State certificate of death for one John Martinez and an authorization for disposal of remains by shipping them back to Antibodies Research, who would return them to the Martinez family. The signature on the line for next of kin was Mary Martinez. It was a name I didn't recognize and apparently wasn't supposed to. There was, however, a notary seal witnessing Mary's signature. The name of the notary was Phyllis Whortley, and that was familiar . . . Whortley—on a nameplate . . . a brass nameplate on a desk: small letters perched on the corner of Gilbert's secretary's desk.

Either Gilbert or her secretary had signed as Mary Martinez, and Phyllis notarized the signature to make everything nice and legal on paper.

It wasn't much evidence to bring into court, but it was one more stitch in the fabric, and it looked as if circumstantial was the only kind of evidence we were going to get.

Bunch had been making calls to the dozen or so air ambulance firms and came up with another tidbit: "John Martinez was flown out on a chartered plane from Arapahoe Airport, Dev. Wings Ambulance Service. He was accompanied by the service's medical flight team."

"Was he on life support?"

"Yeah. That's why booking remembered so easily. Said they don't get much call for long flights with full life support, so it was a big thing. Big cost, too, but the check was good."

"Who paid?"

"Empire State Hospital."

"Was Antibodies involved?"

Bunch nodded. "Mark Gilbert signed the release for the funds; Dr. Morris Matheney signed the medical release."

Matheney's nurse told me he was on afternoon rounds at Warner Memorial and wouldn't be back until around four. I told her I'd wait and settled down to leaf through one of the thousands of *National Geographic*s that find their final resting place in medical offices.

"He's going to be a little late this afternoon," she told me once. "He just called from the hospital."

"I'll wait."

The silence of the small lounge with its half-dozen chairs was broken only by the occasional rattle of the telephone and the distant buzz of voices out of sight down the hallway. It was almost five before the nurse leaned over her office's half-door to tell me the doctor would see me now.

This time there was a definite chill in the air; he neither rose nor offered to shake hands, and the brown eyes above the Lincoln-style beard were defensive and angry. "I've told you before, Mr. Kirk, there's nothing I can do to help you."

I smiled. "But that was before you heard what I have to say."

Matheney leaned back, his beard thrusting out a trifle more. His voice didn't ask what it was, but his eyes did.

"When Nestor Calamaro was officially invisible, he had no existence. But then he became important to some people, and as a result he began to exist."

"Exactly what point are you trying to make?" Matheney's eyes, magnified by their lenses, stared at me without blinking.

"He exists on paper now. As a Mr. John Martinez. He was flown by Wings Ambulance Service to Empire State Hospital in New York. He exists on paper there as a brain-dead organ donor with—you guessed it—extremely rare Rh null blood. He exists on another piece of paper as a corpse cremated after the transplant. And he still exists in the memory of the medical team that did the transplant and who have recognized a photograph of Nestor Calamaro as John Martinez. In fact, Nestor has more existence since he was killed than when he was alive."

The only motion in the doctor's face was his lower lip, which curled inward so he could nip at a spur of dry flesh with his front teeth.

"Nestor still exists in your files, too, doctor."

His head jerked to one side in a quick negative. "Not with that blood he doesn't. The Nestor Calamaro I treated had type A blood. You can look in those files, Kirk."

"But the Nestor who was tested at Warner Memorial, under your authorization, had Rh null blood. What are the odds of that kind of blood showing up in two people named Nestor Calamaro here in Denver?"

The teeth nipped again. "How did you—? You must have broken into my files!"

"Yeah." I placed a photograph on his desk. "Here's a picture I took of Nestor's file—the one sitting in that drawer right now.

If you look closely right here, you can see where someone changed the blood type."

"That's burglary! That's theft—you can't—"

"Before you get too self-righteous, doctor, please remember that the rules against obtaining evidence illegally apply only to public officials such as the police. I'm a private citizen. The evidence I have is admissible in court." It wasn't all that true, but—who knows?—the Supreme Court and its new conservatives could find that way.

"Why are you telling me this? Why haven't you gone to the police with this . . . this story?"

"Because Nestor was murdered and I want to know who killed him. And who killed two pregnant women who have no existence at all now."

Now the eyes only stared emptily.

"And why. Why someone with your ability and achievements would become so greedy as to feed off the lives of the helpless."

Something hardened again in the man's eyes—his professional competence was being challenged, his image of himself as a doctor questioned. "You think I wanted that money for myself?"

"It didn't go to a victims' compensation fund, did it?"

"You know nothing—nothing!"

"Tell me it was for charity. Tell me it was for the advancement of knowledge and the betterment of humankind."

"It was! You with your comfortable ignorance—you have no idea what medical research costs, no idea what thresholds we're on! Thresholds we can cross with just a little more effort!"

"The rats in the Antibodies laboratory? Is that your threshold?"

"Yes! Hybrid protein. If those experiments are successful, transplant surgery can become as routine and as risk-free as tonsillectomies!"

"And that makes it worth Nestor's life?"

He didn't hear my comment. Instead, he leaned tensely across the desk. "My God, Kirk, think what it will mean to develop a protein that kills transplant-attacking cells in human beings! Think of the benefits from eliminating the risk and the cost of all the antirejection drugs that we use today! The protein will not only be more powerful but selective—that's the key. A protein that selectively attacks those T-cells which reject transplanted organs, but that doesn't depress the patient's general immune system!"

"Surely, doctor, there are other ways of getting funding for your research."

"The government funded us for five years and then pulled out when we were this close. Bureaucracy! Some goddamn bureaucrat in Washington said we weren't making satisfactory progress—as if this kind of research could be scheduled like a construction project. It's a dead end, he said. It's not cost effective. That was the term he used: 'cost effective.' He measured the human benefits against dollars and said we weren't cost effective!"

"But you decided to be cost effective," I said. "You took illegal immigrants and sold their bodies to fund your research."

"We used the same criteria to make a decision that Washington used on me. I had no choice! They forced it on me—what else could I do? We're this close to creating the protein, and to quit now—to give up all that we've accomplished . . ." He shook his head. "That would be the criminal act—in the larger scale of things, that would be the truly criminal act."

Behind their thick lenses, his eyes stared at me and beyond. "The wonder of it—the awe-inspiring wonder of that kind of freedom for transplanting. Think what it will mean not just for organ transplantation but cell transplants, too. Islets that can rebuild injured tissue. Even create whole and healthy tissue out of malformed births! Retarded children made normal. Alzheimer's victims brought back to their former abilities, diabetics . . . epileptics . . . Criminal act? No, cost effective—it was cost effective to use two or three marginal individuals for the benefit of the entire human race. Human beings are slaughtered by the hundreds every day—wars, accidents, suicides—every day all over the globe, humans are slaughtered to no purpose or benefit. Three. Three faceless, noncontributive aliens, whose benefit to humanity will far outweigh anything they could ever have achieved in life!"

"The two pregnant women, too?"

He blinked and seemed to recognize my face as someone different from the person he had been arguing with: a face of his own imagining, perhaps the face of his own conscience. Leaning back in his chair, his voice lost its excitement and sounded as flat and factual as a lab report. "They provided intact fetuses near term. Intact fetuses are almost impossible to locate, and even experiments with fetal tissue are no longer allowed. It's insanity. Bureaucratic insanity."

"You needed the fetuses for experiments?"

"I transplanted the fetal kidney into a recipient, using the hybrid protein in conjunction with cyclosporin A. It worked—by God, the experiment worked! And the patient would be alive and healthy today if she hadn't contracted pneumonia. That transplant was a success!"

"The hospital knew of this operation?"

"Of course. But not of the hybrid protein," he added.

"They knew where you got the organ?"

His hand waved irritably, as at a pesky gnat. "Antibodies Research is a clearinghouse for fetal tissue."

"And the second fetus? You experimented with it, too?"

"I don't know what happened there. The recipient's entire immune system collapsed. I've been running various possibilities through the computer for days—weeks—and I still don't know what happened there." His mind drifted off to that problem.

I asked very softly, "What happened to the bodies of the women and fetuses?"

"Gilbert harvested them. To provide funding."

It gave new meaning to the term "operating expenses." We sat in silence. Faintly through the brick walls of the clinic came the sounds of a busy, sunlit avenue pulsing with cars and the shuffle of leather along the sidewalks. Finally, I asked, "Will you tell the police what you've told me?"

"The police?" Matheney sighed deeply, his shoulders weary and sagging against the curve of his padded chair. "Ah yes. The police. I don't know. I need to think about that."

"You've accomplished a lot, doctor. You've made tremendous advances in your experiments. But you see it can't continue."

The shoulders sagged even further. "A little more time. That's all it would take—we're so close."

"There's no time left. You have to make a statement to the police. I have a friend in the police who will listen to what you say. Let's do it now—come with me, doctor. He's a friend. He'll listen."

Another deep breath and his shoulders stiffened a bit. "Don't patronize me, Kirk." A wry twist bent the corners of his mouth. "Why don't you arrest me? That would make a big splash in the papers for you, wouldn't it?"

"That's not important." No arrest, citizen's or otherwise, would do much good in court without a written confession first. "Come on, Dr. Matheney. He's a detective. His name's Kiefer—you'll like him."

"I will, eh? Well, I have things to do first, Kirk. The experiment—I can't leave it the way it is. Records . . . data . . . I have to straighten things out first." He stood, brown eyes once more soft and smiling. "Don't worry, I'm not going anywhere. There's no place I could hide anyway. I'll meet your Detective Kiefer first thing in the morning, and he'll know everything I've told you. But I must make certain the experiments are in a condition to pass on to . . . to whoever will take them over . . ."

He pressed a button on his desk and the nurse, worried-looking but efficient, stuck her head through the doorway.

Matheney rose. "Thank you, Mr. Kirk. It's been an extremely interesting visit. I'm sure you'll understand that I have a tremendous number of details to attend to in a short time. Anne, show Mr. Kirk out and then please come back. I know it's late, but I have a few things I want you to look after."

I went out, but I didn't go home. Instead, I sat in my car and watched the parking lot and the white Chrysler in the slot reserved for Dr. Matheney. On television, this would be the end—the detective would take the good doctor by the arm and walk him down to the nearest police station, saying, as the credits began to roll, "Come on—you're under arrest." But reality wasn't like that. Reality was that arrest was an act loaded with legal freight that could weigh down the arrester in counter-charges and—more important—free the arrestee because of technical violations. What it boiled down to was that I had little choice but to wait and watch, which I did until only Matheney's car and one other remained. Finally the nurse came out, head down as she poked in her purse for her keys.

"Anne!"

She looked up, startled to hear her name.

"When will the doctor be out?"

"Why, he left half an hour ago." She glanced at the white Le Baron and frowned. "I'm sure he left. I saw him going down the walk. But here's his car . . ."

It took us about five minutes to determine that the clinic was, in fact, empty. My guess was that Matheney had gone down the walk, out the alley gate, and over to the street to find a taxi. And then to wherever—though I had a pretty good idea where that was.

"What did he want you to do this afternoon, Anne?"

"Clear up the records. Make certain all the files were up to date. Why?"

"Is that usual?"

"Well, he's very meticulous. But—"

"But what?"

"It's almost as if he's arranging to transfer the files to another physician."

"Did he seem anxious?"

"No. Very calm. Like he always is. Why? What's going on?"

I mumbled something about problems with his experiment at the laboratory and managed to find a phone hood and put in a call to Bunch. He was still in the office, working on equipment for our meeting with Taylor. "Metheney's off and running."

"Where to?"

"I'm betting to Antibodies. That's where his research is. Bunch, he admitted using Nestor and the two women for his research. Now it looks like he's cleaning up his caseload at his office."

"Skipping the country?"

"If he does, so does our case."

"Crap—I'll see you over there, Dev."

I angled onto Valley Highway, which was still choked with the remnants of rush hour traffic, and branched off at the Santa Fe intersection. In the flat gray light of early evening, the blank-walled brick building squatted behind its wire fence, seemingly vacant except for the four cars pulled up to the front door. I parked down the street and waited, figuring Bunch to arrive in a couple minutes, and he did. The Bronco squealed to a halt behind me, and the big man hopped out quickly and slid into the rider's seat.

"Anything going down?"

"No. No one in, no one out."

Bunch leaned on the dash and eyed the building. "You sure he came here?"

"No. But this is where he's running his experiment. I don't think he would go off and leave it hanging—he wants things wrapped up so someone else can take over."

"Wants his money, is what he wants."

"I don't think that's all of it."

We peered through the gloom at the still building as the streetlights began to shine more brightly against the darkening sky.

"I did a little checking on this guy Gilbert," said Bunch. "He came here from LA maybe ten years ago. Worked in commercial real estate until the market went flat. Then somehow he moved over to the private health business."

"Kiefer said he didn't have a record."

"I didn't find one either. He does have a lot of contacts around town from his real estate days. What he did was set up Antibodies and get out a prospectus that promised to pay a twenty percent return on investment the first year, thirty percent the second. He has a board of directors with Matheney at the top and a whole shitpot full of big names underneath." He told me some of them, all recognizable. "It's no wonder Kiefer got pulled."

"Did the company pay off?"

"First year. I hear the returns were thirty-five percent. Now he's got people kissing his ass to take their money."

"A Ponzi scheme?"

"Don't count on it—he made a million off Nestor, didn't he?"

The door opened and two figures in overalls came out. One was tall and thick-bodied; the other was shorter and almost round and had an arm braced with an elastic sling. They stood talking for a few minutes, in no hurry.

"Working late tonight," said Bunch. "Probably had a body to cut up."

There was something vaguely familiar about them. The smaller one. Perhaps a face I'd seen before . . . No, more the shape of the man, his way of carrying himself . . .

"Bunch, those are the ones who broke into our office."

"Say what?"

"The short one. The way he moves, kind of sidling. That's them, Bunch—the burglars."

We watched the big one climb into a Chevy Blazer and back out. The other went to a Toyota pickup and followed. We noted the license numbers as the vehicles turned into the street.

"Think I should follow one of them?" asked Bunch.

I was tempted. "No. Gilbert and Matheney are the ones we want to keep an eye on right now."

He sank back against the seat. "The brown Caddy—that has to be Gilbert's."

The other was a Nissan sedan of some sort. I didn't think it was Matheney's, but the possibility was there. We sat, talking a little bit about one thing and another—the other being the meeting tomorrow morning with Billy Taylor.

"You're all set for that?" I asked Bunch.

"Yeah. I got a camera rig with a remote tripper. We can pick up that goddamn dog at seven and be over there in half an hour."

"It's got to come off, Bunch. I promised Schute."

"Hey, have I ever failed?"

"Yeah. More than once."

"I mean besides those times."

Before I could answer, a hefty, sandy-haired figure pushed quickly through the glass door and half trotted to the brown Seville that sat nearest the entry.

"Uh-oh—here comes Gilbert," said Bunch.

"In a hurry, too." I started my engine." I'll follow him. You sit on the last car."

Bunch slid out and stepped into the shadow of a doorway as the Cadillac's headlights swept across us. I ducked down while it rushed past, then watched the car in the rearview mirror as it rocked into a hard turn at the corner. Squealing the tires, I swung around and followed, staying far enough back so that I had to occasionally guess where Gilbert would turn. But after a couple miles, I thought I knew and dropped back even further. We turned west on Hampden, and Gilbert pushed the speed limit as his heavy car wove through traffic toward Matheney's home.

Off at Sheridan south and a quick turn onto Mansfield. Far ahead, the brown car swung under the iron gateway bearing the ornate *M,* and I slowed to a halt at the entry. Through a screen of blue spruce and elms, I saw the wink of flashing emergency lights, and in the quiet of the peaceful country club neighborhood heard the crackle of official radio traffic with its cryptic, terse messages.

After a while, a blue-and-white coasted down the drive, its flashers dark and the officer saying something into his microphone. I hopped out and waved him to a stop.

"Can you tell me what happened, officer?"

He looked at me for a long moment. "You a reporter?"

"No. I'm a friend of Dr. Matheney's family—I live just down the road. I don't want to intrude, but if something's happened and my wife and I can help . . ."

It wasn't the offer of Christian charity that decided it; rather, it was the idea that I lived just down the road in another of the sprawling mansions that paid so much city tax and had such well-connected residents. He shrugged and scratched at a wing of his mustache. "It looks like the doctor shot himself. You might go up there and tell the detectives you're a family friend—his wife's pretty shook up."

"My God," I said, and I meant it. "All right. Thanks."

The officer lifted a hand and cruised down the lane—his part of the drama was over, and it was back to serve and protect. I sat in the car and thought. Things had, indeed, been put into motion. But as is often the case, the exact direction of things hadn't been foreseen, and this wasn't the outcome I wanted. Matheney was dead. So were the others: Nestor, Serafina, Felicidad. I really couldn't find a great amount of sadness and sympathy for the man, no matter how deeply I looked. What I did find was anger—a dead man couldn't testify, and Matheney's death meant a weak case against Gilbert. He had destroyed himself—fine. But he had also destroyed his usefulness, and that wasn't so fine.

As I pondered, a black Oldsmobile swerved past me and up the driveway; the man behind the wheel had a preoccupied look, and I wasn't surprised to see a medical badge fastened to the car's rear license plate. A few minutes later, Gilbert's brown Cadillac glided down under the branches that shaded the drive.

The headlights caught my face and the car braked abruptly. In the dash lights, I saw Gilbert's mouth twist in anger. The window slid down.

"Matheney killed himself," he said accusingly.

"Maybe you can sell his body."

Gilbert's mouth tightened. "I warned you, Kirk. Goddamn you, I warned you!"

"Going to have your two boys break into my office again?"

The man blinked, anger stifled by caution. "I don't know what you mean. And I don't know what you think you've found out." The thick lips clenched up into a semblance of a smile. "Matheney didn't leave a suicide note. He didn't give his wife any reason why he killed himself. And now he will never testify to one damn thing, Kirk. No one will testify to anything." He pushed a button and the window rose smoothly as he spurted gravel from his rear tires.

I turned, my headlights picking out two or three figures standing in the shadows of trees and staring up the drive. Then I headed back downtown.

A yawning Bunch drove the Bronco toward the mountains, etched sharply by the low morning sun. "I left a note for Kiefer, Dev. He didn't catch the suicide, but he'll learn about it when he gets in."

"We'd better go to work on Chiquichano again," I said.

He nodded, voice stifled by another vast yawn. "That Nissan, it belonged to the secretary. She drove straight home. Still there, as far as I know."

In the far back, Sid Vicious scratched at his carrying case and breathed an unending rumble of growls and doggy curses. On the backseat behind us, the mound of camera equipment jiggled as the Bronco turned off the paved road and started up a dirt track.

"Chiquichano might run now," I said.

"I don't think so. I think as long as Gilbert stays, she'll stay—

he's her golden goose." He added, "I did get party and plate on those two clowns: Earl Vercher and Toby Dunlap. Dunlap's got a jacket for boosting cars and assault. Nothing on Vercher."

"You think they're a better bet than Chiquichano?"

"I think she's a hell of a lot tougher than they are. But she probably knows more about what went on." Another yawn. "The way things are going, we'll be damned lucky to get any kind of hard evidence. You see the paper this morning?"

The headline in the *Rocky Mountain News* said, "Prominent Physician Kills Self," and the article quoted a spokesman for the family who explained that extreme pressures from overwork and depression brought on by the failure of funding for his research contributed to his death. There was no mention of his affiliation with Antibodies Research. A picture of his family— red-eyed wife and two shocked-looking teenaged children—left me staring into space for a long time. "Yeah. I saw it."

Bunch's head wagged. "Too bad he had no guts. He could have done something to straighten things out by testifying."

"Maybe he found out he was only playing at being a god."

"Naw—probably thought he was doing the noble thing. Damn fool."

We rode in silence. The springs of the lurching vehicle creaked with each mudhole and spur of rock. Bunch finally pulled the car into the shelter of a thick stand of aspen, and we unloaded the gear to push through the underbrush. We were going in the back way in case the bikers had sent people ahead to stake out the meeting site. You couldn't trust people like that, Bunch said, because they were sneaky, underhanded, immoral, and sly. So we had to best them in each category.

I followed the big man up a steep hill through a stand of ponderosa and spruce. We crossed a ridge and paused at the edge of a clearing that overlooked another dirt road. It curved around a sharp bluff bitten into the cliff face and narrowed between the rock wall and the rush of the stream that had carved the notch. A barely visible two-rut track branched off toward us through the grassy field, with its orange and white and coral washes of gilia and billows of coneflowers and Indian paintbrush. Across the glade, abrupt against the deep blue sky, a mountain shaggy with black timber gradually lifted to the ragged and crumbled stone of its naked crest.

"Now this is really pretty," sighed Bunch.

It was. But the time was past when a landscape could be admired solely for its beauty; it was useful, too: The open field made it difficult for anyone to approach without being seen, and the steep mountain across the narrow valley blocked anyone from circling around and closing off escape. The trees behind us gave cover and concealment, while the narrow gap the road twisted through meant a bottleneck for vehicles and motorcycles, one that a single rifleman could hold for enough time to cover an escape.

We searched the area carefully with binoculars, finally satisfied that we were the only people there. Then Bunch hefted the carrier with the unhappily muttering Sid and carried him out to the center of the glade. The top of the plastic box was scarcely visible above the grass and flowers; I went another hundred yards and tapped in a stake with a shiny orange pennant and came back to wait. Bunch went back in the trees to set up the cameras and the telephoto equipment.

Taylor was supposed to arrive at ten. About nine-thirty, I hard the distant rap of motorcycle engines somewhere down the canyon. The sound was tossed on the breeze, so its direction was vague, and it quit before coming closer. Then there was a long silence, broken by the occasional tweet of a bird somewhere on the mountain flank and the startled caw of a raven eyeing me from overhead. The muted hiss of the small radio transmitter popped once, and Bunch's voice made a tiny noise: "Can you read me, Dev?"

"Loud and clear. How me?"

"Same. Don't forget to smile for the camera."

Then silence.

At five after ten, a pickup truck ground slowly up the road, nosing for me. It stopped once just beyond the narrows, then came on carefully to stop again where the track branched off. Through the binoculars, I could see that the bed was empty and the front seat held only one silhouette. As instructed, the driver got out and stood with arms lifted to show he was unarmed. I stood up in the grass and waved him forward. Taylor got back in and started up the track.

"Son of a bitch was supposed to ride his motorcycle, Dev. We were supposed to get pictures of him riding his goddamn motorcycle. This isn't working worth a damn!"

"Too damn late now, Bunch."

The truck stopped a hundred yards down the path where the pennant had been driven, and Taylor got out again.

"You Kirk?"

"Yeah."

"What's all this crap about?"

I hoisted the dog carrier. Sid's growls turned into snarls. "Here he is. Come and get him."

The man started to get back in the truck.

"No—leave the truck there. You walk up and get him."

"Well, shit." Taylor, his paunch pushing the T-shirt out between the wings of his leather vest, plodded up the hill.

"That dog all right? That's a valuable dog."

"I can tell you he doesn't have rabies. You were supposed to come on your bike."

"How the hell could I carry a goddamn dog on my bike?"

"Well, judging from some of your girlfriends . . ."

"You're funnier'n shit, ain't you? Want to tell me why you made me go through all this shit?"

He'd find out soon enough if he received a summons from Schute's lawyers; and if he didn't, it wouldn't make any difference anyway. "Your insurance scam. The company wants proof you aren't permanently disabled."

"Is that it? Those fuckers want to get out of paying what they owe me? That what it is?"

"That's what it is." I handed him the carrier and Sid lunged to the grille to bite whatever was nearest.

"Well, shit!" He turned and whistled sharply, and two figures tumbled from the truck cab and sprinted uphill toward me. "Get the fucker—get him!"

I grabbed the transmitter. "Bunch—Bunch, come on!"

15

Taylor hit me first, dropping the dog cage to drive his shoulder into my chest and plunge me backward into the grass so he could aim heavy boots at my head. I rolled, scissoring my legs and clipping him at the knees, and he flopped into a bed of gilia, cursing and swinging at air. The next was Benny, and he was hefting a fighting knife complete with finger guard.

"Bunch, goddamn it!"

He cut viciously at my outstretched hand, and I grabbed his wrist, spun to lever his elbow down across my shoulder, and yanked quick and hard. I wasn't trying to flip him this time but to break the joint, and in the knotted and twisting flesh next to my ear I heard something give with a kind of pop. The hand splayed out in pain, and I stripped off the knife and turned in time to catch a solid punch on the forehead that made me feel ice-cold all over and drove me stumbling backward into a tangle of weeds.

A shadow blotted what was left of the sun and another heavy thud knocked the wind from my lungs. I didn't really feel it with my body, but my mind told me that it was a hard one and that it should hurt. I rolled into a ball, hands clasped at the back of my neck, and tried to focus my strength into my legs, to get my legs under me and lever myself up and away from the stomping boots I knew would be coming.

"Dev—roll the other way!"

"What?"

246 · REX BURNS

"The other way—roll the other way!" The radio squawked. "You're giving me a bad camera angle!"

"Damn your eyes, Bunch—"

A boot whistled past my ear to glance off my shoulder, and I grabbed the toe and heel and twisted sharply, the vague looming shape spinning out of vision. Another body flung itself on me and pummeled at my back.

"That's it, Dev—hold it right there—it's a good shot!"

"Bunch, you son—"

A fist caught my mouth and I felt the numbed flesh split against my teeth. I drove an elbow savagely back to crack against a skull, then looped an arm over enough body to fling Taylor across me with a hip throw and slash at his neck with the blade of my hand as he went past. Somewhere underneath the breathy grunts of the men and the insane barking and snarling of Sid, I heard a roar of motorcycle engines and glimpsed a cluster of bikes rounding the road below.

I saw a face hovering at my shoulder and gave it an elbow and spun to kick at another figure while the third man dived for my leg and began to sink his teeth into my calf.

"Goddamn!"

A kick freed me of that, but Taylor was up again and, head down and fists high, drove toward me in a bloody spew of curses. Crouching, I caught his fists on my forearms and jabbed the point of my knee into his groin. The man made a long squeak as he lifted his head back and fell slowly to one side, hands clutching the spot my knee had caressed. Benny, one arm dangling and the fighting knife clutched in his other hand, was coming at me again, grass roots and mud tangled with his fingers in the grip.

A loud rifle crack fired just over our heads and we stopped, frozen by the sound.

A second round exploded, and I saw the motorcycles slide to a dusty halt and scramble backward frantically, pulling over each other to find shelter behind the shoulder of cliff. A third round whacked into the torn mud and threw gobs of dirt across the beard and eyes of Taylor.

"That's it—party's over, people. Take your goddamn dog and haul ass while you still got one," Bunch yelled.

From the tree line the rifle spoke again, and the three men stumbled down the hill toward the truck, the dog cage banging and barking between them. The pickup truck wheeled around, then dug through the grass and flowers, peeling the earth to bare mud as it fled. I looked at the crushed and torn ground and slowly gathered up the radio and binoculars. So much for peaceful meadows and mountain scenery.

"Not bad, Dev. Not bad at all. I think we got some good shots of Taylor proving he's not disabled."

"Why in hell didn't you help me out?"

"Hey, I'm the cameraman. Besides, you didn't need it."

I rubbed a finger across my split lip, which was puffy and sore and had that metallic taste of torn skin. "The hell I didn't."

"I kind of wish you'd turned toward the camera more, though. The way Taylor was dancing around, I could have got better shots."

I made it to the Bronco in exhausted silence. On the way down the mountain, Bunch said, "Jesus, I hope we don't have to do it all over again."

"What's that?"

"The exposure meter. I had it set for the wrong kind of film."

16

The rest of the morning and well into the afternoon was spent with ice packs and Band-Aids and a long, slow soak in the club's Jacuzzi. I limped back to the office by midafternoon to find Bunch sitting at the desk, which was littered with fresh photographs, and talking on the telephone to Kiefer.

"I don't care if he didn't leave a note, Dan. He killed himself because of Nestor and the two women. He confessed it to Dev."

Bunch put a hand over the mouthpiece. "Kiefer says he still doesn't have enough tangible evidence to move against Gilbert."

"Yeah," he said into the telephone again. "I do understand, Dan. But what happens if that bastard gets away with it? How many others is he going to cut up and sell?"

I glanced through the photographs; they showed Taylor grappling my head under his arm and flailing away with a fist, Taylor hauling back to kick me as I curled on the ground, Taylor using both hands as a club across my shoulders.

"No," said Bunch, "I'm not blaming you. But Gilbert's not going to close up shop just because Matheney's dead. There's too much money in it." Kiefer said something and Bunch answered, "All right. We'll see what we can find out. Tell fucking assistant DA Maddox we'll give him a case so tight even he can't screw it up. Right—good-bye."

He hung up and heaved a long sigh. "They're still not going

to move against Gilbert. Nothing in Matheney's suicide supports a warrant for Antibodies."

"I didn't think it would," I said. "Tell me, Bunch, why couldn't you take at least one shot with me on top?"

"Tell you the truth, Dev, you're not very photogenic." He held up one that showed me struggling to get back on my feet, a close-up from the rear. "That's your best side."

I chose half a dozen of Taylor's most active poses. "Have you faxed these on to Schute yet?"

"No, just got them back from the lab."

I dialed New York, hoping it wasn't too late to catch the man in his office. He was there, his secretary said, waiting to hear from me. I noted the relief in her voice.

"Kirk? What's the story?"

"We have the evidence. Hang on and I'll fax you the stills so you can get started. I'll send the videotape by Fed Ex as soon as it's developed."

"Fine—good work! Do the pictures show him pursuing a normal life?"

"Well, yeah—for a motorcycle gang." I added, "They'll convince a jury he's able to move around."

"Fine, fine! I'll get your check to you in the morning."

On that pleasant note we wished each other long life, the best of everything, and so on. When I hung up, Bunch was standing by the door. "Where are you going?" I asked.

"We. We're going to talk to Gilbert's two minions." Bunch liked that word, minion. And there wasn't much chance to use it.

It was almost quitting time when we made it across town through the afternoon traffic. Bunch drove and I held on, trying not to let the stiffly sprung vehicle stir up the twinges and the bruises that were now turning puffy and discolored. We parked down the block from Antibodies' gate and waited until the Blazer and the Toyota pickup pulled out. One turned north, the other south.

"Which one?" asked Bunch.

"The little guy. I've had enough of big ones for today."

Bunch swung into traffic behind the Toyota. "Hell, Dev, none of those guys were that big."

"All together they were."

We tailed the truck south on Santa Fe into Littleton and an ugly building on South Broadway. It had been converted from a storage shed into a country and western bar complete with sawdust on the floor and wormy barn siding on the walls. Rodeo posters were splotched here and there between wagon wheels, branding irons, and horse tack.

"Is this Vercher or Dunlap?"

"Earl Vercher. Toby Dunlap drives the Blazer."

The short, pudgy man went to the bar instead of to a table and waved a familiar hand at the blonde serving drinks. She bobbed her head, stiff curls twanging. Bunch and I sat on each side of him. The jukebox moaned something about someone whose heart was hung over because it had chugalugged on love.

"Hello, Earl," said Bunch. "How's the shoulder?" I watched in the bar mirror as he turned a startled face toward the big man.

"I know you?"

"You do now. More important, I know you."

The bartender brought Earl his Pabst and asked us what our pleasure was. "Same."

"What you want with me?"

"We want to beat the shit out of you, Earl. Whether we do or not is up to you."

"Hey—what—"

He tried to get up but I gripped the back of his neck and pushed him down onto the stool. Turning, he saw me, and his eyes widened. "Jesus—what happened to your face?"

"That's his war paint, Earl. Always puts it on before he kills somebody."

"Now listen, you people . . ."

"Let's step out back a couple minutes, Earl."

"Hey, now, no—"

We each took an arm and lifted him a couple inches off the floor, striding quickly for the hallway that led past the Pointer and Setter doors to a fire door. It opened to the alley.

"You people, you hurt my shoulder! I'm going to call the—"

He didn't get anything else out. Bunch's fist caught Earl just below the sternum, and he doubled and fell knees first and then face flat onto the gritty tar beside the overfull trash can. A ragged figure poking through the garbage looked at him for an instant and then at us, and turned and hunched quickly away.

"Get up, Vercher. Get up or stay down for good. It's your choice."

"Goddamn, my shoulder!"

"Better make that choice, Earl. Or we'll make it for you."

"What you people want? For God's sake, I ain't done nothing—what you people want?"

"We want you to tell us about Gilbert and Antibodies."

"Oh, man. Oh, no—no, I can't—"

I lifted him by the collar and belt; Bunch hit him again—nothing hard, just scientifically placed. After a while the man stopped retching and looked up from the ground. "I ain't got but one good arm. You people think you're real tough beating up on a man got only one good arm."

I explained things to him. "You're not going to have any good arms in about two seconds."

"Honest to God, I don't know what goes on there, I just work there, that's all!"

"You broke into my office."

He hesitated, peering at me. I hauled him up so he could get a good look. "Yes—yes—we broke in! Gilbert told us to! He wanted us to look for anything you had on the company. Anything in your files."

"You didn't find anything."

"No. But you came by asking questions. Gilbert wanted to know what you were up to."

"You snatched Nestor Calamaro too, didn't you?"

"Who?"

"The guy who worked at the Apple Valley Turkeys plant—you and Dunlap, you grabbed him when he was walking home from work."

"No—nothing like that. We give him a ride, is all. Doc Matheney wanted to talk to him and he asked us to go out and give him a ride over. That's all." He looked from Bunch to me. "You guys ain't the cops. You can't get the law on me."

"We don't need to get the law," Bunch said with a smile. "We've got you."

I leaned over the sweating man, whose skin was now slightly green. "You're going to wish we were cops. We do things cops can't."

"Steady, Dev. Don't get excited, now." Bunch explained to Vercher: "My friend's streak of mean comes out when he really gets mad. You don't want to see that."

"I told you already I only work at that place. I don't know what Gilbert and that other doctor's up to. I swear to God!"

"He protesteth too much, don't he, Dev?"

I nodded. "You know enough to be worried about it."

Vercher's mouth tightened above the bone of his long jaw and the sweat popped out again in the lines of his brow. "I'm gonna be sick."

He was. We waited. Finally, Bunch hauled the soggy face up from the tar. "Gawd, you stink."

"Well, I just been sick!"

"You're going to be a hell of a lot sicker real soon," I said. "In fact, you might get sick enough to die."

"Oh Jesus—don't, fellas."

"I don't know how much longer I can control this rabid animal, Earl."

"What is it you people want?"

"A written statement for the cops."

He looked from Bunch to me. "About what?"

"Just tell the truth about what you do for Gilbert. About picking up Nestor Calamaro in the van. About taking him to the plant. And about what happened to him and the two women."

"I ain't . . . I didn't see them do nothing. We clean up, is all. We help get things ready and then we clean up when the . . . the operation's done."

"You don't help out with the operations?"

"No! Dr. Gilbert and Dr. Matheney, they do the technical stuff. Toby and me, we take care of the shipping and supplies and stock and the janitorial stuff—you know."

"That includes the burner? Putting parts in the burner?"

"Well, yeah . . ."

"Write it down."

He didn't want to, but we convinced him. He wrote it out right there, using a garbage can lid as a desk and our presence as inspiration. It wouldn't be worth a thing in court, but it would provide Kiefer with ammunition to get the assitant DA involved.

"I wasn't around when . . . I mean, they—Gilbert and Matheney and Miss Whortley—they wouldn't let us in the operating room, you know?"

"Just put down everything you know about it. And cheer up," said Bunch. "The first liar always has an edge."

"I ain't lying!"

"You ain't writing, either," I said. "And you'd better."

When he had it down, he signed and dated it, and we drove him to a small tavern near police headquarters and called Kiefer to meet us. The detective slid into the booth and stared at my face. "That something I better know about?"

"Something you'd better not know about."

He grunted and turned his attention to Vercher, and sniffed the sour air around the man. "You're doing this of your own free will?"

"Tell him yes, Earl."

"Yes."

"Earl knows the game is over," I said. "He wants to get a break by making a statement."

"I can't promise a thing, Mr. Vercher. You ought to know that."

"He knows." I handed him the statement. "Read it over. See what you think it's worth."

The sergeant read the handwritten pages carefully, pausing here and there to work through the awkward penmanship. When he looked up, he shook his head. "A lot of this about Matheney and Gilbert is hearsay. He didn't see them actually operate on those people."

"I never witnessed nothing, officer. I told these gentlemen I never knew what Gilbert was doing."

"But it corroborates what we suspect, Dan. And it makes a definite link between a missing man who turned up dead, Dr. Matheney, and Antibodies Research. It's good enough for a warrant," I said.

Vercher had been doing some thinking while Kiefer read. "Toby might make a statement too. Maybe if you can work a deal for us both, you'll have both our statements."

Bunch smiled. "See, Dan? Citizenship at work."

Kiefer finished his coffee and stood, gesturing to Vercher. "Yeah. All right—let's you go call this Toby. We'll see what he has to say to me." He glanced at us. "Voluntarily."

We watched the two men leave the tavern. Bunch sipped at his beer. "You think Maddox will act on Vercher's statement?"

"He won't want to, that's for certain." I drained my beer, keeping my face in shadow so it wouldn't scare the other patrons. "In fact, he'll probably delay as long as he can, and that'll be enough to let Gilbert hear about it and get away."

Bunch rubbed his jaw, the bristles rasping. "Yeah. It would save a lot of important people a lot of embarrassment if Gilbert just disappeared."

"And if they had time to sell their Antibodies stock before the story made news."

"Wouldn't Maddox be popular then!"

"A real boost to an ambitious man's career."

Bunch drained his glass. "Let's go see the Mother Superior. I got an idea." He explained it on the way over.

She did not want to see us. The maid said the senora wasn't home. I recognized her as one of the janitorial crew, and she recognized me too, because a slight tilt of her head told me that Mrs. Chiquichano was listening at the top of the stairs.

"We'll come in and wait for her," I said, and gently lifted the woman aside. "Please tell her we're enjoying her hospitality."

Mrs. Chiquichano came quickly down the stairs, heels driving against the carpet like a pair of hammers. "I want you out of my house. You have no right to be in my house—get out!"

"You know Dr. Matheney committed suicide last night?" asked Bunch.

The woman's black eyes widened slightly and she seemed to hold her breath. "No!"

"It's in all the papers. Got some more good news for you too: Gilbert's two assistants are down at police headquarters right now. They're making statements, lady, to the district attorney, trying to save their asses. Your name'll come up sooner or later."

She shook her head, voice stifled by tension.

"Maybe you and Gilbert should talk things over."

"What do you mean?"

"Call him. Tell him you have to meet him. Tell him it's important."

"He won't come—that one doesn't do what I tell him."

"If he doesn't, say you'll go to the police."

She still couldn't bring herself to agree to that. "Why? Why should I call him?"

"It's you or him." Bunch told her the details of Vercher's statement. "So you better call him. You tell him you want more money to keep silent or you'll go to the police yourself. He'll believe you."

"What do you mean, it's me or him?"

"I mean if you call him, we'll tell the police you cooperated.

If you don't, we'll see that you're prosecuted and sent to jail as an accessory to murder."

It was a good reason. She was vulnerable, and she knew it. But she still wanted some kind of guarantee. Knowing what she herself was capable of, she couldn't trust anyone else.

Bunch sketched in the facts: "Lady, we're not guaranteeing a damn thing. We'll tell the DA you helped us get Gilbert, but that's it. And as far as I'm concerned, we shouldn't be doing that much for you. As far as I'm concerned, we should just call the cops right now and have them nail your fat ass to the wall. But we want Gilbert more than we want you, and you're the way we can get him."

She thought that over and finally nodded. "You will give me time after I call? You will give me time to get my money before you call the police?"

"Yeah. We'll give you time. Now here's what you say." Bunch told her exactly what to say and where they should meet. She dialed and we listened to her follow the script, complete with a few convincing variations when Gilbert, angry and worried, tried to get out of meeting with her. She hung up. "He's coming."

"Fine," smiled Bunch. "And so are you."

Our plan was to use Senora Chiquichano to get Gilbert alone. Gilbert, I was certain, had no intention of volunteering his presence to Kiefer's tender embrace, and when he learned of Vercher's statement, he would be gone. But not if we had him, and especially if we had him on tape talking to Chiquichano about the murders.

The place was a tangle of overgrown riverbank along the South Platte, near enough to downtown for a quick drive to the police station, yet secluded enough that we could handle Gilbert if necessary without witnesses. Chiquichano had told the man that she didn't want to chance being seen with him, and he'd finally agreed, saying he would be there between seven-thirty and eight. That would make it just about dark, and it gave us time to get set up and hidden in the bushes that formed a thick screen between the riverbank and the almost empty railroad yard behind. Across the narrow stream and its banks of dried gray mud, the bike path ran like a ribbon of tar, and the occasional jersey of a cyclist zipped by, a flicker of brightness behind the colorless undergrowth.

"I don't like this place." The woman stood restlessly while Bunch arranged the microphone and transmitter under the light jacket she wore. "I don't like doing this thing."

From my seat behind a thicket of hackberry, I said, "Think of it as another investment, senora—the chance to spend your money in the near future."

She gingerly paced back and forth across the corner of open field and tried not to cut her shoes on the broken glass that always marks forgotten corners of the city. After a while, she said, "I don't think he will come."

"He can't afford not to. Relax."

Bunch, about twenty yards away and hidden in the undergrowth that grew rank along the damp riverbank, gave a low whistle. I peered through the leaves and saw, moving with slow deliberation across the wide and empty rail yard, which was marked here and there with rusty spur lines, a brown Cadillac, lights out and ghostly in the gloom of twilight.

"He's on his way. You remember what to tell him?"

The answer came slightly breathless over the transmitter. "About the two men—yes."

On the horizon, the towers of the city were beginning to light up with glowing windows, and toward the north, a steady river of headlights flowed across the Sixth Avenue overpass. Nearby but elevated out of sight, the traffic on busy I-25 made an unbroken rushing noise that drowned out the feeble sound of the South Platte.

The senora stood and watched the brown car pick its way across the uneven bumps of railroad track to come within fifty yards and halt. She waited. I waited. Bunch waited.

The driver's door swung open; the car's dome light remained

dark, and the fuzzy haze of twilight made it difficult to see clearly. Dimly, I saw a shadow hunch at the car door's hinge and hold still. A moment later, an explosion of flame speared toward Mrs. Chiquichano from the muzzle of a powerful hunting rifle. She gave a strangled, high-pitched noise and flung her hands up to the empty sky as she fell backward and thudded unmoving onto the dirt.

"Son of a bitch!"

I saw Bunch's shape sprint out of the shrubbery toward the Bronco as the Cadillac swung away and started lurching and jouncing toward the city streets.

The woman was dead. The shot had caught her in the throat and sliced an artery, and the gush of blood had sprayed up the side of her face and down across her shoulder and arm. By the time I reached her, only a last tiny pulse or two throbbed out, and, looking at the corpse, I knew that the heavy slug I found in my Healey's fire wall would match the one that had driven like a hammer through the woman's jaw to almost sever her neck.

The straining engine of Bunch's Bronco roared away across the tracks as Gilbert's Cadillac fishtailed in a patch of loose gravel and tried to avoid being cut off. I saw a long arm balance momentarily against the outside mirror of the Bronco, and Bunch's pistol spurted flame as the brown car made a squealing turn for another exit. Bunch floored the pedal and leapt high across an embankment to pancake in a cloud of gravel and weeds and spin toward the heeling Cadillac. Another shot by Bunch, and I saw the windshield of Gilbert's sedan splinter and the car careen wildly in a full turn before aiming back at me. It gained speed and roared, dented and steaming, straight at me. I managed to squeeze off one quick round at the shattered windshield before diving for the thin shelter of a clump of saplings as the straining metal scorched past in an odor of dust and steam and burning oil. It flew by, Gilbert's eyes bulging and his mouth open helplessly. Two hubcaps sprung like satellites as the Cadillac sailed over the bank and plunged with a foaming wash into the shallow river. A broken branch bobbed gently against the windshield, then swirled free to drift downstream.

The paperwork took the rest of the night and once more reminded Bunch and me why we left police work in the first place. Kiefer finally let us go home as the dark towers of the city were being outlined by a sky lightening into gray. It was the same obscure mix of night and day that had seen the beginning of things, and for a moment it seemed as if no time at all had passed, as if we had simply moved in a big circle back to the start. But this time the sun was coming up, and when I reached my apartment, Mrs. Ottoboni's porch light could barely be seen against the growing dawn.

Early the next afternoon, I detoured through North Denver on my way to the office. In the hard daylight the barrackslike apartment house looked even dingier, its scabrous paint and neglected roof no longer hidden in shadow. A clutch of children played in the dirt of the front yard, and as I stopped the car, they fell silent and stared. When I opened my door, they slipped into the dark hallway like timid animals.

A nervous woman answered my knock at apartment 1, her eye and cheek peeking under the door's taut chain.

"Do you remember me? The private detective looking for Mr. Calamaro?"

The answer was a silent half-nod.

"I came by to tell you Senora Chiquichano is dead. No more *mordida*." The rent on the cramped apartments should go down, too, but they would find out about that soon enough. "You understand?"

"*La patrona? Murió?*"

"Dead. Yes."

The eye did not blink as the door slowly closed. A click of the lock. I didn't know if the woman believed me or not.

I hoped to find the check from Security at the office among the letters. Or at least a job offer. But no one offered, and the check was still in the mail. I did have an ornately inscribed letter from El Salvador, however, signed by Felix Frentanes, which, with all the formal politeness a professional scribe could muster, asked for information about his wife. There were no job offers on the telephone either. Instead, a somber little message from Mrs. Gutierrez told Bunch that Nestor's family had received a large check from some company in America and were grateful. The only other message was from Archy. He had transplanted the engine of my old Healey into the body of another one and, if he did say so himself, thought he did a pretty good job.